Always Remembered

BOOK THREE IN THE NEVER FORGOTTEN SERIES

Kelly Risser

Clean Teen Publishing

Cover Design by: Marya Heiman
Typography by: Courtney Nuckels
Editing by: Cynthia Shepp

YA content disclosure

For more information about our content disclosure, please
utilize the QR code above with your
smart phone or visit us at

www.cleanteenpublishing.com.

This book is dedicated to Sharon Eileen Risser. The world took you from us too soon, but you will be always remembered in our hearts.

Chapter 1

*I*f I wondered what a volcano looked like before it erupted, all I needed to do was take one glance at my dad's red face. Wincing, I dropped my gaze to the floor.

"You're grounded for life!" The words exploded from his mouth. My eyes flew back to him in disbelief. He raked his hands through his hair, leaving bits standing on end. Between the disheveled hair and the scowl, anger marred his handsome face. Obviously, he wasn't going to be happy that I went against his orders, but I didn't realize he would get this mad. "How could you? I warned you it was dangerous. Do you have a death wish? If you..."

He continued to yell and pace the floor, lost in his lecture. He wasn't even looking at us. I rolled my eyes at Kieran, who bit his cheek, his shoulders shaking with pent-up laughter. Nice that someone was enjoying this. I, on the other hand, didn't know how to diffuse Dad's anger, and I knew some form of punishment was coming. What it was and when it happened remained to be seen.

The amused expression dissolved from Kieran's face when Dad turned and rammed a long finger into his chest. "And you... don't think that your father won't hear about this. I'll be contacting Stephen just as soon as I figure out what I'm doing with Meara."

Dad glared at me. "I've half a mind to throw you in the dungeon. At least you couldn't escape."

"There's a dungeon?" Once again, I snuck a glance at Kieran. He shrugged. Apparently, he didn't know about it either.

"Of course there's a dungeon," Dad scoffed. "This is a fortress. Where do you think we put our enemies? We certainly don't invite them

1

to tea in the parlor."

My face heated, and my chest tightened in anger. Kieran and I were safe. Why couldn't my dad let it go? Sure, we went against his wishes to rescue my ex-boyfriend from Ken, the evil man who hired Evan for a summer internship. The job started okay, until Ken went crazy and locked Evan in the basement. Definitely not the summer job Evan had in mind. Besides, our mission wasn't successful anyway. Kieran and I intended to free Evan. It was the whole reason we snuck out against my dad's orders in the first place. By the time we got to Ken's house, however, he was already long gone with Evan. Now, every moment we stood here and argued meant Evan could be dead. Fear pierced my heart.

"Tell me what happened," Dad demanded.

"When Kieran and I searched the abandoned house, we found Professor Nolan beaten to the brink of death." I could still smell the metallic tang of blood, hear his raspy, broken breath, and see his bruised skin and broken bones. I knew Evan's professor as a quiet, nerdy college teacher. He wasn't a bad man, or at least, he wasn't as malicious as Ken. Although Ted Nolan brought Evan into this situation, no one deserved to die that way.

"He was locked in a cell in the basement," Kieran added. "It might've been the one Ken used for Evan."

Dad scratched his chin, studying the wall behind us. His eyes narrowed and found mine. "Yes, you mentioned that Evan was being held captive. How did you know?"

I met my father's blazing eyes and lifted my chin. If he was trying to intimidate me, I had nothing to hide. "Because that's what he told me."

"How did you speak to him?" Dad asked me before glaring at Kieran. "I thought you have Meara's necklace?"

During the summer, Evan and I used my grandparents' enchanted necklaces to communicate. When Evan started treating me cruelly, his moods swinging widely out of control, Kieran took the necklace from me for safekeeping. He worried that Evan would be able to hurt me through it.

"He does," I answered before Kieran could defend himself. "I

2

didn't need it. Evan and I were able to talk without it."

I could practically see Dad processing what I told him. I wasn't sure how Evan did it, but the last time we spoke, my necklace was safely stored in Kieran's dresser. Evan reached me without it.

"Okay. What if he lied to you?" Dad asked. "What if he went with Ken willingly?"

"Never. He was being held against his will." He might have broken up with me, but I knew Evan would never betray me like that.

"Can you talk to him now?" Dad asked.

"No. I tried." I managed to keep the disappointment out of my voice. If I knew Evan was okay, maybe the ball of fear in my belly would disappear. Was it the same for him? Was he trying to reach me? How long had he tried the last time before I actually heard him? The questions flew through my mind. I felt guilty that while he was locked in a cell, I was dancing with Kieran at the farewell banquet for my uncle and his family. One of the happiest nights of my life might have been one of Evan's scariest—trapped and alone.

"What reason does Ken have for taking Evan?" Dad asked. "He was Evan's employer, right?"

Kieran spoke before I could. "Ken is the leader of the Blue Men, David."

"He's *what?*"

"Dad, Ted showed us his true form. He was one of the Blue Men, too."

Dad scrubbed his face with his hands, and then lowered them with a sigh. "I think I better sit down." Lost in thought, Dad collapsed into his chair. We stood watching him until he said, "Please join me. It makes me uncomfortable when you hover over me."

I sat on the couch. Kieran sat next to me and rested his arm along the top of the cushion, almost touching my head. His thigh brushed against mine. My dad raised an eyebrow, but he didn't say anything. Mentally, I willed Kieran to move over. I wasn't ready for a relationship with him. Not while I was a mess of nerves and guilt. If Kieran heard my thoughts, he didn't say anything. He didn't move either.

"What else did you learn?" Dad asked.

"Ted gave Meara a package from Evan."

With a question in his eyes, Dad focused on me. I shrugged. "Evan gave me back the necklace, and he wrote something on the napkin it was wrapped in." I pulled the napkin out of my pocket and handed it to him. "Does that mean anything to you?"

"Azuria." Dad read it aloud and frowned. "It sounds familiar, but I can't place it. I'll check the library tonight. See if I can't find a reference."

"Would you like me to join you?" Kieran asked, his tone respectful.

"That's not necessary." The edge was back in Dad's voice. "I'd like you to retire to your rooms and stay there." When I made a noise to protest, he added, "For the remainder of the evening. I'll call a meeting for the morning to determine our next steps."

"The Elders or can I participate too?" I couldn't keep the hopefulness out of my voice. I wanted more than anything for my dad to count me in. In the past, the Elders discussed things, and I got left out.

"You, too." He leaned over and ruffled my hair like I was a little kid, giving me a small smile. "I don't think I could keep you away if I wanted to, could I?"

"No."

"No, sir."

Kieran and I answered at the same time. Dad laughed and waved us out of his room. As soon as the door shut, I collapsed in Kieran's arms. He pulled me close and rested his chin on my head. The adrenaline fled my system, replaced by sheer exhaustion. I could barely stand.

"C'mon," he murmured, his warm breath rustling my hair. "Let's get you back to your room."

I wanted to protest and tell him I could get there on my own, but the truth was, I couldn't. Leaning into his side, I let him guide me with one firm arm around my waist. We moved at a snail's pace. If the dark shadows under his eyes were any indication, he was just as tired as I was.

When we finally reached my door, I invited Kieran in. I didn't want to be alone. What if Evan contacted me again? Last time, his voice dripped with revulsion. I didn't understand why. Did he hate me now? And if so, why did he leave me the necklace and message? His moods were hot and cold with no pattern or reasoning to them. Something was changing him. He told me as much himself when we shared that dream by the pool. His emotions were falling out of his control. Which left one question—who was controlling them?

Kieran pulled off his shirt and tossed it over a chair. He sat on the edge of the bed, taking off his socks and shoes.

"Don't try anything," I warned, forcing myself to look into his eyes. If I didn't, my gaze would be glued to his muscular, half-naked body. Maybe it wasn't such a good idea to invite him in.

"Meara, I'm just as tired as you." He pulled back the covers and climbed into my bed, patting the open space on the other side. "I promise that all I want right now is to sleep."

To prove his point, he lay on his side and closed his eyes. I took that moment to visualize my favorite pajama pants and matching tank top. The soft fabric settled against my skin, providing the right amount of coverage. I ran my fingers through my hair, detangling it, and then crawled into bed.

"Nice jammies." Kieran's hand snaked out and grabbed my waist. He pulled me back against his warm chest, fitting my body next to his. "There is one more thing I want to do," he whispered, his breath tickling my ear. My body tensed slightly while I waited. Tired as I was, if he tried something, I might not be able to resist him. He kissed my forehead. "Relax, Meara. I was only going to say 'hold you.' I just want to hold you. Is that okay?"

I relaxed. The heat from his body melted into my muscles, and his strong arm made me feel safe. "It's okay," I said. "'Night, Kieran."

He kissed my cheek, took a deep breath, and let it out in a contented sigh. "Good night, Meara."

I woke in the early light of morning, Kieran's arm still wrapped around my waist. His steady breathing told me he was asleep. The fortress was quiet, and I hadn't been dreaming. What woke me?

A throat cleared by the door, and I jumped. Kieran reacted to my movement, jerking back and smacking his head on the headboard. "Ow!"

"Good morning." My dad's cheerful tone sounded forced, his expression guarded. "I didn't realize you two were so close."

My face burned. Kieran and I had done nothing wrong, but I

could see my dad's mind working. "It's not what you think," I managed to stammer.

"I certainly hope not," Dad said calmly. "Kieran, would you please go to your own room now? I'd like to talk to my daughter alone."

Kieran sat up immediately. I thought he would just leave, but he leaned over and kissed my cheek, whispering. "I'll see you later."

I nodded, not saying anything. The accusations I saw in Dad's eyes were mortifying. How dare he criticize me when he got my mom pregnant at eighteen! Kieran and I slept together. That was it. *Sleeping.* Not that it was my dad's business anyway. I was eighteen—almost nineteen—which was considered past adulthood in both the human and Selkie worlds. My anger helped dissolve my embarrassment. I pushed myself back and sat upright, leaning against the headboard and awaiting the lecture.

Stepping into the room, my dad sat on the edge of my bed. Kieran gave me an apologetic look before he left, closing the door behind him.

Dad cleared his throat. "So, you and Kieran, huh?"

I dropped my face into my palms, wishing I could drop through the floor instead. "Really, Dad? We're having this conversation?"

He shrugged. "I just want to make sure you're using precautions."

"Nothing's happened between us," I gritted out between my teeth. "Not that it's any of your business, but trust me, if anything does happen, we'll be careful."

Dad was suddenly very interested in the wall on the opposite side of my room. He cleared his throat again, and then nodded. "Good enough."

I waited for him to say more. He obviously had a reason for coming to my room first thing in the morning. My fingers smoothed the blanket that pooled at my waist. Was he going to lecture me more about disobeying his orders? Would he try to punish me? I'd like to see him try. It would give me a chance to put him in his place. We were growing closer, but being in my life for one year did not make him the boss of me.

A gull cried somewhere outside my window. The noise jarred Dad from his reverie. "I came here for a reason."

"I hope so," I joked. He gave me a crooked smile, which I took as a positive sign. If he were going to lecture or punish me, he probably wouldn't look so relaxed.

"I searched the library last night. I didn't find anything on Azuria."

Disappointed, I could only nod. It had to mean something or Evan wouldn't have given the clue to me. *Azuria.* What did it mean?

"Your aunt and I are leaving tonight to search the Minch strait," Dad continued. "Angus will be in charge while we're gone."

I was glad that Dad was taking Aunt Brigid with him. I may not be as close to her as I was with Ula, my other aunt, but I knew Brigid was a fierce fighter. She was the one I would pick to guard my back. Still, they were heading into the heart of the Blue Men's territory. "Have you been there before?"

"No," he said. I caught the worried expression on his face before he turned and looked out the window. "I have no idea what we'll encounter there. We're taking a small team with us."

"Who?" The Selkie scouts who found us at Ken's house seemed competent enough. They were armed with knives and spears. Until I saw their weapons, I hadn't realized that my dad had an army on this island.

"A few of my men, so there will be fewer guards here. You and Kieran will need to help Angus."

"Of course," I said, wondering how many guards my dad had on the island. "Are many of the Selkies trained for battle?"

"About a dozen," Dad said. "I've trained the men who show aptitude. We are a peaceful civilization, Meara. I don't like to focus on war and weaponry."

"I get it, Dad." I moved to stand by him at the window. Outside, people ran and played on the mossy, green grounds. The islanders were getting restless. Per my father's decree, Selkies were not allowed in the water. My entire body ached to change into my seal form and swim, but his ruling had not been lifted. The dangers were too real. While we had a face for our enemy now, we still didn't know where Ken was or what the Blue Men were plotting.

"You can't shelter our people forever," I said. "Not when the Blue Men and others want to harm us. Wouldn't it be best if all of our clan were trained?"

"You'd have women and children fight?" Dad gestured to the

7

families below, roaming the grounds and playing near the shore.

I narrowed my eyes, touching his arm until he looked at me. "I know how to fight. Aunt Brigid fights. How is this different?" I gestured at the families below. "They should know how to defend themselves. Without that ability, they're helpless. A handful of trained Selkies cannot protect an island full of ignorant ones."

"It has worked in the past," he gritted out through clenched teeth.

"Has it?" I asked. "My understanding is that last time you had to retreat."

"Meara!" His voice was sharp with admonishment.

"What? It's true." I refused to apologize. "If you let us, Kieran and I will train them while you're gone."

Dad crossed his arms and stared at me. Finally, he said, "We don't have enough weapons."

"Then I'll conjure them, or make them, or both." When his stubborn expression didn't change, I poked him lightly in the chest. "Lack of weapons is a poor excuse, and you know it. Our bodies are weapons. Knowledge is a weapon."

While I waited for his decision, I rested my forearms on the windowsill. The stone felt cool against my skin. The triplets played a game below. It looked like tag. Their mom stood nearby, talking with another woman. There were so many innocent lives at stake here. My father had to see things my way.

It didn't take him long to decide. "Very well," he said. "I will give you and Kieran the time we are gone to begin your training. You may recruit as many Selkies as you can, but no one will be forced to train who doesn't want to. Understood?"

"Of course," I murmured. My hope was that every Selkie would want to train. Time would tell if that was true or not.

"When we return, I expect a full report and a demonstration of what you have accomplished."

I wrapped my arms around him and squeezed, excited that he was willing to give me a chance. This was my opportunity to prove that I wasn't a little girl, I wasn't helpless, and I was capable of helping others.

He hugged me back before holding me at arm's length. His eyes blazed with pride. "I have faith in you."

"I won't disappoint you," I said.

"I expect you won't." He raised an eyebrow. "I do need one promise from you in exchange."

My stomach sank. *Please don't bring up Kieran,* I thought. I really didn't want to have another awkward talk about my love life.

"I want you to promise that you won't leave the island." He lifted my chin with his hand and stared into my eyes. I wanted to squirm, but I held still. "I mean it. I don't want to worry about you while I'm away on a dangerous mission."

"I won't leave. I promise." I reached up and wrapped my hand around his wrist. "Now you promise me."

"What?" He looked surprised.

"That you'll be careful," I said. "I lost Mom. I don't want to lose you, too."

"Is that all?" He pulled me into his arms again. It felt nice to be held by my father. Once again, I wondered what things would've been like if he'd been in my life all along. Considering I only met him a little over a year ago, we'd already come a long way in our relationship. I loved him and wished I saw more of him. He kissed my forehead. "I'll be careful, Meara. I promise."

Chapter 2

*B*rilliant jeweled colors greeted Evan's tired eyes. The room itself was nondescript, but reds, blues, greens, and yellows highlighted every surface, turning everything to stained glass.

Where am I? Evan thought.

"Finally awake, are you?"

Evan found himself staring into pale green eyes. Eyes that looked vaguely familiar. Long, greenish blond hair floated in his face and tickled his nose. Evan brushed it aside before shifting to sit up on the bed. She quickly moved out of his way and into the shadows.

As his muddy thoughts cleared, details sharpened. The room rippled, not with air, but with water. He was in his blue form, breathing underwater as though he were on land. His chest felt funny, like a bubble of air was contained inside. Other than that and a mild headache, he couldn't complain. Although it would've been nice if Ken hadn't drugged him to bring him here. Wherever here was.

Ken. Evan couldn't think of him as his father, even if biologically it was true. His parents were Darren and Lydia Mitchell, the loving couple who raised him, who didn't even know that he wasn't Darren's son. And... crap! Who were going to be worried sick about him.

"How long have I been out?" His eyes searched the room for the girl. She had to still be here, right? The blinding colors disoriented him. A shadow moved in the corner, but he couldn't make out any details.

"A half days' time."

Damn it! The plane would be arriving in Nova Scotia today without him. No doubt, his parents and Katie were at the airport, waiting to greet him and take him home. What would they think when he didn't walk through the gate? How panicked would they be as they waited, the crowd trickling to one or two individuals, until no more came. Until they realized he was missing. His heart went out to them. He wished he could tell them he was okay. At least for the time being, it appeared no harm had come to him.

The girl continued talking, her voice soft and friendly, "I offered to look after you until you awoke."

Evan squinted in the direction of her voice. It didn't help. He wished she'd move closer so he could see her. Something was nagging at his memory. She seemed so familiar. "Do I know you?"

She came into view, her long hair floating around her pale face. The light mint shade of her hair almost matched her eyes. His gaze moved from her beautiful face down her body, and he jumped. Her waist melded into a tail.

"You're a mermaid?" he asked.

"I prefer Siren." She swished her tail and pouted. "Don't you remember me?" She swam closer, running one finger along his cheek as her eyes searched his. "Not even a little?"

The memory sharpened. Weeks ago, Ken took him to that rundown bar for lunch. What was the name again? The Hideout? No, The Shack. It looked like a rundown shack on the outside, dirty and neglected. The inside was a different story of tasty food and even more delicious entertainment. The girls who waited on the tables and performed there were hypnotically beautiful. One in particular caught his eye. Their waitress. "Deanna?"

Her face lit with pleasure. "You do remember me! I knew you would." She lowered herself next to him on the bed, her tail lightly tapping his leg as she wound her hands around his arm and rested her head on his shoulder. Evan didn't think they formed any kind of relationship that night, but she was being extremely friendly. Friendlier than most people were when they met someone new, even if they had met once before.

Deanna squeezed his arm. "I like you. You're different than most of the others."

"Other Blue Men?" He felt her nod, but she didn't say anything. "Are they all here?"

"Most are here," she whispered. "Some are still in Azuria."

"Azuria!" He recalled reading Ken's mind and hearing that name as Ken told the story of how their queen, or Mother, died. Figuring the queen's name was important if Ken didn't say it aloud, Evan left it as a clue for Meara. Hopefully, she figured it out by now. It was vague, but he didn't have enough time to write anything else. Now Deanna was telling him it was the name of a place. Did he misunderstand? "I thought that was the name of the queen."

Deanna's eyes widened, and she covered his mouth with her hand. "Shhh... you do not want others to hear you. Azuria was the queen's name." Deanna's eyes darted back and forth as though she was confirming they were alone. "Azuria is also the name of their home." She lowered her head, and her voice dropped. "Azuria is everything to them."

"I got that impression from Ken. He hates the Selkies because he thinks one killed her. Is that true?"

Deanna bit her lip and studied him. He watched the emotional struggle on her face. She wanted to tell him, but she was afraid.

"If you can't say..." Evan started.

"I don't know," Deanna admitted. "But some of the Blue Men disagree with Ken."

"I don't understand."

Her eyes grew into two pale green circles. "Please. I've already said more than I should."

Evan felt bad for the poor, scared girl. Funny that he could feel sorry for her when he was the one held prisoner. *Wait.* He was still a prisoner, right?

"Where am I?" he asked.

"My home, Belle Trésor." A wide smile broke across her face and melted the fear. "I live here with my sisters. Of course, now the Blue Men live here, too."

A couple of years of French class in high school paid off enough for Evan to know the name of this place roughly translated to Beautiful Treasure. He shrugged. It made sense, given the stained glass look of everything.

"We're underwater." Evan winced. He hated stating the obvious.

"But where?"

"Off the coast of France." She shivered delicately. "Scotland is too cold for Sirens."

"But you work in Scotland."

Deanna's gaze turned fearful again. "Only when Ken orders us to perform. We'd rather be home." She pushed herself off the bed and swam to the corner of the room where Evan lost her in the colored swirls.

"Are you hungry?" she called. Not waiting for his answer, she brought him a tray laden with food. Rather than the bowls and plates used on land, mesh tents held the food in place. It appeared to be fruits and cheeses. The colors and shapes were different from anything Evan had seen. He eyed it carefully, which made Deanna laugh. "Go ahead and eat. It won't bite you."

"I've never eaten underwater," Evan admitted. "I'm not sure how."

Deanna's expression softened. "It's no different from eating on land. Take a bite. You'll see. It's perfectly safe, I promise you." She reached through an opening in one of the coverings and picked up a small, yellow object. It was about the size of a grape. She popped it in her mouth. Evan watched her chew and swallow. She nodded in encouragement. "See? Easy!"

He picked one that looked the same and tried it. The flavor exploded in his mouth, first tart, and then sweet. "Delicious. What is it?"

"Xi fruit. We grow everything in our garden. The flavors are different from fruits and vegetables on land, but just as good."

"Maybe better," Evan said. He ate another xi, and then tried something that resembled cheese. It was creamy and tangy, reminding him of goat cheese. He didn't ask what animal it came from. He was content to finish the food and quiet his rumbling stomach. Eyes full of merriment, Deanna watched him while he ate. When he picked up the last xi, she took the tray.

"I need to leave for a while." Before Evan could protest, she placed a hand on his arm. "Rest now. You've been through a lot. When you wake, I'll give you a tour." Her face was open and friendly, and Evan noticed how pretty she was. Without the heavy makeup she wore at the bar, she looked much younger. "I'll be back soon."

One swish of her tail, and he was alone in the room. Blinking back sleep, he stood and stretched. He would rest, but first he wanted to see where he was and if he could leave the room. It took little time to explore the room itself, which held a bed, a dresser, and two doors. The door near the dresser was a small water closet with a sink, mirror, and a few unrecognizable fixtures. Briefly, he wondered how underwater plumbing worked, and then decided he probably didn't really want to know. He'd find out soon enough when the need arose. He glanced across the room to the other door. It must lead outside. The room had no windows. What would he find when he opened that door? Was anyone guarding him from escaping?

The door was unlocked and glided smoothly underwater, making no noise. He looked down, jumping back in surprise. His room didn't open into a hallway. There was no floor in front of his door. It dropped off into an enormous cavern. Another building stood across the courtyard. The holes in its tall sides made it look like Swiss cheese. Each hole must be a room. The walls glittered with jewels and sea glass. In some areas, the stones were placed in a mosaic to create scenes—Sirens speaking to dolphins and sea horses, Sirens singing with abandon, Sirens wrapped in the arms of human males—the pictures were bright and detailed. In other areas, the stones were set in no apparent pattern, so their individual beauty stood out against the dark backdrop.

No one swam outside his room or seemed to notice him at all. Blue Men and Sirens went about their business in the cavern below. The Blue Men's rich blue skin contrasted with the muted pastels of the Sirens. Several were pale green like Deanna, but even from this distance, Evan knew none of them was her.

He wanted to explore the Siren dwelling, but his limbs felt heavy. His eyelids drooped. Deanna promised she'd be back later to take him on a tour. If he left now, he might not find his room again. He shut the door and went back to the bed. Lying down, he closed his eyes. He tried to picture Meara. Instead, he saw a girl with pale, celery-green hair.

Chapter 3

I peeked into Ula's room. She was my closest friend here, and also my aunt and confidant. I had so much to tell her. I felt bad about abandoning her at the farewell celebration for Uncle Ren. I couldn't tell her about the plan for Kieran and I to rescue Evan—the more people that knew, the greater the chance that my dad might have found out and stopped us.

At the moment, she seemed to be in a good mood, listening to music and reading a dog-eared Nancy Drew book. Then again, she hadn't realized that I was there yet. I rapped loudly on her door, and she pulled her earbuds out.

"Want to get some fresh air?" I asked.

Her green eyes narrowed in irritation. "Where have you been? You bailed on me the other night."

"I'm sorry." The apology was heartfelt. It was a crappy thing to do. I was so mad at her the first time she left me at an event, and here I did the same thing to her. To be fair, it wasn't as if we were hanging out. She spent the evening with Uncle Ren and his family saying goodbye, so it wasn't like she was alone. I cleared my throat. "I have a good reason."

"I know." Her expression softened. "Evan. Did you find him?"

"No. Ken kidnapped him. They were already gone when we got there."

Ula frowned. "Isn't he the guy who financed Evan's internship?"

"Yes," I said.

"I don't understand."

"I don't either, but I'll tell you what I know." I bit my lip, my thoughts still on my little cousin, Nico, and my uncle and aunt. "Uncle

Ren...they made it home okay? Do we know?"

"They're fine," Ula said. She didn't seem worried at all.

"How can you be sure?" I persisted. It wasn't as though Selkies had phones or even email.

"You know my parents' necklaces and how they work?" she asked. I nodded. "Ren has a similar communication with David. A silver chain they wear on their wrists. Have you seen it?"

"Yeah, I guess." I vaguely remembered seeing a flash of silver at my dad's wrist. It almost looked like a watchband.

"All of us have one. They were gifts from our parents, although Brigid, Paddy, and I don't wear ours since we live here. David keeps his on to communicate with Ren, and our other brothers, Murdo and William."

Murdo. William. I repeated the names silently to myself. It was the first time I heard of them. Two more uncles I hadn't even met yet. I forgot that my dad once told me there were seven children in his family. It was difficult to believe I went from my mom being my only family to this large Selkie family. What would Mom have thought? I guessed she would've liked them. I blinked my eyes and forced myself to focus on something else. Thinking about Mom always made me cry. My uncles... where did they live? Did they rule clans like my dad? Did they have wives or kids? I could ask Ula, but that would sidetrack us into a long conversation about family. There would be time to talk about that later. Right now, I needed to update her on what we learned at Ken's house. I took Ula's book and marked her spot. After setting it on the shelf, I offered my hand to pull her up. "C'mon, it's gorgeous outside. Let's go for a walk."

"Okay." She smiled and grasped my hand. The next thing I knew, we were standing on the shoreline and Ula was beaming at me.

"You're really getting good at transporting," I said. While she grinned, something nagged at the back of my mind. "Ula, why is our family the only one in our clan with powers?"

"I don't know. It's always been that way." She gave me a curious look. "Why?"

"You've been practicing transporting, and your abilities have grown stronger." I paced, thinking about what I wanted to say next.

"Why couldn't we try to teach the others? Maybe they can do magic, and they just don't know how."

She bit her lip, mulling it over. Finally, she consented. "It's very possible, although David may not agree."

"Why not?" I asked. "He's already agreed to let Kieran and I train the clan on weapons and combat."

Her eyes widened. "He has?"

"We're holding a meeting tomorrow. He made me promise not to force anyone, but those who want to be trained, will be."

"I didn't know about it. Why didn't you tell me?" Ula frowned slightly. I didn't mean for her to feel excluded or unwanted. "Can I participate?"

I wrapped my arm around her shoulder and squeezed. "I just told you. Besides, you don't even have to ask. Of course you can participate."

We walked along the shore. The nearness of the water soothed and irritated me at the same time. I could taste the brine. That small sip made me want more. I longed for the freedom of the waves. My dad and aunt left this morning for the strait. With any luck, they'd find Ken, rescue Evan, and put an end to this. I couldn't live my life in fear, and worrying about Evan was giving me an ulcer.

"Will you?" Ula asked.

"Will I what?"

"Will you teach them magic?"

"I'd like to try." The ability to change forms, the most basic of Selkie magic, was in and of itself wonderful. Yet, the other magic I could perform was amazing—influencing the weather, conjuring items, transporting from one location to another, blocking others from entering my mind, and reading other people's minds if I focused hard enough. I had more abilities than most of my clan. On the other hand, the average Selkie could only change form. If I could help them bring out even a little magic, it would improve their lives and improve Ronac. The island and fortress would be better protected if everyone could defend it and not just Dad's guard. Ula seemed worried though, and I wondered why. "What's the harm in teaching them?"

"If you give them power, they may try to overthrow your dad."

"Nonsense." I paused in my pacing and faced her. "You don't

really believe that, do you?"

"No," she answered quickly. "My brother is a fair ruler. There is no reason to overthrow him."

"Exactly." My initial thoughts were of Arren and the other teen Selkies. They were harmless as puppies. I could teach them to fight and protect themselves. It wouldn't hurt to explain about human life, too. Their ignorance made me wince. Which reminded me... "How was the concert?"

I missed the first concert that Arren and his band held at the last Selkie celebration. Given the costumes they were wearing, I could only imagine the probable mashup of songs from Madonna and the Beastie Boys. Not pretty. I wasn't sorry that I missed it, although it might've been entertaining.

Ula shuddered. "As bad as you thought it was going to be. I told you my ears bled the first time I heard them. This wasn't any better. Thanks again for leaving me there."

"Sorry, Ula." I ruined my apology by laughing. The teenage Selkies really had no clue about humans. If I educated them on humanity while teaching defense, we might not have to hide so much. We could blend and, therefore, interact. We certainly wouldn't be just sitting here, waiting for someone or something to attack.

"Meara?" Ula's hand on my arm brought me back to the present. "You were going to tell me something. Was that it? Teaching Selkies magic?"

"You know I went to rescue Evan." When she nodded, I said, "Kieran came with me." Her eyes narrowed, but she didn't interrupt. "We went to the house, but it was too late. They left in a hurry, but everyone was gone. All, except one."

"Who?"

"Evan's professor, Ted Nolan. He was beaten and locked in a cell."

Ula's hands covered her mouth. "Is he okay?"

I shook my head. "He's dead. He died in front of us."

Ula gasped and squeezed my arm. "No! How awful!"

"It was. He looked horrible." Clearing my throat, I added, "He was one of the Blue Men, Ula. He changed before he died to show us."

"What?" Her reaction reminded me of my dad's. She paled in

18

shock and swayed on her feet. "How is that even possible? They can take human form?"

"Clearly, they can," I said. "Ted is the one who told us that Ken has Evan. Ted also said Ken is the leader of the Blue Men."

"Oh, Meara." Ula stopped walking and turned to face me. She searched my face, her eyes full of sympathy. "What are you going to do?"

I shrugged. "What can I do? Dad and Brigid are in the Minch right now. I promised him I wouldn't leave the island. I'm going to do the only thing I can."

"Which is…?" She raised one eyebrow and waited.

"Train the hell out of everyone and build an army." My resolve was set. I would arm our people for success. "The Blue Men won't know what hit them."

Chapter 4

"You're here."

Deanna sounded surprised. Evan sat up and rubbed the sleep from his eyes. He couldn't remember the last time he took such a long nap, well, one that wasn't induced by someone drugging him. He felt refreshed. Giving her a wry smile, he asked, "Can I leave? And if I could, where would I go? It's not like I know my way around the ocean." He glanced down at his blue arms. "And I certainly won't be accepted on land, looking like this."

She ignored his questions and asked, "Are you hungry again?"

"I could eat."

"Good." The tense expression left her face, and she held the door open. "Let's go get some food."

They swam toward the ocean floor. Evan was surprised at how easy it was to swim as one of the Blue Men. Although his form was still humanoid, the longer limbs and clawed hands cut through the water with ease. He had no trouble keeping pace with Deanna. The only time he came up short was out of surprise when they approached the entrance to a large cave. The brightly lit interior showed it was full of activity. To Evan's amusement, it looked like an underwater cafeteria, complete with trays, buckets of silverware, and bins of various foods.

"You can pick what you want to eat." Deanna handed Evan a tray before taking one for herself. "Ask me if you want to know what anything is." She wrinkled her nose slightly in a way Evan found cute. "It's all mostly okay tasting. I tend to stick to the fruits and vegetables."

Evan gestured to the line in front of them. "By all means, lead the way then. I'll mimic what you do."

Deanna seemed startled at first, but she quickly recovered. As they moved through the line, she explained the oddly shaped and colored items to him. He saw the xi fruit he tried earlier. A green, prickly bulb with bright purple flesh looked interesting. He pointed to it and raised an eyebrow.

"Rylotta." Deanna took one and placed it on her plate. "They're yummy when they're ripe and bitter if they're not. These look good."

Evan took one, avoiding the long, needle-like spikes. Opening it would be an adventure. He'd watch Deanna eat hers first.

The next section was fish and shellfish. Most were raw and reminded him of sashimi. He took several pieces before nodding to Deanna that he was ready to go. She led them to a table in the back corner. As they passed other Sirens and Blue Men, a few gave them curious glances. No one stopped to talk or introduce themselves. Evan didn't mind. He wasn't feeling very sociable, especially since no one looked particularly friendly.

He wanted to ask Deanna more about his circumstances. Was he still a prisoner? She didn't answer him earlier, although she did say she was surprised to find him in his room. Did that mean he could've left if he wanted to?

Something told him not to ask her here. He let her carry the dinner conversation, which led to numerous questions about life on land, high school, college, and hockey. Hockey was an easy subject, and he enjoyed explaining the game to her. Deanna was fascinated by the idea of a sport played on ice with sticks and a puck. Every time he tried to breeze over a rule or position in the game, she would stop him to ask for clarification. It surprised him how much he liked talking to her. He was pleased by her interest in hockey, too, especially since he loved it. Meara came to several of his games last year, but he got the impression she only tolerated the sport.

When the food was gone, they took their trays to the front of the cave. He couldn't shake the cafeteria vibe. It made him want to laugh, but he didn't want to offend Deanna. Instead, he asked, "Do you always eat here?"

"A few times a week," she said. "Why? Do you prefer to hunt?"

"I prefer McDonald's," he answered and laughed.

She looked at him quizzically. "Who's Mac Donald?"

"McDonald's is a fast food restaurant. You know, hamburgers, fries…" He tapered off when he realized she had no clue what he was saying. "Don't you ever go anywhere else on land besides that club?"

"Not many places." She tilted her head and studied him, her pale green hair floating in a halo around her head. Although it partially hid her expression, he could see she looked uncomfortable again. He wished he knew what topics were taboo.

Never mind, he thought, *better to just drop it and move on.* "What do you do here?"

"What do you mean?" Her voice sounded guarded.

"Do you have hobbies or interests?" He looked back into the cavern, which was now half empty. "When everybody finishes eating, what do they do?"

"Whatever they want." Her eyebrows drew together in confusion. "Do you want to see the rest of the city now?"

Evan gave up. She didn't understand what he was asking. He wondered how many of the Sirens or Blue Men had never even been on land. Did they all have limited exposure to humans? He shouldn't criticize. He had no experience with sea life. He was just as naïve about ocean creatures as Deanna was about land. With any luck, her tour of their settlement would clue him into the underwater lifestyle. Deanna cleared her throat, and he realized she was waiting for an answer.

"Sure," he said. "I'd love to see the city."

Her smile lit her face. *She's really pretty*, Evan thought before he could help himself. With a shake of his head, he followed her out of the cavern.

His thoughts soon shifted to the world around him. They were deep enough that the water didn't transition from day to night. The sun was too far away. The citizens of Belle Trésor marked the passage from day to night in their own way. The beautiful reds, golds, and oranges of the day changed to blues, purples, and greens at night. It couldn't be a natural occurrence, but their magic was beautiful. From warm to cool, the treasure box that was their home alternated rubies with sapphires. The effect was stunning. It was more beautiful than stained glass in a cathedral because the movement in the water made it come alive.

While scuba diving last summer, Evan wondered what it would feel like to swim unencumbered by heavy diving equipment. He envied Meara's ability to transform into a seal. Now he knew firsthand what if felt like to be a creature of the sea. It was glorious. He would trade television, movies, his car, well, almost anything, for this feeling of freedom. No gravity holding him back, no fear of drowning.

"Evan?" Deanna treaded nearby, wearing a curious expression. "Are you okay?"

"I'm great. Sorry, just lost in my own thoughts."

"No problem. I asked if you want to enter The Chamber." She pointed to a large, glass dome behind her. The smoked glass made it impossible to see in, but it looked like a greenhouse. It was embarrassing that he was daydreaming so deeply that he hadn't noticed the huge structure.

"What is it?"

"It's dry inside. Um..." She bit her lip as she struggled for the words to explain. "I suppose you would say it's the closest we get to living like humans. We grow some food in there. We also have a library, a bowling alley—"

Intrigued, Evan interrupted. "You have a bowling alley?" The thought made him grin. Of all the human things they could do, bowling was a preferred sport for merpeople. Who knew?

"Y-yes." She chewed her bottom lip. Did he make her nervous? Glancing down at the sea floor, her cheeks turned a pretty pink. "You think this is stupid, don't you?"

"What?" He was shocked that she would think that. Moving closer, he placed his hand on her arm. "No, not at all. I'm surprised that Sirens bowl, but I would never say it's stupid. I definitely wouldn't call *you* stupid."

She raised her head. The look she gave him had his heart speeding up. "Do you want to then?" she asked.

Evan couldn't take his eyes away from her mouth. "What?"

She caught his eye, her lips curling up in a slow smile. Clearly, she realized the effect she had on him as she clarified, "Do you want to go inside?"

A quick toss of his head cleared his addled brain. What was the matter with him? He gestured to the dome and said, "Lead the way."

She pointed to a tall door. "We need to enter one at a time. You can go first. It's a drying chamber. I'll meet you on the other side."

Instinctively, he trusted her. He opened the door and swam into the chamber. As soon as the door closed behind him, the water level lowered in the room until he was standing on a wet stone floor. The air grew hot and, within minutes, his hair and clothes were dry. One glance told him that he hadn't changed back to human form. Thankfully, Blue Men had legs and not a tail, so it was more or less irrelevant. He missed being human, though. In this state, he felt like the not-so-jolly blue giant. Big and clunky, especially on dry land.

Stepping through the unlocked inner door, Evan found himself in a wide hallway. The hall was empty, the lighting dim. Music played softly, the instrumental kind heard in elevators and doctor offices.

A moment later, the door squeaked and Deanna came through. She wore fitted blue jeans and a pale pink tank top. Her long hair hung down her back in a braid.

"You changed form." Once again, Evan berated himself for being king of the obvious, but Deanna didn't seem to mind.

She frowned at him and bit her lip. "You couldn't change, could you?"

"No."

With a look of sympathy, she leaned close and whispered. "I was worried about that. Ken did something to you, trapping you in this form."

"So, I can't leave." The dismay was clear in his voice.

"So you can't leave," she repeated.

"I'm a prisoner after all," Evan murmured. How long was Ken planning to keep him? Would he be stuck here forever?

"You're not in a cage," Deanna pointed out. "And Belle Trésor is quite large. You shouldn't get bored."

"It's not that. I want to go home and see my family." His mom was probably frantic with worry. By now, she would have called the police and search parties would be looking for him. It wouldn't do any good. They'd never think to look underwater.

"I'm sorry, Evan." Deanna gently took his arm, her eyes darting from shadow to shadow. "This is not the best place to talk. Perhaps back at your room later?"

Ignoring the sparks that flew when she touched him, Evan let Deanna lead him down the hall.

Chapter 5

A cavern full of Selkies stared at me, expectant expressions on their faces. My people. From the sheer number present, I guessed almost everyone had come to hear what we had to say. It was hard to believe that I stood in this same spot three months ago, frozen in fear, preparing to meet everyone for the first time. Today I felt confident, although I did worry about their reactions to our proposal.

"Do you want to speak or should I?" Kieran's voice was low enough that only I heard him. Apparently, he mistook my hesitation for fear. I wasn't afraid.

"I've got it." I gave him a small smile.

The murmurs of those gathered in the cave grew to a thunderous roar. I spoke loudly, my voice carrying across the large space. "Thank you for coming. I'm sure you're wondering why we called you here."

The silence that followed was encouraging. All eyes were on me again. Many of the Selkies wore bemused expressions. Some looked curious, others worried. No one seemed annoyed or angry. That was a good sign.

Clearing my throat, I continued, "At the beginning of summer, two members of our clan were found dead. We now have reason to believe they were murdered."

A collective gasp traveled through the room. One deep voice called out, "What makes you say that?" The question echoed as others speculated.

"The Blue Men of Minch," Kieran announced, effectively silencing the murmurs. He paused for impact, and then added, "Meara and I met one, and he warned us."

"And you can trust him?" Someone in the back shouted.

"He was dying," I answered. "And angry at being betrayed by his brothers. He had no reason to lie to us."

"Why are you telling us this?"

This came from Arren, one of the adolescents. He was near the front, fear as plain on his face as it was in his voice. His pale innocence made him look younger than me. I knew he was much older in years.

"We can no longer count on a few to protect the many." I said these same words to my father days earlier. "Kieran and I are here to make you an offer." I paused and looked at Kieran. He nodded in encouragement. This was my show, and he was letting me run it.

A sweeping glance told me that I had the attention of every Selkie there. My family stood in the back—Uncle Angus, Ula, and Paddy. They would intervene if necessary, but there was no need. No one spoke. All eyes were trained on the platform where Kieran and I stood.

"We will teach you to fight, to protect Ronac and yourselves. This is voluntary. No one will be forced to participate, although I strongly encourage you to consider it. By show of hands, who is interested?"

For a moment, I held my breath. No one responded. Then, Arren's hand shot in the air.

"Aye," he said. "I am."

Several more followed his lead. I watched in amazement as hands continued to rise. The only ones who didn't volunteer were elderly, young children, and a few mothers.

"When will we begin?" Ula asked. From across the cavern, I could see her huge grin. Her enthusiasm was encouraging.

I turned to Kieran. He crossed his arms and waited, leaving the decision to me. We both faced Ula, and I said, "Now. We'll begin now."

Kieran and I had planned the first session ahead of time. We decided to start with a demonstration. As we climbed down the steps to the main floor, Kieran said, "Anyone not participating may stay and watch this demonstration, if you wish. Otherwise, you are free to leave."

A handful of individuals left. We arranged the remaining crowd in a wide circle, giving us most of the floor to move about. When the space was set to our satisfaction, we faced each other in the center.

"You ready?" he asked with a cocky grin.

I met his gaze with what I hoped was fierce calm and a wicked smile. "Always."

As we sparred, the crowd faded out of my awareness. The occasional gasp or murmur was just background noise. I needed to concentrate. Kieran immediately attacked and placed me on the defense. It didn't last long. I overtook him by adding magic to my moves, throwing energy balls that distracted him. Eventually, I took hold of his arms and flipped him down, placing my knee on his chest and conjuring my knife. I pressed the blade against his throat and smiled slowly. "Do you surrender?"

"Always." He purposely echoed my response from earlier.

I shifted my weight and stood, offering him my hand. "We'll see about that." When the Selkies realized that our battle was over, the room erupted in applause and wolf whistles. We bowed to the crowd.

"Thank you," I said. "That was just a sample of what you might achieve if you listen well and work hard."

"Pair off," Kieran ordered. "Let's start with some basic blocks."

The crowd divided into groups of two. Kieran turned to me once again. "Meara will demonstrate the blocks. Watch her." He spoke to the room, but his eyes never left my face.

On the count of three. His voice slid through my mind, as comfortable now as my own. *One. Two. Three.*

"Inside block."

Striking out with my arm, I hit his forearm and blocked his punch with ease.

"Outside block."

I swept my arm out and knocked his hand down, stopping his next attack.

"High block."

Clenching his hand into a fist, he hammered it down toward my head. My fist flew up and knocked his arm away.

"Low block."

His roundhouse kick aimed at my stomach. I swept my arm down in an arc, hit his ankle, and stopped him before he got too close. We were both breathing heavily when we bowed to the crowd. Once again, our demonstration was met with applause.

Let's show the blocks in slow motion, I suggested.

Kieran gave me a slight nod. *I'll face east, and you take west.*

We repeated the blocks one at a time, and then Kieran said, "Now practice with your partner, and please be careful. We don't want to carry anyone out of here."

The pairs began to practice. It was a sight to behold. Most were clumsy, unsure, and weak. Kieran took half the room and I took the other, helping people move into position, demonstrating the full block, and correcting missteps. After an hour, I was exhausted. Thirty minutes later, it was time to call it quits. I managed to drum up a little enthusiasm, although inwardly, I cringed at how much work we needed to do. "Great work, everyone. We'll practice like this every day. Meet back here tomorrow at the same time."

"Before you leave," Kieran added. "We expect you to practice outside of our sessions. You should also train for strength and endurance—sit-ups, push-ups, running. In battle, you'll be happy you did."

A few groans ensued, but the clapping drowned them out. I smiled at my people. They were tired. It was clear in the way they held themselves as they exited the cavern. Not being able to change and swim took its toll on everyone. Still, they showed up today, they tried, and they would get better. Training would give them focus and purpose. I couldn't ask for more.

"What do you think?" I asked Kieran after the last two left the cavern.

He ran a towel over his face and hair. Dropping it over his shoulder, he paused in thought. "I think," he said finally, "we have our work cut out for us."

Chapter 6

aughing, Evan and Deanna headed back to his room. The evening had been fun. The laughter died on their lips when they opened the door and saw the leader of the Blue Men perched on Evan's bed.

"Did you have a nice time this evening?" Ken smiled, addressing them both. While he seemed nice enough, Evan knew from experience not to trust him. Ken's real mood could be pleasant or foul. Only time would tell.

Deanna remained in the doorway, a slight frown on her face. Her eyes flicked between the two men. It was clear she wanted to escape.

"Deanna, darling, you were due at the club an hour ago," Ken said. "You're quite late, and you know how I feel about lateness."

Her beautiful skin turned a sickly shade of gray as she shook her head vehemently. "I wasn't scheduled to work this evening."

"The schedule changed and now you are." Ken's expression turned dark. When she hesitated, he snapped, "Go!"

She turned and left without another word. Ken watched her leave, a trace of a smile on his face. "Beautiful girl, but flighty. I wouldn't get too serious with her if I were you." He patted the space next to him on the bed. "Sit, son. I want to talk to you."

"I gathered as much," Evan muttered. There was no other reason why Ken would be in his room, unless he was planning to drug him again or lock him up somewhere. It irritated him that Ken had the gall to call Evan 'son' while treating him like a criminal. And yet, Evan dutifully sat next to the man who was a father to him in only one way—genetics.

"How do you like it here?"

"Really?" Evan asked. "That's what you want to talk to me about?"

"It's a valid question." Ken cocked his head and frowned. "Unless you prefer we skip the niceties."

"I'd prefer it." He knew Ken didn't care if Evan loved it here or not.

"Excellent." Ken bared his sharp and pointy teeth. "As you know, you cannot leave. You're trapped in this form."

"I figured as much when Deanna grew legs in the dry dome, and I stayed the same."

"Yes, well," Ken continued, businesslike. "I can't have you alerting your dear girlfriend, Meara."

The way Meara's name slid off Ken's evil lips made Evan tremble with rage. He saw no reason to correct Ken or encourage him to continue talking about her. They weren't dating, but he still felt protective of her. He had been a complete jerk to her this past summer. She knew it, and so did he. Then he made it final by breaking up with her. When they were apart, he loved her. When they were together, hatred overrode his love. He didn't understand it, but he guessed it had something to do with Ken. If Evan managed to escape, maybe they could get back together. Unless that Kieran guy had stepped in and manned up where Evan failed.

Sighing, he ran a hand through his hair. He couldn't do anything about it now. He was trapped under the sea. Ariel had it right. Life was definitely not better where it was wetter. He wanted Ken to leave him alone, but the infuriating man was waiting for Evan's response.

"What do you want with me anyway?" Evan hated the defeat in his voice.

"You're my son," Ken said. "Do I have to want something?"

The son that you trapped here, Evan thought. He didn't say that. Or anything. His eyes were growing heavy. *Make your point and leave*, he silently willed his father.

A sharp laugh burst from Ken, making Evan jump. The man was insane, no question about it. His moods changed with the tides. "It turns out I do want something." He made it sound like the two of them were in on a big joke. Evan wasn't laughing. "Starting tomorrow, we return to the fault and work on finishing what we started."

The mantle plume research—Evan thought their work was done.

He didn't understand Ken's fascination with the fault line. Did it have something to do with being Blue Men of the Minch? Professor Nolan probably knew what made the project significant, but he never told Evan. At least Ken didn't know that Ted spoke to Evan in the basement. Remembering how broken his professor was, there was a good chance that Ted Nolan was dead. Evan wanted to hear what Ken would say about it. "Will Professor Nolan be joining us?"

Shrugging, Ken seemed unconcerned. "Ted's services are no longer needed. I paid him handsomely. He's probably back at that stuffy university, caring for his aquariums."

Ken's blasé response confirmed Evan's suspicions. Ted was either dead or dying. There was no way he was back at King's College. In the beaten condition Evan last saw Ted Nolan, he wouldn't have survived the flight. Ken knew that damn well. Evan had no use for lies. He wanted the man out of his room so he could get some sleep. One last question lingered on Evan's mind. "What exactly is the work we're finishing?"

"Why, we're going to wipe out the Selkies, of course." Ken stood and crossed the room. His eyes glowed with malice, belying the sweetness in his voice. "Pleasant dreams."

Ken left, but Evan couldn't break his eyes away from the door for several minutes afterwards. Ken's plan was to destroy the Selkies. Why? For his age-old grudge? He was truly mad. Evan laid back and stared at the ceiling. How did one deal with a raging lunatic? How was he going to get out of this and protect Meara at the same time?

Chapter 7

The lessons were getting easier. The Selkies advanced from blocks to punches, then to kicks. We had yet to introduce weapons or magic into their training, but progress was being made. They might never be a formidable army, but at this rate, they eventually would and could defend their home.

I arrived in the cavern an hour early to set up. Uncle Angus was already there practicing his punches. He was temporarily leading the clan while my dad was gone, just as he had managed the island while my dad was in Canada last year trying to connect with my mom and me. It was important to my great uncle to lead by example. Although he was the oldest Selkie in the clan, he never let his age get in his way.

"Have you heard from my dad or Aunt Brigid?" I asked him when he stopped to take a drink of water. I didn't want to interrupt his flow.

He wasn't surprised to see me and if he was tired of me asking the same question, he didn't let it show. He came over and pulled me into a hug. "No, child. Not yet."

"What's on the schedule for today?" Kieran asked as he came up behind me. "Are we introducing magic?"

I didn't even hear him enter the cavern, which was proof that my mind was elsewhere. It was almost a week since I last heard from Evan. I was worried. I didn't think Ken would kill him, but I really wasn't sure what he would do.

"I'm not feeling up to this today," I admitted. We talked about starting some basic magic work to assess skill levels. It would never work if I couldn't concentrate. "What if we introduce weapons instead? Then you and Uncle Angus can lead the session."

Kieran's eyes sought mine. "Are you okay?"

At the same time, my uncle mused, "Where will we get so many weapons?"

"I'm fine," I said, answering Kieran first. It was a white lie, and he knew it. We could discuss it later. To Uncle Angus, I said, "Leave the weapons to me. I'll get them."

"So many?" His bushy eyebrows rose in surprise.

"Have you no faith in me, Uncle?" My tone was haughty as I teased. I'd done some research in the library and learned about numerous abandoned fortresses in Scotland and England. I couldn't leave the island, but with my mind, I sought and found the treasure. Even the fortresses that were now tourist attractions had hidden rooms with weapon reserves—secret spaces that were lost to human knowledge decades ago. I didn't need to conjure the weapons from nothing; I just had to transport the supplies that already existed. Time would tell what kind of shape they would be in after being sealed up for a hundred years or longer. Luckily, they didn't need to be beautiful, just functional. A blade, after all, could be sharpened.

"You have that look on your face," Kieran said. He mouth quirked as he tried not to smile. "What are you planning, Meara?"

"I found weapons," I admitted. "A lot of them. I need to transport them here."

"Where are they? Can we help you?" Uncle Angus looked concerned. "You're not thinking of leaving the island again, are you?"

"No, Uncle." Just because I left a few times when I was told not to, were they always going to doubt me? "I have it figured out. I can get them here without leaving this room, but I'll probably be wiped afterwards. That's why I need you to lead the training today."

"Wiped?" Uncle Angus looked between Kieran and me.

"Wiped out. It means tired," Kieran answered him absentmindedly while he scowled at me. "I don't like it. Using too much magic can be harmful."

"I'll be right here when I do it, so you can intervene if you're worried. Just watch." I closed my eyes and envisioned the first castle. Abandoned in a beautiful glen, there was little left to the structure besides crumbling stone. My mind honed in on the weapon reserve, and I transported the supply easily. A small pile of swords, axes, and daggers rested at my feet.

"Well done!" my uncle bellowed. He began to sort and count. Tuning him out, I closed my eyes again. The next structure was in slightly better condition, but still abandoned. The reserve here felt lighter. I transported it and moved onto the next one without opening my eyes. I repeated this four more times, ending with the largest, most-intact fortress. This one was a popular tourist spot. My heart leapt with excitement. The reserve here was huge—at least three times the size of any other. It took some effort, but I transported it.

I opened my eyes and marveled at the pile of weapons in front of me. My uncle and Kieran wore matching shocked expressions. My chest heaved like I ran a marathon. There were enough weapons to outfit the entire clan and then some. "See?" I said. "I told you I could do it."

Then I collapsed.

"She's coming to." Ula's voice spoke near my head. My lashes fluttered before my eyes fully cooperated and opened. I found myself staring into her green eyes. She twisted her mouth into a rueful expression. "You're crazy. You know that, right?"

"What happened?" I tried to sit up, but I collapsed back when the room spun. We were in my room, although I had no memory of getting there. They must've moved me while I was unconscious.

"After you transported enough weapons to outfit the Roman Empire, you passed out." Kieran's voice held reprieve. "I told you too much magic can hurt you."

"I'm fine," I said. "I just needed a little rest."

"Really?" His eyebrows rose, and he crossed his arms.

"Yes."

"Stand up then," Kieran challenged. Ula gasped, but he held out his hand for her to wait.

Sitting up again, the spinning milder this time, I stood slowly. I lasted two seconds before I pitched sideways and Kieran caught me.

As he lowered me back to the bed, his voice was rough with

emotion. "You are not fine. You drained your strength and are lucky you didn't end up in a coma."

He kissed me lightly. I was embarrassed. This was the first time we kissed in front of Ula. I stole a glance her way, relieved to find that her face was only filled with concern for me.

Kieran stood. "Ula, watch her. Do not let her leave."

Ula bristled under his command, her cheeks blossoming pink with anger. She hated being told what to do, especially by Kieran. Over the summer, she finally got over their broken engagement and her bitter feelings toward him, but that didn't mean she liked him. Reluctantly, she promised to stay. I knew the reluctance was for Kieran's order, not because of me. I remained silent. Where would I go? I couldn't even walk. And, if the dark expression on Kieran's face was any indication, I knew a lecture would be coming later.

"You scared me," Kieran admitted. He sat at the end of my bed, my foot resting on his thigh as he worked magic on it. I'd never had a foot massage before. My webbed toes always made me feel self-conscious, that was, until I learned that all Selkies had webbed toes, and many had webbed fingers as well. Kieran didn't. His fingers were long and elegant, and in their current state of massaging my foot, made me want to swoon.

"You turned white as a ghost before you fainted," he continued. "For almost an hour, you were unresponsive. Don't do that again."

"I don't need to," I reasoned. "You said we have more than enough weapons."

"That's not what I mean, Meara, and you know it." He gently placed my foot on the bed, shifted position, and picked up my other one.

Leaning forward, I rested my hand on his arm, waiting until he met my eyes. "I can't promise you that, just as you can't make that promise to me," I said softly. "We're preparing for war, Kieran. If we want to win, we have to take risks."

"Calculated risks, planned risks," Kieran countered. "You were showing off today."

Heat burned my cheeks. He was right. I wanted to prove that I could do it. There was no need to get the weapons from that last fortress. I sighed and sat back. "Maybe," I mumbled. "I'm sorry."

He squeezed my foot. "I care too much about you. I don't like seeing you hurt."

"I'm okay."

Nodding, he said, "You are. It could have gone the other way. Be careful, Meara. That's all I ask."

I promised him I would, although deep down, I wondered if it was a promise I could keep.

Chapter 8

Heavy knocking at the door woke Evan. *Amazing how sound could travel under water*, Evan thought, scrubbing his hands over his face to wake up. He crawled out of bed, thinking coffee would be nice. Somehow, he didn't think he'd find it here.

"I'm coming!" Evan called as the knocking grew more insistent.

Ken's angry face greeted him. "I told you to be ready, Evan. I don't like to be kept waiting." He swept past Evan into the room and eyed the unmade bed. "You just rolled out of bed, didn't you? You're not dressed, and you haven't eaten."

"Not yet," Evan replied cheerfully. Irritating Ken might be a fun new pastime. "Please, make yourself at home."

Ken fumed while Evan got ready. As fun as it was to get under Ken's skin, Evan knew he didn't want to push his luck. He'd seen the result of Ken's temper. There was no point ending up horribly beaten. He could still see Professor Nolan's bloody, bruised, and swollen face. Unfortunately, Evan suspected his professor was dead. Who could survive such a brutal attack?

"Are we taking the boat?" Evan asked as they left his room.

"Don't be stupid," Ken snapped. "Why do we need a boat? We're underwater, and we can travel much faster by swimming." He appraised Evan with barely contained contempt. "Have you even tested your new abilities yet? Are you aware of your speed and strength?"

When he gawked at him, Ken sneered. "Ignorance is a good way to end up dead, my boy."

"I don't know anything about us," Evan admitted. "Will you show me, Father?"

He hated to use that term, but he knew it would soften Ken up. Sure enough, he felt Ken's emotional response at the same time his face softened.

"I'll show you," he said in a calmer voice. "First, let's get some food."

They didn't have coffee in the cave, but they had a bittersweet brew called kaku. Ken explained that it was a cross between coffee and hot chocolate, assuring Evan that kaku was powerful enough to wake the sleepiest of merfolk.

Merfolk. Evan wondered at the term. Was that what he was now? A merman? As a Siren, Deanna had a tail. None of the Blue Men did. They could swim as fast as the Sirens without one.

"Is that what we are?" Evan asked. "Merfolk?"

Ken shrugged and finished the rest of his drink before responding. "It's the easiest way to classify us. Unlike your Selkie girlfriend, the sea is our home. We rarely go on land, and when we do, we take human form. Selkies prefer the land; the sea is their play space. Do you understand?"

"It makes sense to me."

"Good. Then let's get going. We've already lost more time than I like. Tomorrow, I will not be as patient."

"Yes, sir."

Ken seemed pleased by Evan's obedience. They swam out of the cafeteria and through the village. When they reached the open waters, Ken took off. Surprisingly, Evan didn't have any trouble keeping up. They sped through the water, passing sharks and fast-swimming fish as if they were standing still. In no time at all, they reached the mantle plume.

Evan drew short in shock. Death and decay hung in the currents. The rot coated his throat. Trying to clear it did no good. A terrible sense of foreboding coursed through him, causing his body to shudder.

"Magnificent, isn't it?" Ken breathed, coming close beside him. "I'm quite pleased with the progress. At this rate, the Selkies will be dead within weeks."

"What do you mean?" Evan felt sick. Ken was trying to kill the Selkies. Meara was in danger, and Evan didn't know how to reach her.

He tried several times, but he got nothing. Whatever psychic connection they formed on land was lost to him now beneath the waves. He might be able to contact her if he kept the necklace, but at the time, he was more worried about Ken getting it. He had been awfully interested in the gold chain.

"Why do you want to kill them?" Evan asked.

"I told you why." Ken spoke to him slowly as if he were addressing a child. "They killed Azuria. It's time for revenge."

Evan didn't understand. He remembered the story, but it didn't make sense why all Selkies must pay. "Why not find the Selkie who killed her and take your vengeance on him? Why attack them all?"

It was the wrong thing to say. Ken's eyes blazed in anger. His hand wrapped around Evan's throat. He shoved back until Evan was pressed against solid rock, his windpipe crushing under the weight of his hand.

"Do you think I haven't tried for centuries to find him? He is gone, but his descendants are readily accessible and will suffice. Yes, their suffering shall avenge her death. After all, Azuria was not just our queen," Ken grit out. "She was our mother, the heart of all Blue Men. When she died, part of us died, too." Ken glared at Evan, but loosened the grip around his neck. While Evan could breathe again, he chose not to speak. "He killed her. The Selkie seduced her and killed her, so yes. All Selkies descending from that Selkie must die."

Ken released Evan and whirled around, leaving him to rub his sore neck. "Enough of that, we have work to do."

Evan wondered what they could possibly do, but it didn't take him long to find out. Ken traveled along the plume until he found the source, a deeper, wider fissure. Once there, he placed his hands over the opening, emitting a bright blue beam. The fissure steamed, and the ground rumbled beneath them. A loud crack sounded in the distance.

"What are you waiting for?" Ken snapped. "Get down here and cover my hands. Our combined power should extend the damage sufficiently."

Evan didn't want to, but he saw no way out of his current situation. If he swam away, Ken would chase him. He didn't want Meara to get hurt, but he didn't want to die, either.

The moment his hands covered Ken's, a jolt shot up both of Evan's arms and into his core. Power was pulled from his body like his soul was being sucked out by a straw. Too much—it was too much. The scenery blurred and his head swam.

"Damn it!" Ken shoved Evan back, breaking contact. "Pace yourself, son. You're no good to me if you die."

Ken's words echoed in Evan's head. At first, they made no sense, just noise, but he slowly came back to himself as the pain subsided. What the hell was that? Was he at risk of dying? Ken didn't explain anything before he started. If Evan died, it would be his fault—not that Ken would feel any guilt.

"How do I control it?" Evan asked.

Ken made a fist and pressed it into Evan's chest near the bottom of his ribcage on the right side. "Here. Do you feel it? Your power stems from this point."

Evan nodded. Now that he was aware of it, he sensed his power coiled tight in his chest. Ken flattened his hand, and Evan felt a quick tug from behind his ribcage.

"Feel that?" Ken's eyes searched Evan's face.

"Yes. What are you doing?"

With a smile, Ken said, "Drawing on your power. You're like an open vault, giving me full access. I could kill you in a second." Evan swallowed nervously. He knew Ken could do it, too. He patted Evan's chest in a reassuring way like one would with a puppy or small child. "I won't, of course. You're too valuable to me. I'm trying to show you that you can stop me. You can block me and control how much I take."

"How?" If Evan could limit how much power Ken took, it might be possible to delay the mantle plume's growth.

Tilting his head, Ken studied Evan for a minute. "It's funny. I never thought about it before. After all, I have never known life without my power, and I've lived for a very long time. We have never taught anyone how to be one of us, and you know so little. In many ways, you are like an infant." He circled around Evan, rubbing his chin. "Try this. Picture the stream of power in your mind, then imagine yourself blocking the flow."

Evan closed his eyes. In his mind, he saw a faucet, not unlike the stainless-steel gooseneck model in his parents' kitchen. The valve was open, the water streaming out. He imagined turning the valve, shutting off the supply. It worked. He no longer felt Ken's presence.

"Good." Ken grimaced, and his hand shook slightly. Did Evan hurt him when he blocked him?

"When we put our power into the fissure, what does it do?" Evan asked.

Ken surprised him by answering, "It adds our energy to the chaos and speeds up the destruction. Every time we feed the plume, we get that much closer to destroying the Selkies and their precious home."

"Is that all we do? Destroy?" Evan's heart sank. He wanted to save animals, find ways to clean the water, and improve the environment. Instead, he was participating in a plot to wipe out thousands of living things for miles. How many lives had already been lost? Fish could swim away, but plants, coral, and mollusks were all either dead or about to die. They had no ability to escape.

Ken snorted, his expression scornful. "You really like that marine biology nonsense, don't you? Were you planning to save the world?"

"I was hoping to make a difference," Evan countered.

"You are making a difference." Ken's grin sent a shiver down Evan's spine. "Lesson's over. Back to work. This time, pace yourself."

They resumed their positions by the mantle plume. Evan let enough power out to appease Ken, but he vowed to find a way to stop him.

"We were once," Ken said suddenly, startling Evan since he'd been silent so long.

"You were what?" Evan asked, confused. What was Ken talking about?

"Good." Ken's voice held regret. "We were once very good. We protected all who entered our realm."

Evan didn't need to ask what happened. He already knew. *Azuria.* It all pointed back to her.

Chapter 9

My dad and aunt had been gone for three weeks. It allowed us ample time to train the clan. Their progress was impressive. Each session started with sparring. They switched opponents through steady rotations. Young, old, male, female—it didn't matter. They grew stronger, they grew faster, and they had confidence, too. It was in their posture, their focus, and their respect for each other and us as their teachers.

The teenagers were thriving and loved the weapons work. Arren was a natural swordsman. Uncle Angus was so impressed that he chose to train him personally.

We watched the group warm up. They were starting to look formidable. I was sure my dad would be impressed at our progress. My focus didn't stop me from noticing when Kieran came up behind me. He stopped just shy of touching me, although it was only a matter of time until he did. He tried to be casual about it, but there was nothing casual about the way he looked at me. It took all of my willpower to resist leaning back and making contact with him first.

His lips brushed my ear. "Are you sure they're ready for magic?"

Ignoring the tingle that spread through my body from that simple touch, I said, "Of course they are. Look at them. Can you believe how much progress they've made?"

Kieran turned me to him, lifting my chin. "We're a good team."

His eyes burned into mine, making me wish we were alone while simultaneously glad that we were not.

I took a step back and faced the room. "We should get started."

Behind me, he sighed. "As you wish."

"Your attention, please," I called down to the crowd. They stopped sparring and looked up with expectant expressions. "You've been working so hard. Your progress is admirable." I paused and smiled, proud of them. "While I want you to continue to practice hand combat and weaponry, today we'll introduce a new skill. Magic."

A murmur of excitement traveled through the room. Kieran spoke, "We will attempt to teach you what we know. This has never been done before. Magic is passed through the ruling family." He moved behind me, placing his hands on my shoulders. Their warmth relaxed my muscles and calmed my nerves. I appreciated his support more than he knew. "It was Meara's idea to try to teach you. Listen well and maybe you'll learn something new."

"Thanks," I murmured, the sarcasm clear in my voice.

"Too much?" he asked lightly and grinned.

Rolling my eyes, I addressed our people again. "Magic is part of who we are. You use magic whenever you change forms. You probably don't even think about it. As someone who lived eighteen years as a human and only a few months as a Selkie, I have a unique perspective to distinguish what magic feels like. I want to share that knowledge with you."

The crowd grew restless. I could hear them talking to each other, wondering what I meant. Kieran watched me with interest. I hadn't revealed the specific details of how I was going to teach them. After a moment, the room quieted.

"I want you to change into your seal form now. When you do, pay attention to the magic inside of you. Feel it. You must know your own magic before you can call on it for other purposes."

I stopped and waited. No one moved. The faces I saw were unsure and scared. I glanced at Kieran for help.

"We're not asking you to do anything out of the usual," Kieran said. "This is not a test. All you need to do is change forms and be aware as you do it. You can change right back to your human form, too."

Comforted by Kieran's words, the Selkies started to transform. Within minutes, they had all taken their seal form, and then reverted to human.

"Did you feel it?" Kieran asked. The response from most of the crowd was affirmative. "Good."

He motioned for me to continue. I held out my hand, closed in a fist. When I had their attention, I opened it, palm facing upwards. "If you are aware of your magic, you can call on it. Watch."

A small ball of orange light blinked into existence and hovered over my palm. A few Selkies gasped. I covered the ball of energy with my other hand and snuffed it out. "Now you try. Kieran and I will come around to see how you're doing."

At first, I was disappointed. I could see they were trying, but nothing was happening. Maybe it was true that our family had special magic. Then, someone shouted across the room.

Your pal, Arren, just did it, one glowing, yellow ball for the teenager. Kieran's voice rang in my head. He was trying to sound nonchalant, but I heard the pride. He cared about my people as much as I did.

The rest of the Selkies kept trying. By the end of the lesson, Arren was the only one who conjured any magic, outside of Kieran and my family.

The disappointment in the room was palatable. I needed to reassure them. "It's okay. It takes practice. Just because you couldn't call on your magic tonight does not mean that you'll never be able to."

"We'll try again tomorrow." Kieran met my eyes briefly. My heart skipped when I saw the look he gave me—pride, desire, love. His face was an open book. Could he see my emotions as easily as I could see his?

Selkies slowly made their way out of the room. Their mood was slightly better, but they were still disappointed. Their determined expressions told me they'd try even harder tomorrow. I had no doubt the next training session would bring more successes.

When only Kieran and I remained, he asked, "What are your plans for the rest of the day?" His voice was casual, although his gaze was intense.

"I don't know. Nothing planned." I sighed and looked away, blinking back tears. I was worried about my dad and aunt. What was taking them so long? Were they lost or hurt or worse—imprisoned like Evan? Thinking of Evan brought more worry. Was he okay? Why did Ken take him in the first place? Why was Evan so important to him when Professor Nolan clearly had been disposable? I guess I should be thankful that Ken did find Evan valuable. At least that gave him a better chance of still being alive.

"Where are you right now, Meara?" Kieran tucked stray strands of my hair behind my ear, his fingers lingering there, warm against my skin. "You look a million miles away."

I wanted to lean into him, but I stood my ground. "I was hoping today was the day that Dad and Aunt Brigid came back with news. It's been too long. Something happened to them."

"You don't know that. Maybe they found something." He wrapped me in his arms, resting his chin on my head. His strength was my undoing. I let myself relax and be held.

"I'm worried," I mumbled against his chest. His hand stroked my back in a comforting way. The steadiness of his heartbeat soothed my nerves.

"You need to have some fun." When I made a noise of protest, he laughed. "I know you're enjoying training the others, but that's all you've been doing. Training and research."

"Fun won't find Evan. Fun won't keep us safe." I met his gaze with my chin set. "We need to be prepared in case we're attacked."

"You're right." He gripped my chin lightly and lowered his face close to mine. "We do need to be prepared, but you need to relax and de-stress, too."

"How do you recommend I do that? We can't swim."

I didn't mean to sound so bitter, but like everyone else on this island, I was itching to change form. I knew as soon as the threat was over, this island would be deserted for days as we all sought refuge in the cool ocean waters. Just thinking about it brought an ache of longing to my heart.

The tightening of his fingers on my jaw had me snapping back to attention and staring into his eyes—two pools of dark brown framed by thick lashes. It was easy to forget everything as I looked at him. My heart sped up, and my blood heated. Kieran's eyes crinkled with amusement. "What did you do for fun when you were human?"

Human. It seemed so long ago that I was human. Many things

had changed in my life. It was less than one year ago that I followed my father and became a Selkie. A lot happened in a short amount of time. I was no longer the same girl.

"Hung out at the mall, ate at restaurants, and went to the movies mostly." I shrugged. It didn't sound very exciting or fun now.

Kieran nodded, looking thoughtful. He kissed the tip of my nose and smiled. "Give me a couple of hours. I'll pick you up at your room around dinnertime."

I couldn't help it. I grinned. "Are you taking me on a date?"

His eyes danced with mischief. "I believe I am."

Chapter 10

*E*xhaustion pulled at every muscle in Evan's body. Ken half carried, half dragged Evan back to his room. He vaguely remembered the journey home. He was so tired. Shuffling over to the bed, he collapsed on it and fell asleep.

The smell of coffee, rich and strong, woke him. Coffee? Here? No, he must be dreaming. How sad was that? He used to dream about beautiful women, and now it was caffeinated beverages.

The tinkle of feminine laughter startled him. Deanna knelt on the floor near his head, her hands cupped under his nose. Empty hands, he noticed. He tried not to be disappointed that she didn't have a cup of coffee for him.

"I thought that might work," she teased. "Isn't coffee the human cure for sleepiness?"

"Pretty much." He sat up and stretched. It pleased him to see her watching him intently, a slight blush on her cheeks and her eyes on his abdomen where his shirt rode up. He straightened his shirt and ran his fingers through his unkempt hair. "Although the smell is nice, it's really the caffeine that gets you going. Did you bring me some?"

"No." She moved from the floor to sit next to him on the bed. "I created the scent to wake you." She sounded a bit sheepish and wasn't meeting his eyes.

"You can do that? Brilliant!" He rubbed his temples, hoping to relieve the dull ache behind his eyes. "Too bad I can't really have some. I'm craving it right now."

Deanna's face brightened. "But you can! They sell coffee in The Chamber, along with other human foods and drinks."

Pizza? Burgers? Evan's mouth watered in anticipation. "I don't remember seeing that when we were there the other day."

"We didn't go to that floor," Deanna explained. "There are three levels. The first is for growing food and has the bowling alley and library, and the middle floor is shops and restaurants."

"What's on the lowest level?" Evan couldn't believe it was three levels deep. He was impressed. The place was absolutely enormous. No wonder he couldn't see or smell the food during his first visit.

"Storage, and…" She faltered, frowning. "It's restricted. Anyone caught on that floor without clearance is imprisoned."

"Wow. Strict." Evan wondered what could possibly require that much protection. Weapons or military, maybe? His country certainly had similar facilities. He just didn't think he would find one here.

"Will Ken be back? Do you have to work again today?" Deanna swam off the bed and faced him, waiting for his answer.

"What time is it?" Since he crashed as soon as Ken brought him back to his room, he felt disoriented. Without the sun, gauging time of day was difficult.

"It's late afternoon."

He slept through lunch, no wonder he was so hungry. His stomach growled in agreement. "I'm done for the day," he finally answered her original question. "Ken will be back in the morning for me. Do you have to go to work?"

"I have off tonight." She blew out an irritated breath and placed her hands on her hips. "And I double-checked the schedule before I came here, so I'm safe."

"Ken takes some getting used to, doesn't he?" Evan felt sorry for Deanna. She didn't deserve to be treated so poorly. Ken had no respect for the Sirens. To him, they were a means to an end. He had said as much to Evan while they worked. That was probably all Evan was to Ken as well.

Deanna tilted her head and studied him. "You may be Ken's son, but you're nothing like him." She reached out and tentatively placed her hand against Evan's cheek. Her palm was warm and soft.

Evan didn't remember mentioning that Ken was his father. "How did you know that I am Ken's son?"

"Everyone knows," Deanna said. "Ken told us."

"Not sure why he's so proud. He may have given me his genes, but he didn't raise me. Darren did. Darren Mitchell is my real father."

She swam closer, her green eyes wide and trusting. "I'd like to meet your human parents. I'm sure they're wonderful."

His heart raced. This close, he felt the warmth from her body. She smelled spicy and floral, perhaps the remnants of the perfume she wore at the club. His eyes were locked on her soft, full lips. "What makes you say that?" he asked.

"They raised you," she whispered, her arms winding around his neck and pulling his head closer to hers. When her lips touched his, he groaned. Memories from that night in the club flooded his mind as her spicy scent enveloped his senses. He'd kissed her before. A lot. Something, or someone, had made him forget it all. Deanna melted into his arms, moving as close to him as she could. He ran his fingers through her long hair, angling his head to deepen the kiss. It was her turn to sigh. A deep rumble sounded in his gut, and she pulled back, laughing. "We better get you fed. I think your stomach wants to eat me."

Embarrassed, he chuckled and stood, offering his hand. "Let's check out this middle floor you told me about."

They swam to the domed building. This time, she went first. When he came out of the drying room—still blue, of course—she was waiting. He didn't think much of his pale skin and brown hair before, but he was really getting sick of the color blue. He felt so alien. Then again, he wasn't human anymore, was he? He couldn't help smile appreciatively at Deanna. He may not like blue, but he was growing quite fond of the soft minty hue to Deanna's skin and the crisp green of her eyes. The light pink tank top and tan skirt she wore showed off her lithe build and legs, which were long and toned from dancing. He liked her in either form, but her human figure made his blood flow hot.

With a slight smile on her lips, she stepped close and took his hand. She seemed to look for any excuse to touch him, but he didn't mind. With the outfit she was wearing, he wished he could touch her more. Guilt flooded his mind as he briefly thought of Meara. She was in danger. He needed to figure out how to protect her. He had to stop Ken.

Deana tugged his hand and led him down a corridor. "The

stairwell is this way."

They passed a few couples as they walked. Everyone looked human. Everyone but Evan. And yet, no one gave him a second glance. They smiled or nodded and moved on. Polite indifference.

"Why isn't anyone freaked out by my appearance or wondering why I didn't change?" Evan asked.

"They are either Siren or Blue Men." Deanna eyed him with confusion.

"Yeah? So?" Evan persisted. "Aren't they wondering why I can't change?"

"They know why." She leaned closer and whispered, "You are Ken's son. No one would dare insult the prince."

Evan scoffed. "I'm not a prince."

Eyes wide, Deanna turned to face him. "Yes, you are. Like it or not, Ken is in charge. With no queen, as eldest son, he became king. And you are his only son. The first of the Blue Men born in, well..." She scrunched up her brow as she thought about it, and then shrugged. "Well, in forever, really. You're a novelty."

He snorted without meaning to, and for a moment, Deanna looked hurt. "I'm not laughing at you," he apologized. "It's all so strange to me. You have to remember that a few weeks ago, I was just a college student on a summer internship. Hoping to spend time with my girlfriend..."

His words trailed off. *Meara.* Again, she invaded his thoughts. This time he saw her face, as clear as if she was standing in front of him. He loved her so much, but they had both changed. Would he feel the same when he saw her next? Would she feel the same about him? He wished he still had the necklace she gave him, the one that belonged to her grandfather that they used to communicate. It would've worked here, he was sure of it. On the other hand, Ken might have confiscated it. Evan speculated that Ken was beginning to figure out how it worked before they left the house in Aberdeen. He'd commented on it frequently.

"Are you going downstairs or what?" a voice sneered behind them. Evan turned to stare at a guy about his age with mousy, brown hair and glasses. The man's eyes widened comically behind the frames.

"Prince Evan." He dropped to one knee. "My apologies. In the shadows, I didn't recognize you."

"Stand up," Evan mumbled, embarrassed. Others were starting to notice. "What's your name?"

"Dex, My Prince." Dex looked positively scared.

"Relax, Dex." Evan placed a hand on his shoulder and squeezed. "We're cool."

"Cool?" The man glanced from Evan to Deanna and back again.

"It means everything is fine." A line was forming behind them while they exchanged niceties. Several faces looked irritated. "But it won't be fine for long unless we get moving and clear the stairs for others." He let Deanna go first. He tried to let Dex pass, but he refused.

"After you, Prince. I insist." He bowed at the waist and waited. With a sigh, Evan turned and followed Deanna down the stairs, the exchange forgotten as soon as he stepped out of the entryway. It was like walking into any mall back home with bright lights, rows of stores advertising sales, and the tempting scent of fried food and coffee.

A quick glance told him that the stores were not the same as those in Halifax. There was no Abercrombie and Fitch, Victoria's Secret, or Starbucks here. In fact, closer inspection showed that most stores were named by what they sold—Jeans, Hats, Jewelry. *Not the most creative group of creatures*, he thought, finally seeing the sign he was searching for—Coffee and Snacks.

Deanna giggled. "I see you found the food and coffee. Your eyes just lit up." She took his hand again, and he let her. She cast shy glances up at him as they walked to the food area.

Several stands selling drinks and food surrounded a grouping of tables. Only a few people were eating. It was too late for lunch and too early for dinner. Since Evan missed breakfast and lunch, he didn't care what time it was, he was getting something to eat. When they were close enough to read the signs, though, he frowned. The currency was not one that he recognized. How could he forget about paying? He didn't have any money.

"What kind of money do you use?" he asked Deanna, pointing to the closest sign.

"Here, I've got it." Deanna pulled some coins out of her pocket and handed them to Evan. He was surprised by their weight. They were heavy and dull gold in color. Maybe they were made of real gold. Evan wouldn't doubt it. He held one up and inspected it. One side appeared to have a triton carved into it, although the markings were well worn. The image on the other side looked like a pyramid. All the details were rubbed smooth, which made Evan wonder if the coins were centuries old.

"I can't let you pay." While the coins were fascinating, he couldn't keep them. He handed them back to Deanna, deciding he'd rather go hungry. He hated being financially dependent on others. Since his first paper route, he had saved and paid his own way.

"Do you have any okro?" Deanna jingled the coins in her hand, her eyebrows raised. Okro must be the name of their currency. After a moment, he shook his head, and she gave him a sly glance. "Then you have to let me pay, don't you?"

When Evan hesitated, she patted his shoulder in a friendly manner. "Don't worry. You can pay me back."

He relented, but vowed that he would hit Ken up for money the first chance he got. If Ken was going to steal his power and keep him prisoner, then damn it, he was going to pay Evan for it.

At Deanna's suggestion, Evan got a wrap sandwich. It wasn't bad. The outside was seaweed, like the kind used to roll sushi. The inside was a seafood salad of sorts. Similar to tuna salad, but with a fresher taste. It came with French fries, too, and Evan was pleased to discover they tasted like normal fries. Maybe a little soggier, and they definitely needed salt, but close enough.

"Do you like it?" Deanna asked. She leaned on her elbows and watched him eat. She wasn't hungry, since, unlike him, she had breakfast and lunch.

"It's good." Evan sipped the coffee, which was black, thick as tar, and scalding. The flavor was smoky, and he found he preferred it that way.

"What do you want to do next?" She bounced a little in her seat.

He offered her the last couple of fries while he finished his wrap. She ate them, her bites dainty. "Can we talk somewhere?" he asked quietly.

"Aren't we talking now?" She leaned in and matched his hushed tone.

"I mean somewhere private."

"There aren't many places like that here." She slumped back in her chair, lost in thought. A minute later, she popped forward and grabbed his hand. Luckily, it was not the one holding what remained of the hot coffee. "I know where we can go."

He quickly stood and placed the food tray on the garbage can nearby. She danced from foot to foot while she waited. Laughing, he held his hand out to her. Her enthusiasm was infectious.

"By all means, lead the way," he said.

Chapter 11

My first date with a Selkie, and I was wondering what I should wear. I pondered this while staring out my bedroom window. The sun, high in the sky, heated my skin, and a warm breeze caressed my hair. The waves were relatively calm—the perfect day for a swim. Arren and his friends played on the wet, rocky shore, as close as they dared to go these days. The occasional waves rolled over their feet.

How much longer could we endure? Supplies were dwindling. Selkies didn't fish in boats. No swimming meant no fishing. We could conjure a fish or two, but not enough to sustain a whole population for the foreseeable future. Like the last batch of swords that I conjured, that much magic, used consistently, would harm the person who performed it. Uncle Padraic resorted to serving stews and soups, stretching our meager reserves as far as he could. Soon, it wouldn't be enough. We'd need to steal from the mainland by transporting food, or we'd starve.

"Are you in here by yourself?" Ula poked her head in the doorway.

I'd left it ajar to increase the airflow—it was stuffy and hot in my room. Although the weather should be cooling for the fall, we were experiencing an unusual heat wave. The castle was quiet. Almost everyone was outside.

"Why aren't you out enjoying this gorgeous weather? It'll cool off again soon. Fall can be brutal here." She joined me at the window, placing her hand on my arm. "You're okay?" Her green eyes searched mine.

My vision blurred and tears fell when I shook my head. I wasn't okay. I was worried and scared. It was enough that Ken took Evan, and

I had no idea if he was okay or not, but now I was worried about my dad and aunt. Dad said they'd be back in a few days. Now, days turned into weeks and we had no news. Something happened to them, I knew it. We could only pray that they were still alive. After losing my mom less than a year ago, losing my dad, too, would be more than I could handle.

Ula conjured a box of tissues and silently handed one to me. She guided us to the edge of the bed and we sat. With a sharp laugh, she snatched a tissue and blew her nose. "Now you have me crying, too!"

Sniffling, she rested her head on my shoulder. "They'll be okay," she said. I wondered who she was trying to convince—herself or me. "Brigid is tough. Nothing can stop her."

I knew my aunt was a force to be reckoned with, but it didn't explain why they hadn't tried to contact us. "Why haven't we heard from them?"

"I don't know." Ula's voice was quiet. After a moment of silence, she sighed and then jumped up. "Come on. They wouldn't want us to stay indoors and be depressed. Let's go outside and enjoy the weather."

I let her pull me up and transport us to the edge of the water. Arren and his friends were playing a game in the grass. It was similar to volleyball, only they didn't use a net. The guys and girls alike wore swimsuits that showed off their tanned skin. Apparently, I was one of the only ones who spent the last month indoors.

Ula crossed to a large, flat boulder. She sat and removed her sandals to dip her feet in the water. "I sure miss swimming." She patted the spot next to her and looked up at me. "Have a seat."

I slid off my shoes and joined her. The water was cool against my skin. I worried the temptation to dive in was going to be torturous when all I could do was get my feet wet. Instead, I found the ocean soothing. The waves quenched my soul, filling the void and drowning my worry. My dad was okay. He had to be.

Meara, is that you?

The question rang through my head. I'd recognize that voice anywhere. *Dad? Where are you? Why haven't you contacted—?*

Meara, he interrupted. *I don't have much time. They caught us two days into our expedition. We've been imprisoned in their fortress since then.*

Are you hurt? Fear gnawed at my belly, as I imagined all the horrors they were enduring.

We're fine. They have been... He paused, and I assumed he was searching for the right word. *...Hospitable, but we cannot escape.*

Where are you? As I asked, a vision filled my mind of the Minch—the strait between several isles on the north-west coast of Scotland.

We were searching the Isle of Lewis when they found us. They knocked us out, and when we woke up, we were in a dungeon under water. I have no idea where, but we must be someplace in the Minch. Can you see the map?

Yes.

We were in Stornoway, on our way to the Shiant Islands. That's all the information I have. The map vanished from my view. *Tell Angus. Have him send two of my guard—Drust and Judoc. When they arrive at the north end of the Isle of Lewis, they should contact me. I'll try to help direct them to our location.*

What about me? It was always someone else that my dad wanted. I wish he had more faith in me.

Stay safe, he ordered. *I have to go. I love you, honey.*

Love you, too, Dad. My response was lost when the connection broke.

"Meara!"

Ula's hands were on either side of my face. She tapped my cheek lightly with her flat palm when I focused on her. "Good. You're in there. What was that about?"

"Dad contacted me. The Blue Men captured them weeks ago."

"What?" Ula looked shocked. "Where?"

"He couldn't tell me, but he showed me a map. They're in the Minch. The last place they were was the Isle of Lewis."

"Is that where they are now?" Ula nibbled on her nail. Her gaze was distant. I could tell she knew the area, at least a little. "Do the Blue Men live near the Isle of Lewis? We've always known that they live in the Minch strait, but we've searched for their dwelling before with no luck."

"He doesn't know where they are exactly. They were unconscious when the Blue Men moved them to their fortress."

She switched to another nail, lost in thought. If she kept that up, she wouldn't have any nails left. "Why now?" she mused. I raised an eyebrow at her and waited. I didn't know what she was getting at. She sighed in frustration. "I mean, why did your dad wait to contact you?"

I swished my feet back and forth in the surf as I considered her question. Bubbles frothed over my toes. It really went against our nature to stay away from the water. I could feel the energy from it as it coated my skin. The water! Of course! Kicking up my foot, I sprayed us lightly with the salty droplets.

"Hey!" She splashed me back.

"This is it!" I said, tapping the water with my foot for emphasis. "He couldn't contact me until I was touching the water."

Ula's mouth dropped open. "Why didn't I think of that?"

"None of us did, but it makes sense, right? Our power comes from the water." I wiggled my toes to prove my point. "I feel better already, stronger, from only immersing my feet."

"Me, too," she admitted. "What are we going to do now?"

"Go rescue them," I said without hesitation. By the look on Ula's face, I knew I said the wrong thing.

"O-kay," she drawled. "What did your dad tell you to do?"

"Um…"

"Meara—" Her voice held a warning, like any good aunt scolding her niece.

"Fine," I huffed. "He said to send Drust and Judoc." I didn't think much of my dad's guard, especially those two. Drust and Judoc were your typical meatheads, all muscle and no common sense.

"That makes sense. They are two of the most skilled, third and fourth in command respectively. That's why your dad left them here in the first place, to protect us."

"Who's first and second?" I asked.

Ula rolled her eyes at me like 'duh!' "David and Brigid."

"Oh yeah." My dad's guard was small, and he and Brigid were the best fighters that we had.

"You're going to tell Uncle Angus, right?"

I hadn't really planned on it. If I went, the less who knew the better. I would already have to contend with my angry father; I didn't want to fight with my great uncle first.

"If you don't tell him, I will." Ula knew what my silence meant. She crossed her arms and gave me the stink eye. I silently counted the taps of her foot on the ground. I got to twenty when she spoke again, "You need to do as your father asked. Send the guards. I won't let you go and do something stupid."

"You won't *let* me?" I asked dryly. If I chose to go, there was nothing Ula could do to stop me.

She leapt at me and pushed me off the rock. Caught off guard, I toppled back and bumped my head. Her curls fell in my face and tickled my nose. She pinned my arms and grinned at me.

"Ow!" I cried. There were sure to be bruises later. "That hurt."

"Baby," she retorted. Her voice held the irritating singsong tone of winning. "I was proving my point. I can and will stop you. Now, do you promise to tell Uncle Angus and let the guards handle it?"

"Ula, get off me!" I bucked, and she hung on like a burr.

"Promise," she said.

Blowing out a frustrated breath, I gave in. "Okay, I promise. Now, get off me."

She rolled back on her heels and offered me her hand. I eyed it skeptically before placing my hand in hers. She pulled us both to standing, and I winced.

"Head hurt?" she asked, although her voice held no remorse.

"Yes," I bit out, rubbing the back of my skull.

"Shouldn't be so stubborn," she said. "Now, let's go."

"Where now?" I hated the whine in my voice.

She grinned at me, a flash of tiny, white teeth, and I realized she could be fierce when she wanted. "Uncle Angus' room, of course. You've got news to report."

Uncle Angus listened silently as I recounted my conversation with Dad. When I finished he said, "I'll send Drust and Judoc as your father wishes." Rubbing his beard, he hung his head. "I pray they are successful."

"If not, I'm going next." I raised my chin and dared him to

challenge me. He surprised me by laughing and slapping one heavy hand on my shoulder, pushing me down in the chair with more force than he intended, I was sure.

"I'd expect nothing less of you, niece, and it would be stupid for me to argue with you." Another tap, this time it was gentler. "You have that same stubborn set to your jaw as your father."

Ula made a noise of protest, but Uncle Angus cut her off. "It's no use, Ula. If our two best guards can't find them, I will allow Meara to try." He turned and pierced me with his eyes. "But you must promise to give them a fair shot first. I won't have you running out there with them, potentially compromising the mission and risking your life."

I fought the urge to roll my eyes at my uncle's lack of confidence, like I would do anything that stupid. If I said I would wait, then I would. The question was how long. "How long is fair?"

"Two weeks." He rubbed his eyes and sunk back into his chair. "But let's hope they are successful. We could use some good news, eh?"

Ula and I nodded silently in agreement.

"You girls look a little parched. Let me get you a cream soda, and we can discuss happier news." He stood and went to the refrigerator to pull out two cans.

"Um..." A quick glance out the window told me it was late afternoon. In an hour, maybe two at the most, Kieran would show up at my door. I figured there would be plenty of time to get ready. That was before Ula's visit, Dad's message, and now Uncle Angus. If I didn't leave soon, I'd run out of time. Uncle Angus was a talker.

"I insist." Taking frosty mugs from the freezer, he filled and handed them to us. One taste and I was a goner. The sweet, creamy, and cold drink was exactly what I needed at the moment.

"It's good, right?" He winked at me and settled back into his chair. "Your conversation with David got me thinking. The ocean may be the solution to our magic issue."

"How do you mean?" Ula asked.

"I know Arren's an exceptional student." Pride rang through my uncle's voice. "Still, more than one Selkie should've conjured magic today. It's in our blood. What was lacking before was the knowledge, the technique." He turned to me with a twinkle in his eye. "Which you showed them."

"You could be right," I said slowly. "Both Ula and I felt instantly better when we put our feet in the water today. It's not all or nothing, but we've been treating it that way." I stood and crossed to the window. "Arren and his friends were near the water today, occasionally a wave reached them. They've been exposed to the ocean, but the others have not."

Uncle Angus beamed. "Exactly!"

"Tomorrow we'll start on the shore," I said. "Get everyone wading in the shallows first, and then head to higher land to try conjuring again."

"Would you like me to let everyone know?" Ula asked.

"That would be great." I was relieved that she volunteered since I didn't have time. It didn't stop the pang of guilt. Ula didn't know about my date with Kieran. I wasn't hiding the information because it would bother her—she seemed to be resolving her issues with him and getting used to us together. On the other hand, I didn't want to rub our date in her face. Anyway, it was technically a first date. There was plenty of time to tell her.

I finished the last of my tasty drink, licking the sweet foam off my lip. "Thank you, Uncle. That was exactly what I needed." I hugged him, and then Ula. "I need to get going, but I will see you both at practice tomorrow, okay?"

"See you in the morning," Uncle Angus replied.

At the same time, Ula asked. "Where are you going? I thought we could hang out tonight."

With another pang of guilt, I reluctantly admitted, "I have a date."

"Oh," she said, surprise in her voice. Then, "Ohhhhh," as it registered. She sounded disappointed.

"I'd love to hang out with you," I said. "How about tomorrow night?"

She brightened immediately. "Only if you bring strawberry ice cream and promise to tell me about your date."

"Deal."

I left them and hurried down to my room. Showering quickly, I used magic to finish getting ready. I preferred to do things the human way. There was nothing like the relaxing feeling of brushing my hair or even the simple joy of sorting through my accessories and deciding what to wear. Tonight, there just wasn't time. I wore my hair down because I knew Kieran preferred it that way. Visualizing a long, swirling skirt in bright colors and a peasant blouse in turquoise, all that was left were the accessories. The sand-dollar necklace I always wore looked nice, but I refused to wear the matching earrings. Evan gave those to me, and I didn't need a reminder of him tonight. Tomorrow I could worry about him, but tonight, I wanted to relax. It was time I gave Kieran a real chance without the ghost of Evan standing in the way.

I had a pair of pearl earrings that used to belong to my mom. I put them in, running a finger over their smooth surface. *I miss you, Mom*, I thought. *So much.*

A sharp rap at the door made my pulse jump. Why was I nervous? This was Kieran. I trained with him all summer and spent most of my days with him since my dad and aunt left. There was no need to be nervous. Except, there was. Only recently did we start admitting our feelings for each other. This was the first time we were going out on a real date. I hugged my middle—the butterflies were in full force. Swallowing my nerves, I went to answer the door.

Chapter 12

*D*eanna led Evan down a dark corridor. At the end was a secured door. She quickly punched in a code and it swung open. She gestured for Evan to go first, and then secured the door behind them.

The stairs only went one way. Down.

"I thought the lowest floor was off limits?" Evan asked.

"It is." He saw Deanna shrug in the dim lighting. "To most people. I'm not most people." She tilted her head and studied him. "Do you remember the night I met you at the club?"

"Not really." Evan didn't feel bad admitting it. He still didn't understand what happened. "I remember you started singing. I have a few hazy memories in between, but nothing clear. The next thing I knew, Ken was pulling into the driveway, and we were home."

"Ah, that explains a lot." She started down the stairs. Evan thought she would say more, but she didn't.

"What does that explain?" he finally asked.

She reached the bottom step and turned to him with her finger to her mouth. He shut up and waited. Cracking open the heavy door, she stuck her head out and looked both directions before slipping through and motioning for him to follow. The corridor had a bare-bones military feel to it. With utilitarian hanging bulbs, grey walls, and steel doors, it wasn't designed for aesthetics. Deanna kept close to the wall until she reached the third door on the right. She took out a key and opened it, standing back so he could enter.

The interior was the complete opposite of the hallway. It was a fully furnished apartment with elegant decor in a neutral beige and cream color scheme. Tasteful artwork graced the walls, and a plush cream carpet covered the floor.

"This is nice," Evan said hesitantly, wondering why she brought him to this apartment and who it belonged to.

Deanna looked guilty. "We can talk safely here. This belonged to my mother. Now it's mine."

"Belonged?"

Deanna sighed. "Have a seat, Evan. Much of what I'm about to tell you we've already discussed. I thought you remembered our conversation when you remembered me, but obviously, you didn't."

"O-kay." Evan crossed to a plush recliner. Although it looked comfortable, he sat on the edge of it and leaned forward, ready to hear Deanna's explanation.

Instead of sitting too, she crossed the room to a kitchenette. "Can I get you something to drink? Juice, mineral water, or something stronger?" She held up the bottles with an apologetic smile.

"I'll take a mineral water. Thanks."

She pulled two bottles out of a small refrigerator and brought them over. After handing him one, she opened hers and took a sip. Then, she perched on the arm of the chair across from his. Her eyes searched his face. "My mother ruled this city, until Ken imprisoned her and took over."

That was so far from what Evan expected her to say that he choked on his water, the bubbles burning as they went down the wrong pipe.

"Are you okay?" she asked.

"I'm fine." He cleared his throat and took a smaller, more cautious sip. "Where is your mom now?"

"Dead." Deanna's voice cracked when she said this, but beneath the pain was an edge of steel. "Ken claimed she was murdered, but I know for a fact he ordered it." Her gaze sharpened and became shrewd. "You can read his mind, can't you?"

She caught Evan off guard again. Before he could decide whether it was smart to admit it or not, he found himself saying yes. She sat back with a satisfied smile. "I knew it. I sensed it the moment I met you in the club. And Ken has no idea."

"He doesn't? How do you know?"

"I can do the same thing," she said. "This is why I know he ordered that quack of a doctor to kill my mother with a lethal injection. I also know that the doctor worked on you." She leaned forward and touched Evan's arm, her hand warm and soft. "I'm sorry about that. Losing your humanity must be shocking."

"Both Ken and my professor, Ted Nolan, told me I would have eventually died if they didn't intervene."

"It's possible." She shrugged and took another small sip from her bottle. "I know very little about what they did, and you are the first of the Blue Men to be born. Ever. The others are all immortal as I'm sure they've told you."

"That much I knew," Evan said. It was a relief talking to Deanna and knowing there was someone here who could help him. Someone who wanted to help him without ulterior motives. Wait—did she have ulterior motives? "Why are you helping me?"

"I like you." Her response was quick and sounded honest. "I will help you any way I can. In turn, I hope you'll help me."

"Help you how?" Evan tried to keep the suspicion out of his voice.

"The Blue Men are not meant to control the Sirens. I want to free my people. I should rightfully be the ruler now, and I want you to help me overthrow Ken." As she talked, the anger darkened her words. She stood and began to pace the room in agitation. "I want him out."

"I'll help you however I can," Evan said sincerely. Her request was fair. He agreed with her. Ken treated the Sirens poorly. "I need your help first though. Ken is using my power to feed the mantle plume. He's driving the molten lava toward the Selkies. He plans to destroy their island."

She stopped pacing, her face white with shock. "That explains more than anything why he rushed your transformation. What do you want to do? Block him from taking your power?"

"Exactly! Not only do I need to block him, but I also must do it in a way that he doesn't know I'm doing it. He seems to know how much or how little power he's receiving from me."

Deanna frowned. "I don't know much about that. The Blue Men's powers are foreign to my kind. It wasn't until Ken overtook our society that we interacted with them at all."

"How long ago was that?"

"It's been five years, a painful amount of time to us, and merely a blip to the Blue Men." When Evan gave her a questioning look, she shrugged. "When you're infinite, time has different meaning." She sank back into the chair, lost in thought.

"Sirens aren't immortal?" Evan assumed that they were or at least had longer life spans like Selkies. If Meara decided to stay a Selkie, she might live hundreds of years. Evan knew very little about Deanna and her kind.

"I wish." She gave him a sad smile. "Our life span is closer to that of a human, around ninety years."

"Slightly longer than most humans."

"If you say so. With Ken and his gang around, I'd argue that it's slightly less."

"Are any of the Blue Men trustworthy?" Evan asked. "If I could just talk to one and learn more about what I am…" He trailed off, feeling helpless. How could he be one of the Blue Men and have no idea what that meant?

"Some of them seem to be trustworthy. A few of the girls have taken to them. I'll ask around and see what I can find out." She took his empty bottle and, along with her own, placed them in a bin by the sink. When she turned around, she leaned against the counter. "What will you do tomorrow?"

"Tomorrow?"

"When you go back to the plume with Ken?"

"I'll give as little power to him as I can without him noticing. I'm not sure how successful I'll be, but I have to try."

"That's all you can do. Try." She walked over and crouched in front of him, her hands on his knees. "I'm glad I met you, Evan. I know that you're a good person, and I am sorry that this happened to you."

Her pale green eyes were wide and trusting. He felt the need to touch her, so he ran his fingers through her hair. She closed her eyes and leaned her head against his hand.

"I wish we met under different circumstances," she murmured.

"Had the circumstances been different, I'm not sure we would've met." Evan took her hand in his free one. "I'm glad we met as we did."

She opened her eyes and searched his face. "You are?"

Instead of answering, he leaned forward and kissed her. It was slow and sweet. Her lips were soft, and her breathy sighs did things to him. He wanted to deepen the kiss, but he restrained himself. She was special, and he wanted to treat her that way. She pulled back first with a sigh. "I better get you home. Ken will come early to claim you."

"Don't remind me," Evan said.

Chapter 13

"Meara? Are you ready?" Kieran's voice rang through the door. Because he sounded slightly nervous, I relaxed and smiled when I opened the door.

His eyes lit up when he saw me. "You look beautiful." He held out a bouquet of dahlias, a mixture of brilliant purple and peach. "These are for you. I know it's customary for human males to give flowers on a first date."

"They're lovely." I was touched by his gesture. "Where did you get these?" It wasn't like there was a florist shop on the island.

He dipped his head and said, "I picked them on the way here."

I bit my cheek to keep from laughing. He picked them from Ronac's gardens. He was going to pay for that later. Uncle Paddy didn't like anyone messing with his plants, certainly not cutting some of his most beautiful flowers.

I conjured a vase filled with water and placed it on my dresser. After quickly arranging the fragrant blooms, I crossed the room and gave Kieran a kiss on the cheek. "Thank you for the flowers. That was thoughtful."

"It's just the beginning of a magical evening." He wiggled his eyebrows and made me laugh. When he offered me his arm, I took it and followed him out the door.

"Where are we going?" I asked.

"You'll see."

We wove our way down the back staircase and through the hall that led to the kitchen. Were we having a cooking date? A private dinner by the hot oven?

"Seriously, where are we going?" I couldn't stand the suspense.

He turned and raised an eyebrow. "Where does it look like we're going?"

"The kitchen."

After all, it was the only thing down this corridor, unless he was going to pass through the hall and go outside.

"Very good." I heard the humor in his voice. "Don't worry; it's not our final destination."

The kitchen was bustling with more workers than I'd seen in a long time. Then again, I tended to avoid this part of the castle unless I needed a snack. Uncle Padraic knew better than to put me to work. I was an awful cook. He tried to teach me when I first came to Ronac and failed. If it didn't come from a jar or a can or it required more than heating, I wasn't the girl for the job.

Uncle Paddy lorded over a large kettle housing his latest soup or stew.

"What's on the menu for tonight?" I asked, and he looked up in surprise.

"Gumbo." He held out a spoon to give me a taste. It was smoky with a little spice.

"Delicious," I said.

"Good." He smiled. "Too bad you're not having any." I pouted, which made him laugh. "Don't worry. Kieran's got it all planned out."

The guys shared a companionable look. Unlike Ula, my uncle seemed happy that Kieran and I were together. From the beginning, he encouraged it. It could be because they were friends, which somewhat surprised me. Paddy was shy and usually kept to his kitchen, where Kieran was outgoing. And yet, I often saw them shooting hoops or racing across the flat, open ground. I was glad Kieran had a friend here.

"It's ready then?" A pleased expression crossed Kieran's face.

"Right here." My uncle patted a large, wicker basket before handing it to Kieran. "It's everything you asked for."

Kieran was taking me on a picnic! It was such a romantic thing to do that it shocked me. I was all about the romance, but Kieran never struck me as a romantic. Truth be told, I thought he was more the love 'em and leave 'em type. That was, until recently. If he weren't interested in me on a more permanent basis, he never would have risked his life for mine. I never wanted to see him lying cold and still like that again.

"Thanks," Kieran said after peering at the contents. "What do I owe you?"

"Nothing." My uncle put an arm around us and guided us to the door. "Just get out of my kitchen and go have fun."

After giving us a gentle shove, my uncle headed back to his kettle. Kieran took my hand. I had a moment to register how nice it felt to hold his hand before he transported us.

We stood on an area of the island that I hadn't visited, which surprised me, since I explored the entire thing and thought I saw it all. The island wasn't that big, really, so this confused me. "Where are we?"

Rich green moss dotted with tiny, yellow flowers covered the rocks, softening their sharpness and creating a plush, natural carpet. The air smelled both sweet and clean.

"This cove is reserved for the ruling family only," Kieran said.

"Really? Why don't I know about it?" My dad didn't mention it as far as I could remember. It was one more thing to add to the ever-growing list of withheld information.

"They would've told you when you made Elder." He sat and pulled me down next to him. "I guess it's more of an Elder thing than ruling family. I'm not sure if Paddy and Ula know about it."

That made me sad. Aunt Ula and Uncle Paddy did so much for the clan, but they weren't held to the same esteem as my dad, Aunt Brigid, or Uncle Angus, simply because they weren't powerful. It wasn't their fault. They were born that way. Maybe I could help them change that with training.

"They told you about it?" I knew Kieran was growing closer to my family, but was he close enough to know about the secret family hangout?

"I heard them talking about it during an Elder meeting. I asked where it was, and Brigid showed me."

"Brigid showed you?" I tried to keep the sarcasm out of my voice. I knew I failed when Kieran gave me a confused look.

"Yeah? So?"

"Brigid doesn't really do things like that," I said.

"Like what?"

"Help others."

He laughed. The sound was rich and smooth. He didn't laugh enough. I loved the sound of his happiness. He quieted into a smirk. "She's not that bad. She's proud of you, you know?"

"She is?" She never said anything to me. I thought she saw me as a disappointment or a burden.

"Sure. She's always talking about how much you've learned in such a short time. You've impressed her."

"Hmm..."

"Would you rather sit on a blanket? The ground is kind of damp." He opened the basket and pulled out a blue woven throw. When he stood and attempted to lay it out, the wind lifted the edge and folded it over. I stood and took the other end to help him. Once the blanket was down, he began unpacking the basket.

"What made you think of a picnic?" I asked.

He glanced up and gave me a sheepish grin. "I've seen picnics in movies and watched families at the beach. It seemed like fun." He cleared his throat, and his face grew serious. "Plus, I wanted to spend time alone with you."

Leaning forward, his lips touched mine, soft at first, but with growing urgency. I broke the kiss and placed my hand on his chest. "I'm not ready for... that... you know?"

His lips quirked in that lopsided way that I loved. "I know. It doesn't mean we can't still have some fun, does it? Even if I can't ravish you on the picnic blanket?"

I rolled my eyes. "Have you been reading romance novels?"

"What? No! This is all me." He gestured down his body, which I had to admit looked really nice in dark blue jeans and a white polo. The white shirt set off his dark, tanned skin and clung to his muscles. The jeans were a nice change from his usual basketball shorts.

"You should wear jeans more often," I blurted.

He watched with amusement as my face heated. "Whatever you like, Meara."

Why did I blush so easy? I busied myself picking at the edge of the blanket. He reached over to still my hand, and with his other, lifted my chin. "I like it when you blush," he said. "I find it adorable."

He brushed his lips over mine, and then he returned his attention to the picnic basket. Watching him set out the food, I realized how hungry I was. Ula and I went straight to Uncle Angus' room after I spoke with Dad, and I didn't have time to eat after.

"Are you zoning out on me again?" Kieran teased.

"What? Oh, sorry." I twisted off a small cluster of red grapes and popped one in my mouth. It was ripe and sweet. "Mmm... these are good. Try one."

I fed him a grape. His eyes heated when my fingers brushed his lips. "That is good." His voice was low and husky. Was he talking about the grape? Before I could move my hand, he grabbed my wrist and kissed my fingertips. Butterflies awoke in my belly, and I shivered involuntarily. "A picnic was a good idea, yes?"

"A wonderful idea," I agreed. It came out a little less enthusiastic than I intended, and of course, Kieran noticed.

"What's going on, Meara? What are you worried about?" I started to say I was fine, but he interrupted. "Don't tell me you're fine. I'll know you're lying, and I'll read your mind to find out the truth."

"I can block you." My response was automatic.

"Can you?" he murmured, eyes smoldering. "I'll take that challenge."

He pulled me into his lap, and I yelped in surprise. That was all the invitation he needed to devour my mouth. My hand slid into his hair. He gripped my hip with one hand, while the other slid up the back of my shirt. His kiss was demanding, but I met his passion with my own.

It ended as abruptly as it started, both of us struggling for breath. Kieran's face was scrunched up, and he pouted. "Your dad contacted you, and you didn't tell me?"

Damn. That was twice today that I lost a battle of wills. I ran my fingers through my hair. "I wanted to, but you planned this romantic date. I didn't want to spoil the mood."

"Too late," he muttered under his breath, but I heard him.

"You're the one who invaded my thoughts," I said. "It wasn't nice to kiss me to get information." I picked up some cubes of cheese and crackers. If Kieran planned to be mad at me, that was fine. I wasn't letting good food go to waste.

He blew out a frustrated breath. "I'm sorry," he said. "I'm hurt that you felt you couldn't tell me. We can reschedule a date. I know you're worried about your dad and Brigid. I wish you would've told me right away. This is big news."

"It is," I agreed, relieved he wasn't upset. Ruining our first date hadn't been on my agenda today. "I can't do anything though. Uncle Angus made me promise to wait."

"You didn't promise you'd stay away completely, only that you wouldn't accompany Drust and Judoc on the mission."

I winced. "You saw that?"

His face broke into a full-toothed boast. "Honey, I saw it all. Your shield didn't even exist while I was kissing you."

"I'll work on that."

His eyes crinkled with humor. "I'm sure you will."

"It won't happen again."

He made a noncommittal noise and bit a piece of cheese. His eyes grew distant, and I knew he was thinking about rescuing my dad. The amount he cared continued to surprise me.

"What are you thinking?" I asked.

Ignoring my question, he handed me a sandwich. "Eat up. We need to get going."

"Where?"

"To find Drust and Judoc before they leave. Weren't you listening to me?"

"I was," I said, confused. "But why are we finding them?" If we couldn't go with them, I didn't see the point in tracking them down.

"I agree with you," he said. "Those guys are meatheads and doomed to fail without our help."

"And with our help?" I asked skeptically.

"They have a slightly better chance." He shook his head. "I still don't place high odds on their success."

We ate the rest of our food in silence, lost in our own thoughts. The date had not turned out how I expected, but for the moment, it was perfect.

Chapter 14

"How do you do it?" Evan asked. He convinced Deanna to spend another hour at the underground apartment so she could try to teach him how to access and control Ken's thoughts.

"Let me ask you a question." She leaned forward, her forearms resting on her knees. "When did you know that you could read Ken's mind?"

"He was telling me the story of how their mother was killed. While he didn't say much out loud, I heard him say Azuria in my mind. I felt his rage and vengeance too."

"He spoke in your mind?" she asked.

Evan shook his head. "He didn't intend to. I'm sure that he has no idea that I heard what he was thinking. Do you hear his voice, too?"

"Yes." Deanna sat back. "My experience is similar to yours, which is good. This might work." She took a breath and blew it out like she was nervous or anxious. "The only way we can practice this is if I try to get into your head. Are you okay with that?"

"Yes," Evan said automatically. "I want to learn."

"Let's start then." A slight pain in his temple was followed by an image of a young girl with pale green hair. She swam alongside a beautiful woman with olive skin and dark blue, flowing curls. "My mom," Deanna said. "You see her, don't you?"

"Yes."

"Did you feel when I entered your mind?" Deanna asked. Evan nodded. "Perfect. That means you'll feel something similar when Ken tries to tap into your energy."

"I have," Evan said. "That's why I was able to limit how much energy he took."

"Good. To trick him, you need to create a false feeling, make him think he's taking your power when he's not."

"Won't he feel something when I enter his mind? Like the pain I felt when you entered mine?"

She tapped her lip with her fingertip and considered his question. Finally, she said, "I don't think so. When I placed those fake memories in his head, he didn't even react. I don't think he feels it. And I slip under his radar now, for the most part, so I know it worked."

"Slip under his radar? How?"

"He remembers me as one of the weakest of my people. Sure, I have to endure his abuse, but he does not recall my true identity."

"Wait." Shocked, Evan wanted to make sure he understood. "You mean, he doesn't remember that your mom was the leader of the Sirens?"

"That's what I mean exactly." She gave him a confident smile. "He thinks I am an orphan, an outcast among my people."

Evan was impressed. It probably took a lot of magic and skill to fool Ken. "Who does know your true identity?"

"The other Sirens, but they keep my secret. It's in their best interest to do so." Her features darkened as she scowled. "We all want to regain control of our lives."

"Can they do what you do? Can they read minds?" He was intrigued. It was strange that he had been down here for several days, but the only people he interacted with so far were Ken and Deanna. He wondered what the others were like.

"Not that I know of," she said. "However, I'm not sure they've ever tried. They're scared. For the most part, they follow orders and try to stay out of Ken's way." She settled into her chair and gave Evan an encouraging smile. "Enough small talk. It's your turn now."

"To do what?"

"Practice. You don't think you're going to crack Ken's head first try, do you? You need to practice. I'm the perfect option." She grinned. "I'm here, after all. And willing."

"What do I do?"

"First, see if you can get into my head. It would be ideal if you can do it without me noticing."

He frowned. She was so beautiful that it was distracting. "Can you close your eyes or turn away or something?"

Her smile was indulgent. "Sure."

She closed her eyes, and her face took on a peaceful expression. After a moment, one slim eyebrow rose. "Are you trying?"

"No." He cleared his throat.

"What are you waiting for?" Her tone was a mix of humor and impatience. While she spoke, he focused on the sound of her voice, the lift of her chest as she breathed in, the curve of her cheek, and the slender line of her neck.

He's so adorable. Does he realize how much he affects me?

Evan heard her voice, cool and smooth, in his head. He saw himself, only more handsome and stronger. His muscles were sculpted, his eyes glowed a sapphire blue. Then he realized that he was seeing himself as she saw him. Too perfect. He remembered when he was ten years old and showing off on his bike, trying to jump a ramp to impress Becky Martin, the freckled-faced girl with the braids who was staying at the inn that week with her parents. He missed the landing and chipped his tooth on the handlebar. Deanna's giggle distracted him, and he was once again in his own head.

"Oh my! I hope that first kiss was worth the pain," she teased.

"It was." He grinned. "Did I do okay placing that image?"

"Okay? You were better than I was. I didn't even realize you were in my head until I saw that sweet little boy tumbling head-first over his bike, and what could only be Becky falling down laughing, tears in her eyes."

"She teased me about it," he said. "But she still kissed me."

Shaking her head in amazement, Deanna stood and offered him her hand. "You're going to do fine. I don't think Ken realizes that by creating you, he created his match."

"You think I stand a chance?"

"I really do." She nodded as a smile slowly spread across her face. "I think you might just save us, Evan."

He let her pull him up to standing, their bodies almost touching. "A hero," she whispered, stepping forward and closing the distance.

"You're certainly mine."

Her lips brushed over his, light and teasing. Winding her hands into his hair, she pulled him closer. The sweet, warm scent that was her surrounded him, causing a deep ache in his chest. She slid her tongue along his mouth, encouraging him to open it. He did, and she deepened the kiss, showing him with her thoughts what she wanted to do. His breath caught, and his own thoughts disappeared. Her throaty laugh filled his head. *Are you willing?* He made a noise in agreement, unwilling to break contact with her.

She slid her hands down and took his hands in hers, walking backwards and leading him to the leather sofa. Lowering herself onto it, she pulled him down with her. *You're an excellent student,* her voice whispered through his head, *and a fast learner.*

Chapter 15

Kieran seemed to know where he was going. I followed closely behind him. I had no clue where Dad's guard trained. I didn't even know how many men he had in it. He took four with him and Brigid on their mission, and I assumed they were all captured and imprisoned. Dad didn't say when I spoke to him, and I never asked. Two others were already dead. They washed ashore at the beginning of summer. We never determined the cause of death. Now, it was safe to assume the Blue Men killed them. How many more would die before this was over?

"They're in the room up ahead," Kieran said. As we drew closer, he straightened his shoulders and lifted his chin. Was he even aware of the shift in his stance? He went into warrior mode so naturally.

"Drust. Judoc." Kieran addressed them upon entering the room. He was their equal, if not their superior. "I take it that Angus filled you in on the details?"

"He did." Judoc, the taller of the two men, spoke first. "Are you coming with us, Kieran?"

"No." Kieran gestured to me. "We came to ensure you had everything you needed for the journey."

"You? Son of the Alkana clan, and you, human daughter of David?" Drust snorted his disgust, and I fought the urge to slap the ugly smirk from his face. "What can you offer us?"

"Are those the weapons you're taking?" I asked, pleased that my voice stayed calm. My hands shook with anger, so I clasped them behind my back. Each man held a small dagger, no more than four inches long. "Are you planning to give the Blue Men paper cuts?"

"Insolent brat," Drust spat and flexed his muscles. "We are the weapons."

I almost rolled my eyes when he confirmed what a meathead he was. Judoc had the decency to look unsure and a little embarrassed at the antics of his companion.

Should we show them? Kieran's voice slid through my mind. I loved his confidence in me. He didn't see me as just a girl; he saw me as his equal.

Please, I said. Together, we conjured swords at the same time. The guards dropped their sorry excuses for weapons. Shock clear on their faces, they raised their hands in surrender.

"You lasted two seconds," Kieran said dryly. "And we are not your enemy. So let's try this again. Do you want our help?"

Drust eyed the swords with suspicion, maybe even fear. "Where did you get those?"

"Meara found them." Kieran's voice rang with pride, although I recalled that his first reaction was anger when I depleted my energy to bring them to the island.

Three pairs of eyes focused on me. I shrugged. "They were hidden in castles on the mainland. No one was using them, so I figured there was no harm in taking them."

"Can you teach us?" Judoc asked, looking at me specifically.

"Of course," I said.

None of my dad's guard had attended any of our training sessions. At the time, I assumed it meant they were already well trained. Now, I knew that it was pride that kept them away. As much as I wanted to go and rescue my dad myself, I couldn't refuse to train these two and risk their lives, even if they were arrogant and rude.

Kieran and I each conjured an additional sword from our supply. He paired off with Judoc, a closer height match, and I with Drust. Drust was several inches taller than I was and about fifty pounds heavier, but I made up for the size difference with speed. We spent the remainder of the evening showing the guards how to use the weapons, both offensively and defensively. The moon was high when our session finished. Kieran and I could still best them, but they made remarkable progress in mere hours.

"Will you leave in the morning?" Kieran asked.

Drust shook his head, and Judoc said, "We'll leave now under the cover of night."

"You must contact my dad when you get to the isle," I said. "That was his specific order."

"We will." Drust bowed and took my hand, kissing the top of it. His earlier attitude was gone. "My apologies, Meara. You honor your father and the clan."

Judoc bowed as well, and then shook both of our hands. "Thank you both for sharing your knowledge. We cannot repay you."

"You can," I said. "Bring them and yourselves back safely."

"We will do our best."

With curt nods, they turned and strode away from us. I prayed they would find success, though I had my doubts.

Chapter 16

Evan hummed as he dressed. Ken would be knocking at his door soon. Evan wanted to be ready. He was nervous about trying to trick the leader of the Blue Men, but he was experiencing some level of giddy excitement. If it worked, Evan could slow Ken's efforts. With any luck, he could be stopped, which would be tricky to do without Ken becoming aware of his motives.

Once again wishing he had a hot cup of coffee, Evan decided to convince Deanna to go back to the mall with him that evening if she wasn't working. He needed to learn her work schedule.

Should he feel guilty for what happened between them last night? At first, he thought so, but he found that he couldn't muster up the emotion. His body was relaxed and his heart full. Deanna made him feel alive. They parted ways a few hours ago, and he couldn't wait to see her again. He hadn't felt that way with Meara in a long time. Most of last summer, he was tense and angry. Whether it was Ken's influence or not, the distance in their relationship seemed real to Evan. Meara felt it, too. Otherwise, she would've fought him more when he broke up with her. She took the news almost too easily, like her heart reached the same conclusion. No, he didn't feel guilty. If anything, he was sad. What they had together was great while it lasted.

Evan opened the door to Ken's raised hand.

"You're up!" Surprise was clear in Ken's voice.

"I'm ready to go." With a wide smile, Evan crossed his arms and leaned on the doorframe.

Ken's surprise gave way to suspicion. "That's a change from yesterday."

"I do have an ulterior motive," Evan said, knowing that his choice of words would intrigue Ken.

"Oh?" Ken chuckled, but the sound was menacing. "Let's hear it."

"I want you to pay me for the use of my power. I can't live here on my good looks alone, and I'm quite fond of coffee."

Ken's laugh was more genuine this time. "You found the mall then."

"I did," Evan said. "And I've got a bit of a caffeine addiction."

Scratching his chin, Ken considered Evan's request. Finally, he said, "Fair enough. I will pay you, so long as you cooperate."

"Cooperation's my middle name." Evan stuck out his hand. "Deal?"

Ken gave him a searching look, then, apparently satisfied, he shook Evan's hand. "Deal."

Evan paid closer attention this time as they swam to the mantle plume. He knew they were getting close when the water took on the putrid taste of death and decay. Shortly after he began to taste it, Evan noticed the destruction. The half-rotted skeletons of decomposing fish that couldn't swim away fast enough. Further along, he noticed greyish-black slime that might have once been an anemone. The water was murky, black, and thick with loss, only Evan's sharp, supernatural sight allowed him to navigate through the sludge. To a human, it might've appeared to be a man-made disaster like an oil spill. As one of the Blue Men, Evan was immune to Ken's magic and could see the mantle plume's destruction for what it was—evil. Ken might be able to accept murder as a means to his goals, but Evan never would. Killing was immoral. Flora or fauna, innocents shouldn't have to die for one man's mission.

"How much farther until the fault reaches the Selkies' island?" Evan asked. The deep crack in the ocean floor stretched beyond his sight. Billows of steam rose from the fissure where the hot lava, glowing red, met the cold ocean water.

"I don't know exactly," Ken admitted after a moment's silence. "I've never been there, but I know the general vicinity."

"Wouldn't it be helpful to find it first?" Evan hoped Ken might bite at this idea. If they swam close enough, Evan might be able to warn Meara if their psychic connection still worked. He couldn't reach her from Belle Trésor. Perhaps the Siren settlement was too far away or warded against that kind of magic.

"It would make sense, if we could find the island. The Selkies have encased it in their magic. We've yet to discover it." Ken sounded bitter. "I've been searching for several decades."

"It's warded against our magic?" That surprised Evan. Ken made it sound like the Selkies didn't stand a chance against the Blue Men. Maybe the Selkies were stronger than Ken thought. For Meara's sake, Evan hoped so.

"I will find their island using the mantle plume," Ken said. "Magic cannot stop a force of nature. When we've properly fed it, the plume will destroy them."

"How?" Evan asked. Ken explained the day before, but Evan didn't fully understand. To be honest, he had only half listened. At the time, he was more worried about losing his power or dying at Ken's hands. Now, Evan focused on Ken's response.

"It's simple really. The mantle plume is an underwater volcano. Our power feeds that volcano, increasing the friction, which generates more heat and melts the rock beneath the ocean's surface. We're also growing the fault and moving the hot magma closer to the Selkies' island."

"Because you know the general vicinity where the island exists?"

"Exactly!" Ken's voice rose in excitement. "The destruction will have massive reach. They will burn in fire and ash. When the eruption is complete, their home, their people, will exist no more." His sharp teeth gleamed in the water, and his gaze drilled into Evan. His eyes, Evan noted, were those of a madman. "This event will make Pompeii look like child's play."

Evan's blood froze as dread settled in his stomach. How was he—a human-turned-supernatural being—in any way equipped to stop this? This was something that Ken must have plotted for centuries before finally executing on the idea.

Finally, they arrived at the spot where they were the day before. Evan recognized a small rock formation nearby. Ken immediately crouched down and placed his hands in the thick, gray silt. The ground began to glow a soft blue.

"Join me."

It was a command, not a request. Evan dropped beside Ken. This was it. The true test of whether his practice with Deanna would pay off. He placed his hands over Ken's and felt the immediate tug on his energy. He let Ken siphon some, although he limited the flow to a trickle.

Entering Ken's mind was easy, because the man was so focused on his task. Once Evan knew that he was in, he began to feed Ken a vision—Evan's power flowed into Ken's and, together, they grew the plume, stretching the destructive fissure another twenty yards. In reality, Evan used his power against Ken and siphoned some of Ken's energy for his purposes. While Ken saw the plume expand, Evan knew that it really receded a foot. Not much, but with practice, Evan was confident he could do more.

By the end of the day, Ken's brow was pale and his breathing was gurgled and uneven. He clasped Evan's arm, straightened slowly, and smiled. "Well done, my boy. We made good progress today."

As a last move before he got out of Ken's head, Evan made Ken see that Evan was as dirty and tired as he was. It would not be good for Ken to notice how unaffected he really was.

"I agree, sir." Giddy with his success, Evan struggled to keep his voice calm. He couldn't wait to tell Deanna. "We'll return tomorrow?"

Ken agreed, and they swam out of the muck and grime, back to the jeweled beauty of the Siren lair. It was a small victory, but a win all the same. Evan held his own against Ken today without him knowing. Evan felt something flutter in his chest. That flutter was hope.

Chapter 17

All around me, I watched Selkies play in the surf. It was nice to see them lighthearted and having fun, especially after I worried that they wouldn't go in the water. When Kieran and I first told them our theory that we needed the seawater to recharge before we began working magic, they refused to transform or leave the safety of land. I knew they were hesitant to disobey their leader, even if it meant they were following the orders of his daughter.

To encourage them, I said, "It's okay. Yesterday afternoon, my dad contacted me this way. That's how we learned where he is and where to send Drust and Judoc. We are water creatures. We need to be in the water."

When they still didn't move, Kieran and I went in first. Wading into the cool water, I fought the urge to change. The frothy waves caressed my calves. I went deeper until the water was chest-high. The current rocked me back and forth, a gentle lulling. Kieran stood next to me, motioning to the others to join us. One by one, they came until we were surrounded by our people, their faces cheerful and relaxed.

I heard Uncle Paddy whoop in excitement. He lifted a net full of fish into the air. "They swam right to me. We'll have fresh fish tonight!"

Cheers and applause broke out around us. Paddy grinned at me, more relaxed than I had seen him in months. "I need to go and begin preparing these."

"Off with you then!" I called back to him, laughing.

We played in the water. It was nice to forget my worries for a while. Well, maybe not forget them, but let them float, buoyant and light. Life was bigger than my fears. We were bigger, and we would get through this. We would.

Kieran moved closer, his warm, smooth skin sliding against mine. His lips caressing my ear, he asked, "Should we get started?"

I ignored the shiver that traveled down my spine and the urge to sink into his arms. With a small sigh, I nodded. Kieran clapped his hands loudly. Bobbing heads turned to us. Their quick response told me that we had their trust. The Selkies were ours to command. In only a matter of weeks, we had built an army.

Anxious to begin training, I was the first one out of the water. I wanted to see what happened next. Would the pre-training swim result in more successes?

One by one, they exited the surf. It was difficult to leave the comfort of the ocean. I knew that they felt the pull as much as I did and fought the urge to stay in the sea.

We moved to the mossy bluff, and the group settled into neat rows facing us. I held my hand out, palm up, and waited. The rowdy crowd grew silent.

"We begin where we left off in our last session, a ball of energy." I searched through the faces before me, my eyes settling on Arren, the only one to manifest his energy last time. He nodded, and I continued my scan. I noticed that people seemed to be more relaxed and optimistic. Again, I chalked it up to the water, wishing we'd realized it sooner, but glad that we now knew how important it was.

"Focus on your core source of power. Visualize the ball of light in your hand. Make it be." I closed my hand into a fist and then reopened it. An orange ball of light hovered above my palm. I blew on it lightly, and it doubled in size. The collective gasp made me smile to myself. "Breathe it to life. You can do it!"

Focusing on the light, I drew it back to me and squeezed it between my palms until I reabsorbed the energy. "Begin," I said when everyone continued to stare at me in awe.

Have I told you how amazing you are? Kieran's voice whispered like silk through my mind. *I want to kiss you.*

Desire, raw and needy, clawed at my insides. I hated that his voice made me lose control. Frustrated with myself, I snapped, "Not now! Focus."

86

I felt him chuckle, a thrumming in my chest. Moments like this, it felt like he was a part of me, as familiar as my own body. At least my exasperation at his inappropriate timing tamed the butterflies in my stomach. He loved to get a rise out of me, and he was usually successful.

"You take the front this time," I said, acting as though nothing passed between us. "I'm going to work with Arren and his friends."

"Trying to make me jealous?" Kieran wiggled his eyebrows, and I laughed despite myself.

"Just go," I called over my shoulder, already on my way to the back of the crowd where the teenagers stood.

Like last time, Arren was the first to be successful. The light flickered in his hand, and then steadied. The blonde girl followed, her energy glowing pink. Go figure. She grinned at Arren, and then met my eyes with a shy smile.

"Great job," I told them both. To their companions, I said, "Keep trying."

I moved quickly through the rows. Ula grew a rather impressive ball of purple light. Paddy rejoined us after assigning fish duty to his kitchen help. His energy was the color of rust. At least a dozen more Selkies were successful. With each success, my pride grew. They were doing it. They were starting to conjure magic. This proved it. With practice, they would be unstoppable.

I felt Kieran's strong arms around my waist before he spoke. "Keep practicing. Meara and I will be right back."

I didn't get a chance to ask him where we were going. I had enough time to notice Ula's curious expression before Kieran whisked us away, back to the private cove.

"What are you—?" My words were lost in his kiss. His hands were everywhere, and my brain couldn't keep up. It was enough to keep from drowning in his arms.

When he pulled back, gulping air, he rested his forehead against mine.

"What was that?" I asked.

"You're amazing," he said. "You don't even know it. Do you realize you just broke down one of the biggest barriers to our people?" He stopped and shook his head. "No, you didn't break it down. You smashed it to pieces."

I struggled to follow what he was saying. His voice was deep with emotion. When I placed my hands in his, I realized his were shaking. "Are you okay?" I asked.

He responded with a short laugh before saying, "No. No, I'm not." He stepped closer and kissed me again. His lips were gentle this time, the kiss tender. "I'm not sure I'll ever be okay again."

"Kieran…" My voice trembled. "You're scaring me."

He pulled me so tight against him that I could barely breathe. His hand caressed the back of my head, smoothing my hair. Leaning down, he spoke softly in my ear. "You changed their lives, Meara. Our Selkies can conjure magic because you believed in them and showed them. That's something that no one else has done."

"You're making it sound much bigger than it is." My face grew hot. I wasn't used to flattery, much less the intense focus Kieran gave me. "I may have taught them how to do it, but they already had the magic within them."

"It is a big deal. For centuries, only the ruling families used magic. Why no one thought to teach the others, I don't know. You did it, though." He ran his hands through his hair, his eyes dancing with excitement. "When word gets out, clans everywhere will be changed."

I hadn't thought about that. It worried me. Would they hate me for the change? Would I be known as the human who destroyed the Selkies' way of life?

"Never!" Kieran must've read my mind. He kissed my forehead, then lifted my chin and stared in my eyes. "You will be revered. What you've done is amazing."

It was easy to lose myself in his dark eyes. Intense emotions crossed his face. Before I could consider what they meant, he locked me in another passionate kiss.

"Kieran!" I laughed once I broke away and pushed on his chest. "Shouldn't we go back? You pulled me away from our training session!"

He moved his lips to my throat, finding a sensitive spot that made me cling to him and bite back a moan. "Do you really want to?" he asked, his voice a tempting baritone.

"What I want is irrelevant," I said, barely above a whisper. It was difficult to concentrate with the magic he was doing to my ear.

"Not to me." He lifted his head and met my eyes, then sighed. "Fine. We'll go back."

Taking my hand, he transported us. We appeared in the front of the crowd. I patted my hair, wondering if we looked guilty. We must've looked slightly rumpled, because Arren raised his fingers to his lips and gave a shrill whistle. It was followed by cheers and applause from the others. *If the ground would open up and swallow me, that would be nice,* I thought. That, or in another minute, I was going to combust if the heat coming off my face and neck was any indication.

"Back to practicing!" Kieran called. He didn't seem embarrassed at all. In fact, he grinned like a proud fool. Shaking my head at his bizarre behavior, I switched my concentration to the crowd. Thoughts of Kieran could wait until later.

By the end of the training session, more than half of the Selkies were able to create and sustain a ball of energy. The colors were as unique as the individuals who wielded the magic. Ula's light was a lovely lilac purple, while the male Selkie next to her held a vivid yellow ball. The remaining Selkies who couldn't manifest the sphere were able to generate sparks of colored light.

"Excellent," I spoke as I moved through the group. "You are doing amazing. Now that you can physically manifest your power, you can begin to learn how to harness it to both protect you and defend our home. Are you ready?"

Shouts of confirmation and excited cheers broke out around me. "First, I want you to learn how to create a shield. It can protect you if your enemy tries to use magic against you." I held out my hand and once again, my light appeared. For me, it happened almost instantaneously. I thought it into existence, and it was there. With slightly more concentration, I was able to shape it and grow it around me into a pulsing shield of light. "Focus on your energy. See the ball of light grow and blanket you. You will need to keep some focus on it to hold that form, but as you practice, the amount of concentration required will lessen. Why don't you give it a try?"

Arren and a couple of others managed to create a shield first try, although they each blinked out of existence rather quickly. With satisfaction, I watched the successful attempts increase until almost every Selkie could create and hold the shield for a few minutes.

"Wonderful!" I shouted to be heard above their shouts of joy and excited chatter. "Now, I want to show you how to use your magic in combat. Release your shields, please." I motioned for Kieran to join me, and the Selkies surrounded us in a tight circle. With a laugh, I asked them to back up a little. "I know you're eager to see our demonstration, but I don't want anyone to be hurt by accident."

They backed up quickly, leaving us with an adequate amount of space. Kieran faced me and winked. I pretended to ignore him, although my mouth twitched in the corner.

"I'm going to throw my magic at Kieran. Watch what he does."

A large, pulsing globe of orange light floated in front of me. I pushed out with my hands and drove it toward Kieran, assuming that he would block it with his shield. Instead, he concentrated the shield around his right hand like a catcher's mitt and captured my energy, absorbing it into his own.

"Whoa." Arren's voice was louder than the others, although several gasped in surprise. "Teach me how to do that."

Show off. I scowled at Kieran. *What if they hurt themselves?*

You did it first try without even knowing what you were doing, he countered. *They'll be fine.*

Kieran moved to work with Arren. The other Selkies paired off and started practicing. Most kept to the basics of shielding, but a few started lobbing small energy balls at each other. They were learning fast, much faster than before. It was happening. The magic was growing. I could feel it in the air, heavy with power. One more success for us. One more show of strength. We were going to do this. We were going to defend our home.

Chapter 18

"It worked!" Deanna swam into Evan's arms. Her fragrant hair tickled his nose. She moved back, her bright eyes focused on him. "And Ken didn't notice?"

"He was oblivious, although I didn't make much progress." Evan worried about getting his hopes too high. Deanna was excited enough for both of them.

"No matter. You made progress, and it was your first time at that!" She smiled and patted his chest. "I'm treating you to dinner and coffee."

Dinner sounded great. Evan was starved. Ken didn't believe in breaks or stopping for lunch. Come to think of it, Evan hadn't even eaten breakfast. "Can we go now?" he asked, rubbing his stomach.

"Why not?" She shrugged her slim shoulders. "It's your night, after all."

They swam out of Evan's room, heading toward the dome. This was Evan's third time going there. He was relatively sure he could find his own way if he needed to. Considering that Deanna was with him whenever one or the other of them wasn't at work, though, it didn't seem like a big concern.

He let her go through the drying room first, anticipating what outfit she would pick tonight. It was always fun to see her looking like a human. With the exception of her pale green hair and green eyes that were decidedly not human-like coloring, she could pass for one when she had legs. Some hair dye and contacts and she'd blend right in. He wondered if she had any interest in living on land, or even if Sirens could live on land for extended lengths of time. He planned to ask her once they got their dinner. Hopefully, she would answer him.

She was tapping her foot impatiently when he opened the door. Her slight scowl quickly turned into a grin when she saw his T-shirt.

"Blue Man Group? That's a real thing?"

"It is." Evan smirked a little at his own choice of clothing.

She pointed. "And they're blue like that?"

"Well, they paint their skin blue, yes."

She looked up at him, her expression puzzled. "Why would they do that?"

"Part of their show. They're performers."

"Like me?" She seemed pleased by that.

"Like you," Evan confirmed. Taking her hand, he headed to the stairwell. They could talk and walk at the same time. He was getting hungrier by the minute. "If I joined them, I have a built-in costume."

He meant to be funny, but it must've come out bitter since Deanna made a dismayed noise. "I'll help you get back to your human form, Evan," she said. "I know you're not happy like this."

"It's okay." It was an automatic response, but he realized that he meant it. Down here, it didn't really matter what color he was. Around him were beings of all colors and shades. Some of the Blue Men chose to take forms that were more human, others did not, but all the Sirens kept their soft pastel coloring, even in human form.

They walked the rest of the way in silence, lost in their own thoughts. When they reached the food court, Deanna bought a salad and got Evan a personal pizza. He had no idea how deep sea pizza would taste, but he found it tasted a lot like the pies on land. Delicious.

"Can I ask you a question?" Evan asked after he'd eaten half his meal and took the edge off his hunger.

"Of course," Deanna said. "You don't have to ask for permission. I think we're beyond that point in our relationship, Evan."

His heart jumped a little when she said relationship. Was that what they were doing? In some ways, he knew her intimately, but so much about her was a mystery. He realized the question he was about to ask her made him nervous. Would she read something into it? Did he want her to? With a sigh, he asked it anyway. "Do Sirens ever live on land? I mean, if you wanted to, could you?"

She gave him an appraising look before answering. "Some have.

A few Sirens have married humans, raised families, and died on land. Most don't though. The sea calls to us."

"Would you lose your essence the way Selkies do?" He remembered Meara telling him about the strong pull of the ocean. It was a rare Selkie that could give up the ocean to live on land with a human. If they did, they gave up their powers and essentially became human. That meant a much shorter life span too. He wondered why Selkies were so limited when other species weren't. "I mean, why can't they live with humans?"

A dark expression crossed Deanna's face before she changed it to something more neutral. "You're thinking about your ex-girlfriend, aren't you?"

"Yes," Evan admitted. "Meara was told that if she lives with humans for longer than a year, she'll lose her magic."

"That's my understanding, too," Deanna said. Her voice softened with sympathy. "Their magic is different than ours. I don't claim to understand it, but they live in groups. They need their people. Somehow, each individual's essence nourishes the masses. And, like us, they are tied to the sea."

"But they live on land," Evan said, confused.

"Yes," Deanna said. "Like I told you, I don't understand it either."

In some ways, Evan was relieved that he broke up with Meara now that he understood how critical her clan was to her. He couldn't make her choose between her family and him. If they stayed together, wouldn't that have been the ultimate result? Of course, now that he was one of the Blue Men...

"What about the Blue Men? Can we live on land?"

Deanna quickly scanned the crowd and gave him a nervous laugh. "You're asking a lot of questions tonight."

"I'm sorry. If you want me to stop—"

"It's okay." She covered his hand with hers. Leaning across the table, she whispered in his ear. "I'm worried that we're being watched."

She brushed a kiss on his lips, and then sat back with a smile. If anyone were watching, they would only think that they were a cute couple, exchanging a few words and affectionate moments.

"Dee! Is that you?"

A young Siren with a bright purple pixie cut ran over to their table.

Following behind at a slower pace were two Blue Men and another girl with long, curly red hair. The red was as bright as a fire hydrant. Apparently, siren coloring was not limited to pastels.

"Krystal and Melody!" Deanna stood and hugged them. "I thought you were working tonight."

The girls shook their heads in unison. "Ken sent us home early. He was holding a private celebration and didn't want any of us there."

A private party without women? It didn't sound fun to Evan. What was Ken up to? Evan wanted to ask, but he didn't know these people. Luckily, Deanna asked for him, "What kind of party?"

The girls glanced over at their dates, who had walked away to stand in line for food. When the women started talking, they stared at Evan as if considering.

"He's safe, Krystal," Deanna said quickly.

"Blue Men only," Krystal reluctantly answered in a whisper. "It had something to do with capturing two more Selkies."

Deanna met Evan's eyes. Hers were filled with sympathy and something more... a warning?

"Two more?" Evan asked before he could help himself. "How many does he already have?"

Krystal's eyes grew round. "You're familiar with Selkies? I thought you only recently found out about your heritage. Weren't you living as a human?"

"I was," Evan said, catching himself before he said 'I am.' He still thought of himself as mostly human after all. "I was dating a Selkie, though."

"You dated a Selkie?" The redhead, who Evan deduced was Melody, asked this question. She barely got it out before erupting into a fit of giggles. Krystal joined in. Deanna didn't laugh, but she seemed amused.

"What's so funny?" Evan looked at the three women. He was obviously missing something.

"They're so ugly," Krystal managed between her snickers. "They turn into seals, for goodness sake."

"Yeah, and you are part fish," Evan bit back before realizing that he shouldn't have said anything. The girls stopped laughing and stared at him.

"Careful," Krystal drawled with an undercurrent of steel in her tone.

"You're lovely, of course," Evan said. "I just don't think it's nice to make fun of another species. It's not like they can help who they are or what they turn into."

"Well said, Evan." Deanna looked at her friends with reproach. They sobered up and cleared their throats. At least they had the decency to look a little embarrassed.

The guys returned, their trays piled with food. They sat down and started eating, not offering anything to their dates. Evan found this rather rude.

"Would either of you like anything to eat or drink?" he asked the Sirens, giving the men a look of reproach. It was wasted, since they didn't even acknowledge him. Of course, when the women shook their heads, Evan sighed with relief. If they had said yes, he would need to borrow money from Deanna again. Ken hadn't paid him anything yet.

Evan sat in silence while the girls gossiped and the guys ate. He wanted to hear more about the captive Selkies, but he wasn't sure if it was a safe topic with this group. He glanced around the food court and realized there was a rather noticeable absence of Blue Men tonight. The only ones here were the two at their table. Were these two left behind as guards? Out on a date? Or was there another reason that they couldn't attend the celebration?

Who could Ken have captured? Evan's gut told him that it wasn't Meara, but it could be someone from her family or Kieran. *Maybe that wouldn't be such a bad thing*, Evan thought before chastising himself for being cruel. Just because Kieran liked Meara and was probably pursuing her right now didn't mean Evan needed to wish bad things upon the Selkie.

"You're quiet," Deanna said, moving her chair closer to rest her hand on his arm. "Did you want to leave? I know you have to go to work early tomorrow."

When she asked the question, she nudged his foot with her own. Funny that underwater, the nudge was still the universal sign between a couple that it was time to go. He faked a yawn and stretched, irrationally pleased to see Krystal and Melody eye his body with interest while

Deanna's face flashed with jealousy. "You're right. I didn't sleep well last night. I better get some rest tonight or work will be brutal."

The guy with black hair and a considerable amount of facial piercings looked closer at Evan. "I didn't catch your name."

"It's Evan."

"Ken's son." The guy shook his head almost sadly. "He's got you working on that mantle plume. That's brutal, man. I don't envy you."

Evan didn't know what to say. Luckily, the dark-haired man reached across the table and offered Evan his hand. "I'm Vesh."

"Vesh?" It wasn't a name Evan heard before.

"Short for Veshian, but yeah, everyone calls me Vesh. This is Slate." He nudged the other guy in the shoulder. Slate grunted in reply, not looking up from the last of his food.

"Nice to meet you both." Evan stood, following Deanna's lead. "Well, see you around."

Vesh gave him a cheery smile. "We're usually here, so you'll know where to find us."

Chapter 19

I paced in Uncle Angus' room while he and Kieran played chess. The silence and waiting was killing me. I couldn't take it any longer. "How can you two sit there so calmly? It's been two weeks since Dad contacted me, and we've heard nothing else."

I knew this for a fact. Every morning, I watched the sun rise while wading in the surf. I prayed my dad would contact me again so I could have some news. Any news. My prayers had yet to be answered.

"What can we do, Meara?" Uncle Angus looked at me with sympathy. I'd been getting that look a lot lately. I was a wreck. I couldn't sit still, barely ate, and woke up several times at night. Each day that passed with no news made me lose a little hope that we would find them. If we didn't rescue my dad and aunt, then how would we ever save Evan? Ken could be torturing Evan right now. Would he hate me when, or if, I did find him?

Now both men were watching me pace, the game momentarily forgotten, concern on their faces. I didn't want them to worry about me, and I certainly didn't want their sympathy. I wanted my uncle to believe in me and let me go rescue them.

"How much longer do we wait?" I asked, stealing a glance at Kieran. He was unusually quiet and averted his eyes to analyze the chessboard. It wasn't like him to stay out of a conversation. Did he agree with my uncle? "You told me two weeks."

Uncle Angus heaved a great sigh and sat back in his chair. He stroked his beard while he studied me. "So, I did, Meara. So I did. You feel that you can succeed where two of your father's best guard did not?"

"Yes," I said without hesitation. "They were completely unprepared,

Uncle. Ask Kieran!"

"She's right," Kieran said. I was relieved that he decided to speak. "We trained them for a few hours, but it was certainly not enough to prepare them."

"Why don't Ronac Selkies know how to fight?" I asked. "Kieran does. Dad and Aunt Brigid do. Why wasn't Dad's guard trained properly?"

Uncle Angus shook his head sadly and with a grunt, rose from his chair. "I'm getting a drink. Can I get you anything?"

He was avoiding my questions. Sometimes, my great uncle needed a little time to formulate his thoughts. I could let him have that. At least it meant he was considering my questions. "I'll have a Diet Coke," I said.

"Nothing for me," Kieran replied.

I waited while my uncle went to the fridge and got two cans. He chose a ginger ale. Handing me my drink, he said, "You must understand. Your grandparents died over a hundred years ago, Meara. We battled the Blue Men, but we had to retreat. We lost many of our strongest fighters in that battle, including my mother." His eyes grew distant, filling with sadness. "Before we could regroup and try again, the Blue Men simply disappeared. We've lived peacefully since then. I believe your father thought the threat had passed." He patted my hand and sat back down. "The last eighteen years, your dad's been preoccupied in his search for you and your mom. Not that you are to blame in any of this," he quickly added.

As far as explanations go, it felt weak. In a matter of months, I'd learned to fight, and, in turn, train the majority of our people to defend themselves, too. I preferred not to go to war or risk innocent lives, but I also knew that we were heading toward a battle with the Blue Men. It was ignorant to think that we were safe on this island. Dad should have known better.

A knock at the door disturbed my thoughts. Before my uncle could answer it, it burst open and a tall man strode in. He looked familiar, but he wasn't one of our own. I glanced at Kieran. By his broad grin, it was obvious that he recognized the stranger.

"Cole!" Kieran met the man halfway, pulling him into a manly hug. "What are you doing here, old friend?"

Now I remembered how I knew him. He was one of Kieran's buddies at the dance club. The one who danced with Val. My stomach tightened, and I fought back tears when a wave of homesickness hit me. I missed my friends and my grandparents. If I thought about it, I could picture them clearly—Grandma Mary's springy curls and smiling face and Grandpa Jamie's stern, but no less loving, demeanor. The year at their house was one full of love, hugs, and home cooking. I longed to see them again and hoped someday I would.

What would my life be like now if I had not gone with my dad? If I stayed in Nova Scotia, then Evan may not have taken the internship. He could be home and safe. We'd probably still be together. Would I have been happier? I certainly wouldn't feel the knot of worry eating at my gut and making me clench my teeth. On the other hand, I wouldn't have Kieran either. It wasn't wise to dwell on what could have been when there was nothing I could do about it now.

Kieran and Cole watched me with odd expressions. "I'm sorry. Did you say something to me?" I asked.

"I was introducing Cole," Kieran said. Cole extended his hand, and I shook it. He was as tall as Kieran, but fair where Kieran was dark. His eyes were a lovely shade of hazel.

"Nice to meet you, Cole," I said. "Although I do remember you from the club."

"Do you?" Cole shared an amused look with Kieran. It was nice that they enjoyed themselves that evening at our expense. At least Kieran eventually apologized to me. If he hadn't, I might not have gotten past thinking he was a conceited jerk.

"Your friend was delightful. I enjoyed meeting you as well." Cole turned back to Kieran, his expression changing to all business. "Is there somewhere we can go to talk?"

Kieran moved next to me and reached for my hand. The gesture was not missed by Cole, who raised an eyebrow at him. "We can talk in front of Meara," Kieran said. "And Angus. He is in charge while David is away."

This news surprised Cole, if his wide eyes were any indication. "David is gone? Where is he?"

"Long story, my friend." Kieran led us to the couch. He gestured to a chair and said, "Why don't you sit, Cole, and tell us why you're here. After, we'll send for dinner and fill you in over the meal."

Uncle Angus sat in his recliner, and Cole took the other chair. I sipped my soda, waiting for Cole to begin and noticing how he eyed the can with envy.

"Cole, can I get you something to drink before you start?" I asked.

"Please," he said. "Water would be great."

My uncle moved to stand, but I waved him off. "I got it," I said. "I know where you keep the glasses." I moved quickly, adding ice and water, not wanting to miss the story.

Cole smiled at me gratefully when I handed him the glass. I returned to my spot beside Kieran. He rested his hand on my knee. A casual gesture, but I wondered why he was touching me so much. Was he making a point to Cole that I was taken? That was ridiculous. We went on one date. We weren't betrothed or whatever it was that Selkies do.

After a long drink from the glass, Cole set it on the table and began, "Your father sent me to check on your welfare. He was expecting you back shortly after the Dispute Moon."

This was news to me. So Kieran was supposed to leave the same day as my Uncle Ren's family? Why didn't he say anything to me? Was he in trouble with his dad? Cole didn't appear to be upset, more curious.

"When you didn't come home and didn't send word, understandably, Stephen grew worried. That's when he sent me." The reproach was clear in Cole's voice, but Kieran didn't look troubled.

"How is my family?" Kieran asked.

Cole smiled. "Tyrese is obstinate as always. Your father is trying to convince her that it's time to consider a mate. She will have nothing of it."

"Good for her," Kieran said with a laugh.

"Who's Tyrese?" I asked.

Kieran avoided my eyes. "My little sister."

"You have a sister? Why didn't you tell me?" I glanced at Uncle Angus. He watched the three of us with amusement.

You never asked. His words flowed calmly through my mind, but they had the opposite effect on my emotions. I was furious, especially when he added, *I have a brother, too.* Out loud, he said, "How's Alexios?"

"Worried sick, of course, and following your father around, trying to console him and stand in your place," Cole said. "Not that anyone could," he quickly added when Kieran glared at him.

"You have a brother *and* a sister?" I couldn't hold back the hurt in my voice. "And you didn't mention anything to me?"

"Kieran and Alex are identical twins," Cole said, looking surprised. "Kieran never said anything?"

"It hadn't come up," Kieran said. He squeezed my hand right before I pulled mine away and moved to the other side of the couch. He scowled at me. "Really, it's not a big deal. Alex and I aren't even that close."

"So that makes it okay? There are two of you, yet since you aren't close, it's not worth mentioning?"

Cole laughed, clearly enjoying the sight of Kieran uncomfortable. "I would never say there are two of Kieran. The gods help us all. Kieran and Alex may look identical, but their personalities are as different as the sun and moon."

"Does your brother keep secrets from the girl that he proclaims to care about?" I asked. My words were snippy, but I didn't care. This wasn't something small, like, "I forgot to mention I hate peas." This was huge. It made me realize how little I really knew about him. I only knew the facts in the context of our small little island. I'd let that go to my head.

Disillusioned—that was how I felt at the moment.

Kieran scrubbed his hands over his face. *I'm sorry,* his words whispered through my mind. *I'll tell you anything you want to know about me later, but for now, can you please let it go? It's important that I present myself appropriately in front of Cole.*

Fine, I said. *But this hurts, Kieran. I don't really know you.*

How well do you think I know you, Meara? That's what the human ritual of dating is about, right? Getting to know each other? You can't assume after one date that we would know all there is to know about each other.

Damn it. Why did he have to make so much sense? We became friends, and before that, he was my trainer. I hadn't told him everything about me. It just felt like he knew more about my life since he had been with me almost the entire time I had been a Selkie. He knew very little of my life as a human. We had a lot to learn about each other.

You're right, I relented. *But we are talking later.*

I look forward to it. His tone made me shiver. *One more thing, can you move closer so I may hold your hand again?*

I relented, scooting over and taking his hand. My uncle and Cole watched us with bemused expressions. "Is your lovers' spat all settled?" Uncle Angus asked.

My face heated up about two hundred degrees in response.

"Please continue," Kieran said. His tone was cool, yet pleasant. If he was embarrassed, he didn't show it.

Cole shrugged. "That's about it, I guess. Your father is worried, your brother worries for your father, and your sister fights for her freedom. Everyone else is the same. Bryce asked me to tell you hello. She looks forward to your return."

Bryce? This time I kept my face neutral, not even turning my head. I was proud of myself.

She's hot for my body, Kieran answered. *Can you blame her?* He gave me a sexy grin. When I didn't return it, the teasing expression melted away. *Honestly, Meara. I don't feel that way about her at all. I never have. There's nothing between us.*

"We can leave the room, if you two want to keep talking." My uncle sounded more amused than offended, but I figured it was time we stopped talking telepathically. It was rude, especially if they were aware of it. We must be ignoring them.

"Should I see about having dinner delivered?" I asked. It seemed only fair that Kieran spend time with Cole since he traveled so far, and this was my uncle's room. I was the most ideally suited to the task.

"I can go," Kieran volunteered.

"Stay and visit with Cole," I said. "It's no trouble."

I squeezed his hand and stood, transporting to the kitchen. It left Kieran no time to argue with me. Uncle Paddy stood by the stove as usual, his face flushed from the steam. He looked happy. I know he would worry less now that he once again had a supply of fresh fish.

"Hi Paddy." I walked over and looked in the pot. The thick, creamy soup emitted an herbal scent. "Is that chowder?"

"It is." He picked up a clean spoon from the counter, dipped it in the kettle, and handed me a taste. "What do you think?"

A myriad of flavors danced on my tongue. I tasted fish, but also chives, dill, and butter in the rich broth. It was delicious, as all of Paddy's concoctions tended to be. "I love it. What is it?"

"Cullen skink."

"What?" That did not sound appetizing at all.

I must've made a face, because Paddy laughed. "Cullen skink is fish chowder made with haddock. It's a traditional dish."

"Huh. Strange name, but I like it." Remembering that I was here for a reason, I added, "Kieran has a clan member visiting. His name is Cole. We'd like to eat in Uncle Angus' room tonight."

"Cole?" Paddy's eyes looked distant for a moment, and then he smiled as recognition dawned on him. "Ah, yes. Tall chap with blond hair, right? I remember him from my youth."

It caught me off guard when my aunts and uncles talked about their childhood. Except for Uncle Angus, everyone looked young, much younger than their actual ages. I forgot that with my dad and Kieran's dad being close friends, the two families must have socialized frequently.

"Did you visit Kieran's home often when you were young?"

"Enough," Paddy said. "Until our parents were killed." He paused, and then asked, "Why is Cole here?"

"Checking on Kieran from what I gather."

Paddy nodded. "I imagine Stephan is concerned. Kieran stayed here longer than he originally planned." Paddy gave me a long look, and then cleared his throat. "Of course, no one planned on David and Brigid getting captured."

"Right..." The conversation was starting to feel awkward. I was ready to get back to the others and see if I was missing anything. "Do you want me to take the food with me?"

"No, I'll send someone up in a few minutes."

"Will we get to eat some of that?" I asked, pointing to the chowder.

"Of course," Paddy said. "Now, out of my kitchen so I can finish the preparations."

I transported back to Uncle Angus' room. The men sat in the

same positions, although now they all held beers. "Dinner is on its way," I said. "Cullen skink."

I took their murmurs to be sounds of approval and sat next to Kieran again. "Did I miss anything?" I asked.

"Not unless you enjoy a rousing conversation about basketball," my uncle said, pursing his lips and wiggling his eyebrows to make me laugh.

"I'm not much of a sports girl," I admitted.

"What?" Cole looked at me in mock horror. "And Kieran is interested in you?"

Kieran was about to retort when a knock at the door interrupted him. He moved to open it and let in the Selkie carrying a tray of food. Paddy wasn't kidding! The food almost beat me back to the room. He sent up four large bowls of the soup, a loaf of warm bread, and crab cakes. For me, he included greens since I mentioned last week how much I missed a tossed salad and ranch dressing. I was touched that he remembered.

We sat at my uncle's table and ate. The three of us took turns telling Cole about our current situation and how we got here. The more we talked, the more concerned Cole looked.

"And now? With the additional guards missing, what are your plans?" Cole's gaze moved between Uncle Angus and Kieran. I tried not to be offended that he wasn't addressing me.

"I go next," I said. "Uncle Angus promised me."

"*We* go next," Kieran countered.

"And I arrived just in time," Cole said. "Stephen is not going to like this. Not at all."

"He doesn't have a say in the matter!" Kieran snapped back, shocking me with the venom in his voice. Didn't he get along with his father? He always spoke of him warmly.

"What should I report back?" Cole asked. His tone this time was mild and respectful.

"The truth," Kieran said. "Tomorrow, Meara and I will leave to rescue the elders, possibly fight the Blue Men. We will return victorious."

I choked on a spoonful of chowder. A sip of water managed to cover it up, so no one else noticed. I was no longer hungry. What was the matter with me? This was what I wanted. To take action, to fight, but now that the moment was upon me, fear constricted my throat and filled my belly.

Would we, could we, find success where others failed?

Chapter 20

The swim home was excruciating torture. Every muscle ached in Evan's body. For the first time in months, he had a beast of a headache. After the success he experienced yesterday, he was expecting to make progress again today. It took everything in him to keep Ken ignorant of the plan. The mantle plume didn't grow, but it didn't shrink either. They were at a standstill, and today, there were no winners. Both of them looked like death warmed over on the swim home.

Usually, Ken made sure Evan went back to his room. Not today. They parted ways as soon as they crossed into Belle Trésor grounds. Evan assumed Ken planned to take a nap, too. At this point, he didn't care what Ken did. Eyelids heavy like lead weights, the only thing Evan wanted was sleep.

When he woke and stretched, the blue and purple jewels of evening told him he'd slept for hours—most of the day, actually. The good news was he felt completely recharged. Now that the day was almost done, he wasn't sure what to do. Getting food was probably a smart idea. He hadn't eaten since breakfast.

The decision of cave or dome was easy. The cave reminded him too much of a high school cafeteria, and it would have way more prying eyes. He was really starting to enjoy the mall at the dry dome. Ken paid him today, too. A good thing, since Deanna was working tonight. She worked most nights this week. For a second, he wondered if Ken was trying to keep them apart. Then he decided that Ken was too busy trying to destroy the Selkies to worry about Evan's love life.

He reached the doors of the glass structure without even realizing it. Who knew that he would become so comfortable with his new home that he could find his way while daydreaming?

Relaxing in the dry room, he let the heat ease his aching muscles. When he'd loitered there long enough, he chose jeans and a plain green T-shirt. No one here would appreciate any of the witty sayings he might otherwise pick. The humor was lost when you had to explain it.

The first floor wasn't too crowded tonight. Usually, groups of Sirens and Blue Men mulled about, getting drinks in the bar area or crowding the bowling alley. Tonight, these areas were quiet. In fact, on his walk to the stairwell, he didn't see another soul. A little odd, Evan mused, but maybe something was going on somewhere else.

When he reached the second level, he heard voices before he exited the stairwell. There were definitely more people here. The room was alive with the smell of fried food, strong coffee, and the mingled, heady scent of too many perfumes in one place. Sirens loved to lay on the perfume, especially when they had to work.

"Evan! Hey, Evan! Over here!" The Siren with the bright purple hair waved to him. What was her name again? Kristin? No... Krystal. It was Krystal.

"Hi, Krystal." He smiled at her, and then nodded at her companion. "You're Vesh, right?"

"You remembered. I'm touched." Vesh leaned forward and shook Evan's hand. "Have a seat. We're about to get some dinner."

Evan sat across from the couple. It was crowded. There were more people in the mall than he had ever seen before. "Is something going on tonight?"

"A band," Krystal said with a sparkle in her eye. "I hope they play good dance music."

"Doubt it." Vesh laughed. "It's Slate's band. They're pretty hardcore."

Krystal pouted her lips and crossed her arms, but her face brightened considerably a moment later. She started waving frantically like she had at Evan.

Evan turned, expecting to see the other Siren, Melody, but the person approaching their table was another one of the Blue Men. He looked familiar. When he was only a few feet away, Evan realized why. This was the guy from the stairwell. The one he met the first time Deanna brought Evan here.

"Dex!" Krystal squealed and threw her arms around his neck. He hugged her back, a wide smile on his face, until he saw Evan and his expression turned nervous.

"Prince," Dex said with a nod of greeting.

Evan winced. "Please don't call me that. Where I'm from, that's the name of a flamboyant singer, or rather was, until he changed his name to a symbol."

Three blank faces stared at him. Finally, Vesh asked, "Why would someone do that?"

"I—" Evan had no reasonable answer. He decided to let it drop. "Never mind, just call me Evan."

"Evan," Dex said. "I can do that."

"Want to get a pizza?" Vesh asked. "I'm starved."

Evan shrugged. "Pizza sounds good." Anything sounded good at this point. Hunger gnawed at his insides, making him queasy.

"Why don't you order, sweetheart?" Vesh handed Krystal money, giving her a playful slap on her curvy backside when she turned. Krystal giggled as she walked away, which surprised Evan. *Human women,* he thought, *would get annoyed or feel degraded by that gesture.* Apparently, the exchange worked for Vesh and Krystal.

When she was out of earshot and waiting at the pizza stand, Vesh leaned forward, an inquisitive expression on his face. Evan looked at Dex, who shrugged and leaned in, too. Curious, Evan joined them.

"Can we trust you?" Vesh asked. The question was directed at Evan.

"With what?" Evan replied, genuinely surprised. What was this guy going on about?

Vesh leaned back and crossed his arms. He exchanged a look with Dex, and although neither spoke, some agreement must've been reached. "Deanna trusts you?"

"I assume so. I mean, we're kinda..."

Vesh snorted. "Sex is not trust. Don't confuse the two."

"No," Evan said, feeling dumb. "I mean, we're more..."

"He's just giving you a hard time, Evan," Dex chimed in, his voice soft and level. "What Vesh is trying to ask is, are you loyal to Ken?"

Speechless, Evan swallowed hard. They were seriously asking him that? Here? In a public place where Ken or any of his lackeys could hear? Evan also didn't know where these guys stood. They watched him expectantly, waiting for his answer. Clearly, there was a right one and a wrong one. Going with his gut, Evan gave them a vague truth. "If you ask him, I am."

"Good answer." Vesh seemed pleased. "Yes, I think we can trust you."

"Great," Evan said. He felt relieved, but he still didn't know why. Had he passed some kind of test? It felt like it. Who were these two? What about Slate? Was he part of their group? Were the Sirens, too? "Maybe you can fill me in on what you're talking about then."

Dex laughed, and Vesh flashed his teeth in a quick grin. "In time, my friend. This is not the place for it, and oh, our pizza is here. Thanks, love." He kissed Krystal's cheek when she leaned over him to put the pizza on the table. The smell made Evan salivate.

"Dig in, boys." Krystal smiled and straightened. "I'll get some drinks. Be right back."

The sauce burnt the roof of his mouth, but Evan didn't care. He was tired of feeling hungry. One meal a day didn't cut it, and while the Siren food was okay, he missed his mom's cooking. Meatloaf, mashed potatoes, and buttered rolls sounded good right now. His mom made great meatloaf. He could almost smell it. Heck, he'd even eat the broccoli she was always coaxing him to finish.

"You want anymore?"

Vesh pushed the tray over. Only two slices remained. While Evan was daydreaming, they almost polished off the rest of the pizza. He grabbed one and slid it onto his plate. "Thanks."

"Is this like the pizza you ate on land?" Dex asked.

"Similar," Evan said. There were vegetables on this pizza he didn't recognize, but the sauce was red and tasted like normal pizza sauce. The cheese seemed a little more creamy, but overall, it tasted good.

Hanging out with Dex and Vesh, Evan could almost pretend he

was back at home hanging out in the Halifax mall with the guys. That was, until he looked down and noticed his blue arms and clawed hands. The other two looked human. Dex, with his glasses and mousy, brown hair, would blend in anywhere. Vesh wore his black hair spiky. He had a ring in his nose and another in his eyebrow. The look was a little edgier than Evan was used to, but it seemed to work for the guy. The Sirens certainly appeared to like Vesh's looks. They might like how Evan looked too if they saw him in his human form. Would Ken ever let Evan return to it? He missed being human. As much as he was envious of Meara's ability to swim unhindered, and now he could, too, he'd trade it all to go back to life the way it was before.

"You alright, Evan?" Vesh shouted to be heard above the band. They were on their second song. Evan guessed that they recently formed the group. The band members were still feeling out each other's style.

Evan shrugged. "I'm okay. Missing land, I guess."

"Want to get out of here?" Vesh asked.

"Don't you need to wait for Krystal?" Evan asked. He wondered if Vesh and Krystal were dating. They didn't really act like it. After she served them pizza, then brought over a pitcher of something that was green, but tasted fruity, she headed over to the space in front of the stage. All the girls were currently dancing there, waving their hands in time to the music.

"She's fine. We're not together, if that's what you're thinking." Vesh wiggled his eyebrows and flashed his teeth in a devilish smile. "I don't like to get attached. We hang out sometimes, but that's about it."

Evan let it drop. The whole relationship slash dating process was confusing at best on land, and down here, he had no idea. There were very few couples that he could see. At least, monogamous ones. If he saw two individuals together one day, the next day they might be with someone else. The lifestyle was completely foreign.

"What do I owe?" Evan asked and pulled out his wallet.

Vesh waved him off. "I got it. You can pick up the tab next time." He turned to Dex, who had been sitting quietly this whole time. Presumably, he was listening to the band. "You coming, Dexter?'

It was odd that Vesh used his full name, but Dex didn't seem to notice or mind. He shook his head. "I want to catch the set. I'll see you later."

Vesh patted Dex's shoulder, then stood and motioned for Evan to follow. They headed up to the first floor. "Have you been to the gardens yet?" Vesh asked over his shoulder.

"Briefly," Evan said. "Well, I walked by them when Deanna gave me a tour of the dome."

"Then you haven't really seen them." Vesh took the remaining stairs two at a time. The guy had a lot of nervous energy. Maybe all Blue Men were like that. Evan used so much power earlier today that he was already starting to feel tired again.

Once upstairs, they walked past the bowling alley and down the back hall to the gardens. There were three different rooms, mimicking various climates on land. One was tropical, one dry like the desert, and the last one was somewhere in between.

Vesh headed to the tropical room. "I work in here. The money's not bad, and the view can't be beat," he said. "I think you'll like it."

Evan stepped in, and the hot, humid air took his breath away. For a moment, he closed his eyes and tilted his head toward the ceiling. Pretending the bright, intense light was the sun shining down on him, a sigh escaped before he could stop it. How he missed the feeling of the sun on his skin.

Vesh cleared his throat, and Evan opened his eyes. His embarrassment was overshadowed by the pure comfort of the warm light and dry land. "Sorry," Evan said automatically. He didn't feel apologetic, but he didn't know what else to say.

"It's okay, man. I thought this might remind you of home. Was I right?"

Evan nodded. "Where I'm from, it's rarely this hot but, if I close my eyes, the light does feel similar to the sun. Have you been on land?"

"Not for a long time." An unrecognizable emotion crossed Vesh's eyes. Was it sadness? Wistfulness? "Since Azuria died, very few of us have been out of the sea. Ken controls who can leave the ocean, and mainly, it has been only those closest to him." Vesh walked further into the room, and Evan fell into step alongside him. They were the only two people in the bright, quiet room.

"Where are we going?" Evan was curious more than anything.

"There's an area in the back I want to show you." Vesh smiled at him. "Do you recognize any of these plants?"

Evan glanced around. He wasn't much of a plant expert. A few things looked familiar. Were those bananas? And pineapple? The air was heady with the exotic perfumes of brightly colored blooms. Most of the plants did not look like anything he'd seen before.

"Some," Evan said. "But not most."

"That makes sense." Vesh's eyes lit with amusement at Evan's confusion. "Centuries ago, the Sirens cultivated plants from the land, but most of those plants required sunlight to live. They did not do well with the gases down here. Most of the vegetation you see is a hybrid of land and sea plants. They are hardier, yield more, and thrive in these specific conditions."

"Fascinating." Evan didn't care much about horticulture, but it was interesting that the Sirens would think to blend land and sea plants together.

"This is it." Vesh stopped suddenly and stepped to the side so Evan could see around him. The view was breathtaking. Palm trees, sand, and crystal blue water. It was an underwater oasis in a deep-sea dome.

"Why is this here?" Evan asked.

"Irrigation system," Vesh explained. "Too much salt kills the plants, so we pump it in and filter it. This is the reservoir used by all three rooms." Vesh grinned. "Some of us also use it as a swimming pool. Fresh water swimming is so different from salt water."

"Tell me about it." Evan longed to sit in the sand and put his feet in the water. "Can we sit here for a while?"

"Sure." Vesh took off his shoes and sat down. "You can go for a swim if you like."

"I've done enough swimming," Evan said, and then regretted the edge in his voice. Vesh was trying to be nice. It wasn't his fault that Evan was stuck here. "Sorry, man."

"Stop apologizing. You have nothing to be sorry for," Vesh said. "C'mon and have a seat."

Joining Vesh at the water's edge, Evan put his feet in the water. It was cool and refreshing. The sand was warm, but not too hot underneath him. He laid back and put his hands behind his head, once more closing his eyes. This time, he felt Vesh lie back next to him.

"Can you tell me about modern life on land?" Vesh asked. He sounded hesitant, like he was worried that Evan would say no.

"Yeah," Evan said. "Yeah, I can." This was a topic Evan was comfortable with. "When did Azuria die, if that was the last time you were on land?"

"I can't tell you the exact year. We don't track time like mortals do." Vesh pursed his lips in thought. Then, he said, "It was the seventeen hundreds. Maybe 1728?"

Evan stared at Vesh, struggling to comprehend his age. He looked about twenty-two, and with the earplugs and pierced eyebrow, he could pass for a modern teen. Then again, from what Evan had seen in the city, piercings were common amongst the Blue Men. Maybe early human tribes actually learned about decorating their bodies with piercings from the Blue Men. That was wild to consider. After all, Vesh had lived for a very long time, so it was entirely possible.

"Evan?" Vesh frowned at him. "Are you still with me?"

"Yeah, sorry. Just thinking about where to start."

If Vesh had been undersea since the eighteen century, he missed a ton of advances.

"What might surprise you the most," Evan said when he figured out where to start, "is that man can fly."

"Those metal contraptions," Vesh murmured. "Yes, I've heard of them from the others. They are called aero planes."

"Airplanes," Evan corrected.

Vesh sat upright and stared down at Evan. "What magic moves them?"

"Not magic," Evan countered. "Technology and mechanics. We built machines that can carry us through the air."

"They are like sky boats?" Vesh asked.

"Something like that," Evan said, picturing a Viking ship sailing through the sky. Then again, a blimp looked a little like a boat. Vesh's analogy wasn't too bad.

They spent the rest of the afternoon lying under the bright lights. Evan described life on land and answered Vesh's questions. They compared similarities and differences of their worlds. Evan kept waiting for the light to dim, to change, but it never did. He was anticipating the sunset, he realized, something that would never happen here. An ache filled his chest and spread. Would he ever see the sun rise or set again?

Chapter 21

Uncle Angus hugged me tight, then Paddy, followed by Ula. They embraced Kieran too. The way they were treating us, it was like they were sending us off to our funeral. Honestly, I found it rather depressing. Thankfully, Cole was already gone, so that was one less set of mournful eyes. He left right after breakfast to report to Kieran's dad.

Kieran and I needed to talk about his brother and sister. He had an identical twin. How crazy was that? I knew nothing about his family before yesterday. He never mentioned his mom. Was she alive? I assumed that Ula knew about Kieran's family—they had been betrothed, after all—but she never mentioned an identical twin. Was I the only one who thought that was big news? Whatever, I needed to focus if we were going to rescue my dad, my aunt, and the guards successfully. We were it, the last chance for our clan. If we didn't return... No, I wasn't going there. Success was the only option.

Kieran was discussing our travel plans with Uncle Angus. We were taking a risk by changing into our seal form and swimming to the Shiant Islands. Since neither of us had been there before, we couldn't transport. The only other option was a boat, and Ronac had none. Under normal circumstances, Selkies would never use one. Conjuring a vessel would deplete our energy and delay us for at least a day, if not more. We already lost too much time waiting for Drust and Judoc to return. Swimming was the most efficient mode of transportation, given our limited options. I prayed that we weren't heading into a trap.

Ula hugged me again. "I'll be in the surf every morning. Contact me if you can. If it's safe."

"Of course." It was my turn to blink back tears. Leaving was harder than I thought, although my love for family diminished my fear of the unknown. I prayed we would see everyone again, and then said an extra prayer that the island and our Selkies would be safe while we were gone. Ronac was dangerously low on defenses.

"You'll keep training with the others?" I asked.

"We will," Uncle Angus answered. "Don't worry about us. Focus on the rescue."

"Meara," Kieran's voice was warm, but firm. "It's time."

I wiped my eyes and gave them a wide smile. It felt more like a grimace. I wanted to appear brave, but I was sure it came across as nervous. Taking a deep breath, the resolve settled in. I could do this. I had to do this. "Let's go."

I felt their eyes upon us as we changed into seals and dove into the water. My fear disappeared as the utter joy of swimming in the ocean overtook me.

I missed this, I admitted.

Me too, came Kieran's deep reply. *I wish we had time to enjoy it.*

We've got at least an hour or two, I replied. *It's better than nothing.*

"What's the plan?" Kieran strode to the edge of the cliff and peered down before turning back to me. "Where do we start looking?"

We had arrived at the Shiant Islands exactly where my father told us to go. Rain poured down, a wet, cold curtain. With my hair plastered to my forehead, it was difficult, if not impossible, to see beyond a few feet around us. The water chilled me to the core.

So cold.

So alone.

The thoughts drifted through my mind, though they weren't my own. Before I could give the words any consideration, my vision went black.

I stood alone on the shore. The ocean was calm, the sky clear. Where was Kieran and when did it stop raining? As I watched, the water iced over. Crystals danced outward, forming a lacy, solid surface. The latticework spread as far as I could see. In the distance, a shadowy figure glided toward me.

The figure drew near, and I realized it was a woman. She wore a beaded, strapless gown that sparkled as she floated on the ice. The fabric looked heavy, but the way it swirled at her ankles told me it was not. Her feet were bare, though she seemed unbothered by the ice. Like the ground beneath her feet, her skin was a pale aqua. Her long. wavy hair appeared white in the bright sunlight, though by the time she stood before me, I could tell that it was really a very light blue. Her eyes, the brilliant turquoise of the Caribbean Sea, mesmerized me.

"My child." She reached out to embrace me. Her touch burned, and the kiss she placed on each cheek bit like frostbite. "The time has come for the truth to be revealed."

"Truth?" What was she talking about? What truth? It was difficult to think in her presence. Where was Kieran? Where was I for that matter? I started with the most pressing question, "Who are you?"

"If you look within, you'll find the answer." Her finger touched my collarbone. Through the icy spark that followed, I knew.

"Azuria," I said. "Queen of the Blue Men of the Minch."

"Queen Mother," she corrected with a soft smile. "My sons have been without their mother's influence for too long. A change is overdue. You must help me."

Her bright eyes shimmered with unshed tears for her sons. She was not requesting my help. She demanded it.

"What can I do?" I asked.

"Make them see the truth. My son, Ken, thinks I was seduced by a Selkie, which resulted in my death. He'll stop at nothing until he feels he has avenged me. Selkies are not our enemy. I did not die at my lover's hand." She closed her eyes, a trail of tears glistening down her cheeks. She opened her eyes again, twin pools of sadness. "I will show you the truth."

Placing her slender hands alongside my face, she tilted my head down. She was a few inches shorter than I was. A faint floral smell enveloped us. Water lilies, maybe? Standing on the tips of her toes, she kissed my forehead. I had the strangest feeling of falling, although my feet were planted on the ground. The world spun. Light and color flashed by in a dizzy array. When the motion stopped, I stood on the same shore, but the landscape looked different. The queen was gone. A man sat on a boulder in the distance, watching something out at sea.

Movement in the water caught my attention. A slim arm cut through the surface, followed by a thick ribbon of light blue hair. Was it Azuria?

The swimmer drew closer to the man on the rock. That was when I knew it was Azuria because I could feel her emotions and understand her thoughts. She was joyful and exhilarated from her swim. She did not notice the man sitting on the shore. It wasn't until she emerged from the water that she saw him. She jumped back in alarm, covering her exposed flesh with her arms.

"Who are you?" she asked. "And why are you in my cove?"

The man turned away when he saw she was naked. His face slightly red, he stood and murmured, "My apologies, m'lady. My name is Zane. I did not realize this land belonged to anyone. I was simply looking for a place to rest."

"You were mistaken, of course, for it does belong to someone. It belongs to me." She strode toward him, a simple gown forming over the curves of her body, her hair dry by the time she reached him. Standing regally before him, she offered her hand. "I am Queen Azuria."

"Your Majesty." Zane bowed, took her outstretched hand, and kissed it lightly. "Your loveliness knows no equal. I am at your mercy and pledge you my loyalty."

"I know not if you mean what you say, but your words flatter me all the same." Her eyes softened at the beautiful man before her. When he smiled at her words, Azuria gasped at the way it lit his face. He was truly lovely with dark, wavy hair and sapphire blue eyes.

He bowed again before offering her his arm. "Then allow me the opportunity to prove myself to you."

The scene faded out. Azuria's voice filled my mind. *That is all you will learn here. Let us travel ahead to another critical moment. This is the moment that changed everything.*

The sun rising and falling rapidly as time moved forward. A sense of foreboding filled me, and once again, I found myself on the same shore watching a scene unfold. Azuria and Zane were wrapped in each other's arms. Neither looked happy.

"You must stay." She clung to him and cried. "I love you."

"And I you," he whispered into her hair. "But staying means death. I am a Selkie. Your ways are not mine. I must be with my own kind."

"What if my ways could be yours?" She clenched his shirt between her hands, her face turned up to his with hopefulness. "What if I used my magic to change you? Would you join my men?"

"I would do anything to be with you forever." He lowered his head and kissed her. "Nothing would make me happier."

"Lie down," she commanded. He obeyed. The trust and hope on his face matched the determination and love on hers. She opened his shirt, laying her hands flat on his chest over his heart. Chanting in a language I couldn't understand, the words formed a haunting melody. Blue light flowed from her fingers into his skin. The color spread out, staining him, and his eyes closed, a small smile on his face. She continued her song. It was working. He was changing. Then something went wrong. Zane's eyes flew open, and he gasped for breath like a fish out of water. The blue receded, leaving his skin ashy gray. Azuria's chant turned to a wail of agony. She tried everything to revive him. It was too late. With one last shuddering breath, he died. She collapsed to her knees, crying on his dead body. Whether it was her tears or the remaining magic, his body rapidly decomposed. The ashes blew away in the wind. Soon, there was nothing left of Zane except Azuria's grief.

No. No. No. No. No. No.

I didn't know if they were her words or mine. Her grief overwhelmed me and drove out my own sense of self-awareness. Heartbreak was a knife in my chest. I couldn't breathe. I couldn't think. How did she live with this agony? Then I knew the answer. She didn't.

Throwing her hands skyward, Azuria screamed a curse. Nature responded. Dark clouds gathered, turning the blue sky an ominous black. A bolt of lightning cut through her. When the smoke dissipated, the queen lay dead in the spot where her lover died only moments earlier.

The voices of men shouting grew loud behind me. I turned to see a wave of blue soldiers running at me. Then everything went blissfully dark.

"Meara!"

Kieran screamed my name, his face buried in my neck. Where was I? My body shook uncontrollably. I was so cold.

"Oh god. Oh, thank god!" He kissed me, his mouth hot against my icy lips.

"Wh-where, wh-where are we?" It was difficult to speak through my chattering teeth. The shaking was getting worse.

"In a cave. I noticed it on the way in." He rubbed his hands up and down my arms, trying to generate heat. A fire blazed nearby, but the heat didn't reach me. "Change, Meara."

"What?" I traced his mouth with my fingers. Why was he frowning? What was he telling me to do? My brain was fuzzy. I couldn't focus on what he was saying. Sleep, I needed sleep.

"You can't sleep," he said as if he could read my mind. *Oh right, he could.* "You have to warm up first. Change."

The command echoed through my brain, and my body responded. The fur flowed over my skin, bringing welcoming heat. Once my change was complete, Kieran followed. In his seal form, he stretched next to me. I nuzzled against his warmth and fell asleep.

When I woke, Kieran was gone. The fire still blazed, only now I could feel it. The cavern was comfortably warm. I stretched and yawned, my body relaxed. Realizing I was vulnerable in seal form, I changed back to human, visualizing myself in a warm hoodie, jeans, and hiking boots. I felt better fully dressed and prepared should anyone come by. Where was I and what happened?

Azuria, the queen of the Blue Men, contacted me. How? She was dead. I saw her die in front of me. Was she a ghost? The visions she showed me reared to life. Image after image woke my sleepy brain. Azuria asked for my help. The problem was that I wasn't sure how to help her.

"You're awake."

Kieran stood in the cave entrance holding several large fish. He seemed relieved and happy to see me awake. Holding up the wiggling fish, he said, "I figured you'd be hungry."

"Famished."

"Raw or cooked?"

Wrinkling my nose, I said, "Cooked, please. I can eat raw in seal form, but as human, I like my food unrecognizable from the animal it once was."

"As you wish." He winked before busying himself with our meal preparations. He had a pan and a small spatula.

"Did you bring those with us?" We didn't bring backpacks. If he brought the pan, I had no idea where he kept it.

"No," he said. "I found it in the corner of the cave, along with a tea kettle and other random dishes. Someone must've squatted here for a while."

"Lucky for us." I scooted back to give him room to move around the fire. My hair was a mess. I self-consciously ran my fingers through it, wincing when I hit a large snarl. Visualizing an elastic band, I pulled my hair into a ponytail. It wasn't my most glamorous look, but it would have to do.

"Have you recovered?" he asked.

"I feel fine." I frowned, remembering everything Azuria had shown me, but not how I got here. "What happened?"

"All I know is that we were standing on the shore trying to decide which area to explore first. Then you collapsed. I tried to revive you, but nothing worked. You started to shake and your lips turned blue." He flipped the fish, and then stared into the fire. I knew that look. He was fighting to control his emotions. His face was carefully blank, but his voice betrayed him when it trembled. "I brought you back here and started a fire. The cave grew hot, but it had no impact on you."

"You told me to change." I remembered his voice, scared but firm.

"It worked." He sat back and looked at me. His eyes shimmered in the firelight. "In seal form, with me beside you, you finally warmed up."

I scooted closer to him. He watched me advance, but he didn't move. When I was directly in front of him, I rose up on my knees, leaned forward, and kissed him. The kiss was slow and sweet. With a sigh, I lifted my head and searched his eyes, seeing nothing but love and concern. "Thank you for taking care of me."

With a low growl, Kieran pulled me into his lap and drew my mouth to his. This time, it felt like he poured all his fear and worry into the kiss. It was intense and passionate. I wrapped my arms around his neck and pulled him closer.

The smell of acrid smoke permeated the air. Kieran leapt up, dumping me off his lap.

"The fish!" we cried at the same time.

Lifting the pan off the fire, he grabbed a plate from the small pile next to him and flipped the fish onto it. The skin was black. Neither of us said anything. We stared in dismay at our partially burnt dinner, then we looked at each other and started laughing. Using a fork, Kieran scraped the charred skin off the fish. The flesh underneath was edible, maybe a little dry and tough, but I was hungry enough that it didn't matter. We split the fish between us, polishing it off.

"I could use a drink right now," I said.

"The water is hot," he said, nodding to the kettle. It was warming on some embers near the edge of the fire pit. "I found some tea leaves in a tin. I'm not sure what kind or how old. Are you feeling brave?"

"Why not?" Old tea wouldn't hurt me, right?

He laughed. "I'm only kidding. You think I'd let you drink something unknown and mysterious? No way. You gave me one scare already since we've been here."

He poured a cup of hot water, waving his fingers over the top before handing the mug to me. "Try this."

The steam was thick and fragrant. I blew on the surface to cool the hot contents. Cautiously, I took a sip and grinned. "Hot chocolate?"

It was creamy and rich with a hint of cinnamon. He nodded. "My mom taught me how to make it."

I drank a little more, the comforting beverage warming my insides. "You never talk about your mom," I said quietly.

Kieran poured his own mug, did the finger wave over it, and sat down next to me. He blew into his mug, and I waited for him to say something. "She's a great lady," he said after a moment. "You will love her." He cleared his throat. "I don't talk about her because she no longer lives with us."

"Where is she?" I searched his face, trying to see if this conversation was upsetting him. He didn't seem sad or angry, although he squirmed a little.

"She left my dad for someone else." The confession came out in a rush. "She was banished from our home."

"Oh." No wonder he never talked about her. The burning wood sparked and crackled, filling the silence between us. I wanted to say something soothing, but no words came to mind.

Kieran saved me by changing the subject. I guess he didn't want to talk about his mom anymore either. "What happened yesterday, Meara? Do you remember?"

"I didn't at first, but it came back to me." I scooted closer to the fire and leaned back against the cave wall, getting comfortable. Kieran moved beside me and waited for me to continue. "It was Azuria. She wanted to show me what happened. Ken thinks the Selkie seduced her, and then killed her. He didn't. They were in love. His name was Zane. Azuria accidentally killed him first."

"How'd she do that?"

"She loved him, and he couldn't stay with her as a Selkie. She thought she could use her magic to turn him into one of the Blue Men. At first, it looked like it was working but then." I stopped, my eyes filling with tears. "It was awful. He couldn't breathe. She couldn't help him. He died right in front of her."

Kieran wiped the tears off my cheek and took my empty mug, setting it to the side with his own. When our hands were empty, he clasped mine in his. His thumb lightly caressed the back of my hand. "What did she do next?"

"She killed herself." I shuddered. "I watched her do it. Then, I saw the Blue Men running toward us and shouting. That's when I woke up, or returned here, or whatever happened." I took a deep breath. "That's all I remember."

"Why show those visions to you?" Kieran's brow knit together. "What was her motive?"

"I don't know." Only certain parts of the conversation were clear in my memory. "She said something about helping her and the truth. I don't understand how I can help. She's dead."

"At least you're safe." Kieran put his arm around my shoulder. When I leaned into him, he kissed my forehead. "What do you want to do? Should we continue the search or return to Ronac?"

I pushed away to stare up at him. "We have to continue searching. My dad and aunt are out there, held captive. Evan is still missing. We can't give up."

"Relax, Meara." His hand pressed into my shoulder, urging me to rest my head against him again. Reluctantly, I complied. "I was only checking how you felt. You had quite an experience. I wanted to make sure you were okay."

"I'm fine. We'll start again in the morning."

He chuckled, the sound vibrating through me. "I'm glad you're at least willing to wait until the morning."

"Kieran—"

"I'm kidding!" He lowered his head and kissed me lightly. When I relaxed against him, he laughed again. "Sort of."

I pretended to punch him, and he responded by tickling me. "Stop!" I gasped between giggles, which only encouraged him. When I didn't think I could take any more, he stopped. As I struggled to catch my breath, he lowered his forehead to mine.

"I was really worried about you, Meara." His voice was husky with emotion. "I felt so helpless."

I stroked his cheek, and then lowered my hand to rest on his chest. His heart beat erratically, causing mine to do the same. "You helped me. More than you think."

Our lips met in a long, slow kiss. One kiss led to another. The fire dimmed, and shadows grew long on the cavern wall.

I love you.

The words penetrated my mind along with the image of a woman, her beauty primitive and fierce. It took a moment for me to realize that I was seeing myself.

"Is that how you see me?"

With firelight dancing over his features, I saw his face redden. "Oh, you saw that?" His expression was rueful. "That's never happened before. You make me lose control."

"I can't believe that," I said lightly.

His face remained solemn. "It's true."

"You think more of me than I am," I murmured. "But you make me want to be the woman you see."

With a sudden certainty, I knew what I wanted. There was no way to tell what tomorrow might bring, but tonight we had each other. I unbuttoned his shirt and slid my hands beneath it, running my lips over the smooth skin on his shoulder, kissing the sensitive spot where shoulder meets neck. Sensing the change in my mood, his muscles tensed.

"Are you sure?" he whispered in my ear.

"I'm sure," I whispered back, and then sighed as his tongue teased my earlobe. I ran my fingers through his hair, and then down his back.

"There's no going back," he warned. "After this, I won't settle for being your friend." His lips moved from my ear, down my neck, to trace a path on my collarbone.

"I don't want to go back," I said. "I love you."

With a groan, he rolled onto his back, taking me with him. My hair fell like a curtain around his face. Desire burned in his eyes, sending a thrill through my body. He was strong, powerful, and he loved me. More than once, he'd risked his life for me, and he would do it again. I would do the same for him. He was mine, and I was his.

A loud pop from the fire woke me up. The cavern temperature dropped rapidly, and I watched as my breath puffed out in a visible haze. My body was warm against Kieran's, but if the temperate kept dropping, it wouldn't be that way for long.

Azuria materialized at the cave entrance. Icicles formed where she leaned against the stone. "It's good to see the color return to your skin." Her mouth lifted, but the expression was more sad than happy. "I apologize for harming you earlier. I was not aware that my touch would have that effect."

"I'm fine." I struggled to sit up without waking Kieran. His deep, steady breathing told me that I'd succeeded. Visualizing a sweatshirt, long pants, and warm socks and boots, I stood and crossed to her.

"Why did you contact me?" I asked.

She reached toward my face, then caught herself and lowered her hand. "You have a strong connection to one of my children."

"I don't see how. I've only met two of them, Ken and Ted." Unless the butler was also one of the Blue Men. At this point, it wouldn't surprise me.

She looked over my shoulder. Kieran was mumbling in his sleep. "Come," she said. "Let us walk. The night is clear, and this way, we will not disturb your friend."

I followed her out of the cave. The moonlight cast the landscape in pale silver, and the queen's dress glowed. It wouldn't be farfetched to assume she was an apparition, yet I knew she was as real as I was.

"I speak not of Kenneth or Theodore, though I'm sad that one saw the need to kill the other. My eldest son is so full of hate and vengeance. It breaks my heart." Her voice caught, and she wiped her eyes. Grief rolled over me in waves. In that current of emotion, however, was a spark of hope. Eyes piercing mine, she said, "It is the newest child, my first grandchild, who has the capacity to save us all."

A child? A child was going to stop the Blue Men and prevent a war? I could scarcely believe it, and yet, if it was true, then Kieran and I had to find him. Had I met him already at Ken's house? I didn't remember any children being there or Evan talking about a child.

"What is this child's name?" I asked. "Where is he?"

Azuria moved closer to me, searching my face. "You know him as Evan."

I stared at her. My mouth was probably hanging open, gaping like a fish. She couldn't mean my Evan. He was human. His parents were Lydia and Darren Mitchell. They ran a bed and breakfast. He'd lived in Canada his whole life. Evan wasn't Azuria's grandson. That would make him one of the Blue Men, and that was impossible. "Evan is human. He can't—"

"He can, and he is," she said gently. "Evan is Ken's son. Granted, he was conceived under nefarious circumstances. Ken tricked a human female into thinking that he was her husband. I am not proud of my son's behavior. I am, however, pleased with the result. As I said, Evan will save us all."

"How?" My mind was whirling. The headaches, the glowing eyes, the mood swings... it all made sense now if Evan went through some kind of change. Did his blue form look like Ted's? Did he hate me? Would any of the love he had for me remain or was it replaced by the anger and repulsion he felt for me last summer?

"Meara!" Kieran called for me, the panic clear in his voice. Instinctively, I turned at the sound of his voice, but I couldn't see the cave from where we stood. When I turned back, Azuria was gone.

Find Evan. Find our savior.

Her voice whispered through my mind along with an image. She showed me a map, the western coast of France. Below the waves, a jeweled dwelling appeared.

He awaits you here.

Meara! This time, Kieran's voice rang through my head. The map disappeared, and I no longer sensed Azuria's presence.

I'm okay, I responded. *I'll be right there.*

Walking quickly, I made my way back to the cave. The entire time, I weighed our choices. Did we stay here and try to find the Blue Men's keep, rescuing Dad and Aunt Brigid? If a battle was coming, the Selkies needed them back at Ronac. On the other hand, Azuria made it clear that finding Evan was imperative. Somehow, Evan could end this threat. If Ken realized that Evan was the key to his undoing, he'd never let him live, son or not. Both tasks were critical. Both tasks were treacherous, requiring that we prepare for the unknown. I kicked a rock and let out a frustrated cry. I had no idea what to do first.

Chapter 22

"Ken seriously called in sick?"

Evan tried to figure out if Vesh was telling the truth. He didn't look like he was joking. Of course, in Vesh's blue form, Evan couldn't read his expressions that well. A smile or snarl both looked creepy on Vesh's elongated face.

"What are you complaining about? You get a free day." Vesh's large form filled the doorway. He was neither moving in, nor out. Loitering. That was probably the right term for it. Waiting. "So I was thinking..." He paused and this time, Evan knew Vesh was smiling at him. "We spent yesterday afternoon experiencing your world on land. Today, I want to show you our world."

Evan didn't agree with Vesh. While The Chamber's tropical dome with its warm light was similar to being on land, it wasn't the same thing. Not even close. How did you describe the feeling of the sun on your skin to someone who has not felt it in centuries? Evan didn't want to learn about sea life. He was tired and wanted coffee.

"I've been living in your world for a couple of months now," Evan said, trying to keep his voice neutral. He wasn't a morning person, and Vesh was too chipper for this hour of the day. "I think I know what it's like."

"No, you don't." Something like anger flashed in Vesh's eyes. Evan took a step back. Vesh sighed and ran his fingers through his hair. "Look, all I'm saying is that you only know what Ken showed you when it comes to our abilities, which isn't much, right?"

"Right," Evan admitted. "Although Deanna showed me some stuff."

"I bet she did," Vesh leered. Evan kept his gaze steady and waited.

After a moment, Vesh rolled his eyes and continued, "You're no fun. Anyway, whatever Deanna showed you is only what she knows as a Siren. She doesn't really get us, you know, being a different species and all."

"Okay." Evan's stomach tightened. Was it excitement or hunger? Shouldn't he be able to tell the difference? "What do you have in mind?"

"We can grab some food first," Vesh jabbed Evan's side. "Your stomach is yelling for food, and I know you'll be more pleasant after you've eaten. Then, we'll head out to sea, and I'll show you a few things."

They went to the cave instead of the mall food court. No one seemed to notice them or care. Bustling about on their way to work or home, the other Blue Men and Sirens barely acknowledged them with a nod. Vesh ate more than any living creature should be able to fit in its stomach, and for the first time, Evan didn't feel so bad that he was hungry all the time. Maybe the voracious appetite came with the territory.

"Where are the others? Slate and...?" Evan couldn't remember the other guy's name. Sure, he met him twice, but he was quiet and reserved, blending into the background. In some ways, the quiet guy reminded Evan of Professor Nolan.

"Dex," Vesh supplied. "I don't know what they're up to. I didn't bother asking them. Figured you might not like an audience."

Evan blanched at Vesh's words. What exactly was he going to show Evan?

Vesh stood. "You're ready then?"

"Sure." Evan didn't know what he was getting ready for, but he was hoping that he might learn something new at least. Possibly something to help him with his fight. Once again, he wondered, was Vesh on his side?

They slid the trays into the compartment by the entrance and swam out. Vesh headed out of the city, in a direction that Evan hadn't gone before. It was the opposite way that he went every day with Ken.

"Where are we going?" Evan asked curiously.

"Nowhere in particular. I wanted to get out of town, away from prying eyes. The waters are fairly calm out this way, and there's a trench up ahead. We'll try there."

While he talked, Vesh kept up his speed. It wasn't hard for Evan to pace him, but he wondered why Vesh was in a hurry. Was he really worried about others following them?

He dipped down, and Evan saw the trench. It was a wide chasm in the ocean floor. Plants and fish abounded in the area, their colors bright in the dark water.

"Close your eyes," Vesh commanded. "What do you feel?"

Evan obeyed. The current rocked him gently. "Water," he said with his eyes still closed. Silence ensued. He wondered if Vesh left, but when he opened his eyes, the other man was staring at him, an incredulous expression on his face.

Skin bristling, Evan asked, "What?"

"Water? That's the best you got?" Snorting derisively, Vesh turned to swim away. "If you're not going to take this seriously…"

"Wait." Evan reached out and caught Vesh's arm. "I don't know what I'm supposed to feel. Give me a chance. Remember, I was human for twenty years first. Tell me what I'm supposed to feel. What do *you* feel?"

Vesh closed his eyes. His features smoothed, his expression growing peaceful. "A tiger shark is terrorizing a school of fish, and two dolphins are playing in the currents nearby…" Vesh turned his body, eyes still closed. "Further out, a whale is swimming with her calf." His nose wrinkled and his lip curled in distaste before his eyes flew open. "That horrid mouthful of decay must be Ken's project."

"You picked all that up?" Evan was amazed. The mantle plume was miles in the other direction. How far did Vesh's senses reach?

"You could, too," Vesh said. "If you tried." He swam closer, stopping in front of Evan. "You'll need to, if you want to realize your full power. The ocean sustains us, but we must be one with it. Only then will you be able to pull energy from the living forces around you." He paused again, considering Evan. In a lower voice he added, "You'll need to, if you want to have any chance of defeating Ken."

"What? I—" Evan's first instinct was to deny what Vesh was saying, but Vesh brushed off his protests with a quick shake of his head.

"You better damn well be trying to defeat him. We're counting on you." Vesh motioned angrily. "You don't agree with what he's doing, do you? You can't possibly like the fact that he's torturing your girlfriend's father."

Evan felt the shock of Vesh's statement rivet through his body. "Ken has David?"

"He does. David's sister, too. The hot one with the purple eyes."

"Brigid." The name came to Evan immediately. Although he'd only met her once, Meara mentioned her aunt often enough. "But how?"

"They were looking for you." Vesh sat on a rock, idly sifting sand and silt through his hand. "Ken caught them over a month ago, and four others in their rescue party. Two more were captured recently."

Eight Selkies. Meara must be worried sick. She was coming next. He knew it. It wasn't in her to stay behind and let others fight. Knowing her the way he did, the situation would be killing her right now. He thought she had given up on him. She hadn't. If David and Brigid attempted to rescue Evan, it was at Meara's request. Although the rescue attempts failed, he felt better knowing that they tried. They cared enough to risk their lives.

"What is Ken doing with them? Are they okay?"

"The last I heard, they were alive. My brothers are not the most hospitable of folk." Vesh shook his head. His eyes filled with regret. "We don't all feel the same, but it's not safe to argue with Ken. He's quite mad, you know."

"I know," Evan said softly. In his mind, he saw Ted Nolan, swollen and bloody.

"He killed our brother."

When Evan met Vesh's eyes, he nodded. "Ken killed Theodore. We are immortal and connected. All of us. When one dies, we feel it." He put his hand on Evan's shoulder. "I'm sorry, Evan. I know he was your professor, and you were close."

Evan's throat tightened. He was surprised how much it affected him to know that Professor Nolan was dead. Guessing was one thing, knowing was another. Ted Nolan was a flawed man, but he meant well. Ken had no right to kill him. "Why didn't I feel it?"

"I don't know." Vesh frowned at him. "Maybe you haven't honed that ability yet."

"Ted wasn't a bad man. He apologized for bringing me into this," Evan said. Perhaps his words might ease Vesh's pain too. After all, he lost a brother. "He tried to help me in the end. With any luck, he got my message to Meara before he died."

"He was one of the gentlest of my brothers when my mother was alive," Vesh said. "But Ted was also one of the most loyal to Ken after her death. Look where that loyalty got him."

"How many of the Blue Men think like you?" Evan asked. He assumed Slate and Dex felt the same, but were there more?

"Slate and Dex," Vesh said, confirming Evan's thoughts. "Potentially a few more. It's risky to talk about it. We don't know for sure. If I can help you harness your power, that might get us the furthest at this point. We won't revolt against Ken on our own. We're not strong enough."

There was an apology in Vesh's voice, but Evan didn't acknowledge it. Vesh didn't need to apologize to him. Evan knew Ken's wrath all too well. He wouldn't wish that on anyone. As Ken's son, though, perhaps he did stand a chance against him.

"I'm ready to try again," Evan said. Closing his eyes, he let the moving water settle him first. A peace flowed through his veins, and he became part of the ocean. He felt the moment it happened, like every pore in his body opened to the life around him... so many sounds, so many smells and feelings. He breathed it all in, and the power thrummed through him. His chest expanded and his eyes flew open. "That's freaking amazing."

Vesh grinned, his sharp, white teeth glinting. "Now we're talking. You're glowing, man. Looks like you got a rush of power."

"I did!" Evan felt like he could swim the Atlantic and back. "Is it always like that?"

"Pretty much, if you're open to it. The ocean sustains us. If we accept her gifts, our power grows." Vesh stood and stretched. "Child's play, my friend. That was only step one. Now that you have the energy, you need to learn what to do with it."

Evan listened as Vesh explained the basics to him. They could control the waves, the rise and swell of the water. Blue Men sunk ships, but raised them too. It was all in the will of the wielder. They could also speak to the animals, although they could not control them. Ocean dwellers varied in intelligence, the same way that living beings did on land. Fish were not that bright, while great white sharks and humpback whales were very intelligent.

"If they like you," Vesh explained. "They are an asset to have on your side. They bring news from far away, especially the humpbacks who travel great distances. They are the eyes and ears of the ocean, and most will talk to us."

"We sound almost invincible." It was both thrilling and scary to Evan. What chance would the Selkies have against them?

"In the water, we more or less are," Vesh agreed. "Land is a different story. Without contact with the ocean, our powers are considerably less." Vesh placed his hand on Evan's shoulder and gave him a reassuring squeeze. "I don't want to see the Selkies destroyed any more than you do, my friend. Ken is bent on revenge and hatred. Our mother would not agree with that."

"Your mother was killed by a Selkie?" This was the story that Ken told Evan during the summer. How their queen, their mother, was left heartbroken by a Selkie and committed suicide.

"She died at her own hand." Vesh sounded bitter, but not angry. "I cannot say whether the Selkie was to blame or not. Ken is convinced, of course."

"Azuria," Evan said. It was the name Evan remembered Ken thinking when he told Evan the story. It was the clue he left for Meara on the napkin. Hopefully, Ted was able to give it to her, and she learned by now what it meant.

"Azuria," Vesh repeated quietly. "Our mother and our home."

"Your home?"

Vesh nodded. "Our fortress is also called Azuria. It was named after her. She was everything to us. When she died, a part of us died with her."

"You don't seem evil," Evan said without thinking. He winced when he realized what he said. "Um, sorry."

"Don't apologize. Some of us have turned to evil. Like Ken. He's the oldest. Azuria's death impacted him the most. He is full of hatred. As you progressed down the line, well, the impact lessened." Evan raised an eyebrow questioningly, and Vesh continued, "Right. I'm sure you've guessed then, that Dex, Slate, and I are the youngest. Well..." He paused and gave Evan a crooked smile. "Before you, of course. You're the baby of the group."

If Ken was his father, then all the other Blue Men were uncles to him. He could barely fathom. There were so many of them. It would make for interesting family reunions back in Nova Scotia.

"How old are you?" Evan asked. "If you don't mind me asking."

"I don't mind." Vesh shrugged. "I'm over eight hundred years old. As I said, we don't really track to an exact year."

"You don't look a day over twenty-two," Evan said dryly.

Vesh laughed, a deep, throaty gargle that startled the small silver fish around them. "We don't age, Evan. That's what immortal means."

"So, I'll stop aging, too?" Evan didn't know how he felt about that. He'd never considered it before. Who would've thought that he would find himself immortal?

"Probably. Hard to tell since your mother was human." Vesh slapped Evan's back in a friendly gesture. "I guess we'll have to wait and see. Now, how about we get back to training, shall we? None of us will be immortal if Ken succeeds in his plans."

"You think he'd wipe us all out?"

The smile disappeared from Vesh's face. "I don't think. I know. If Ken succeeds, we're all dead."

That left Evan with one option. He had to succeed.

Chapter 23

"Where the hell did you go this time?" Kieran was waiting at the entrance to the cave, his hair mussed and eyes alert. "You're seriously going to give me a heart attack, Meara. I might need to strap you to my side."

"I'm fine. Azuria contacted me again."

A frown line formed between Kieran's eyes. He was not happy with that news. "What did she want this time? Did she come to finish making you a Selkie popsicle?"

"She kept her distance," I said. "And apologized for freezing me earlier. She didn't realize that her touch would have that effect on me. No, she told me that she contacted me because of Evan. Evan—" I lost my words and swallowed. Evan was one of the Blue Men of the Minch. Azuria explained how it happened, that Ken tricked Lydia, but I struggled to accept it. It didn't matter what I thought anyway, Azuria was adamant that he was one of them.

"Evan...?" Kieran prompted, raising his eyebrow.

"Evan is one of the Blue Men, Kieran." I started pacing and rubbing my arms. The early morning air was chilly. "Azuria said so. He's the key to stopping Ken, and she showed me where they are."

"Where?" Kieran took the news about Evan better than I did. Maybe he saw the signs over the summer. I didn't, although now it made sense. The headaches, the mood swings... I knew he was struggling with something. I just didn't know what.

"Off the coast of France." The map came back to me, clear in my mind. I could see the dwelling and even determine the approximate location from the coast. Azuria would guide us there; I was confident that she was sharing the vision with me now. Somehow, we'd made a connection.

His mouth fell. "France? Are you sure? That seems far away considering they're trying to destroy our home in Scotland."

"I'm positive. I can get us there. Azuria is helping me."

"Helping you how?" He moved closer and looked into my eyes. "Are you sure you're okay?"

"I feel fine. She connected to me psychically somehow."

He rested his forehead on mine and sighed. "As long as she keeps her distance. I prefer you warm and not frostbit."

"Ha, ha." Stomach rumbling, I moved into the cave. "Do we have anything to eat?"

"The fish is gone. Do you want me to catch another?"

"Can't we conjure something? I'm starving." I also really, really did not want fish for breakfast. A bagel and cream cheese sounded heavenly.

"I was trying not to use too much magic, but there is a village not too far from here." Kieran closed his eyes and held out his hands. "This shouldn't take too much effort."

The cave filled with the yeasty smell of fresh bread. I almost drooled over the delicious aroma. He split the loaf in half and gave me the bigger piece, fragrant steam was rising from the middle.

I tore off a chunk, closing my eyes as I chewed. "Thank you," I said after I swallowed. "This is delicious."

He laughed. "You look like you're having an experience over there."

"I am," I said with a wink and sat by the low-burning fire. It chased the damp and chill from my skin. As I ate, I thought about our options.

"What are you thinking?" Kieran asked, sitting across from me. In the firelight, his eyes glowed like the brandy my dad sometimes drank.

"Who do we rescue first?" I didn't share what I was thinking. I let the question hang between us. Kieran chewed silently, his face deep in thought as he stared at the crackling embers.

"Evan." His voice was resigned, but firm. "We know where he is, and that's what Azuria more or less told you to do, right?"

"Yes." I hugged my knees, grateful that he confirmed what I already decided. "Who knows, maybe he knows where Dad is being kept."

"Maybe." Kieran didn't sound very confident. "Maybe he's made some friends in his new world. He was a popular kid, right? Good-natured, except when he was being an ass to you."

"Kieran." My voice held a warning. I wasn't sure how I felt about Evan anymore, but I didn't want to hash it out with Kieran.

"At any rate," Kieran continued as if I hadn't spoken. "At least we know why he was being an ass to you. He was becoming one of them."

He said the last word with contempt. I agreed. Becoming one of the Blue Men of the Minch was the last thing I would want. The last thing I imagined Evan, human Evan, would want. Was he a monster now? Was he working with Ken? Trying to destroy us? I hoped not... or Azuria was sending us to our deaths.

"When do you want to leave?" Kieran asked. Once again, he left the planning to me. He would support whatever I decided and back me up as needed.

"As soon as we put out this fire and pack up the camp."

I knew it was hard for him not to be in charge, especially after I listened to Cole talk about how Kieran headed his father's guard. He successfully led dangerous missions, and now he was taking orders from me—the girl who was not even a full Selkie. Did he regret the last few months that he spent training me? Did he miss his family?

He stood and walked around the circle of the fire, offering his hand to me. I took it and stood. "You might want to shield some of those thoughts, Meara." His voice was rough with emotion, and my face grew hot. He tilted up my chin and stared into my eyes. "I don't regret one minute of time spent with you, and I have no problem following your lead."

The intense emotions behind his words left me stunned. I pressed a soft kiss on his lips. "Thank you."

We swam fast and didn't take any breaks, but it was late by the time we arrived in the waters near France. Azuria was showing me images more frequently the closer we got. I couldn't hear her voice, but I sensed her intent. We were almost there, and she wanted us to proceed with caution.

We're getting close, I told Kieran. *Ken will have scouts, so we need to be alert.*

I'm watching, he said. *The waters are quiet now. Did Azuria say how much further?*

No, only that we're almost there. He knew that she had been communicating with me most of the way. Now she was showing me an underwater cavern, several meters to our right. *She's showing me shelter where we can rest for the night.*

Kieran stopped and let me pass him. *Sounds good to me. I'm exhausted.*

The idea of remaining underwater did not appeal to me. While at Ronac, I hated that we were forbidden to swim in the sea. But, I didn't want to live in it either because we had to stay in seal form. In our human bodies, we couldn't breathe underwater for more than an hour or two. I didn't understand it, but I wasn't about to argue with Selkie magic.

This isn't my favorite form, I complained.

It's not my favorite form of yours either, Kieran said. I heard the laughter in his words, and he sent me a few steamy thoughts. If I could blush as a seal, I would.

The rock formation that Azuria assured me was the cave came into view. I was thrilled that we found it. If we didn't get settled in the cavern soon, I was going to sleep float—possibly right to Ken's door.

We found the entrance easy enough. Though it was hardly more than a hole carved into the rocks, it would sleep the two of us with a little room to spare. Kieran swam up to me with a large fish in his mouth, offering it. I closed my eyes and bit off half, trying to ignore the crunch of bone and the metallic aftertaste. I was not a fan of scaly, raw fish. He ate the other half with gusto. Unlike me, he enjoyed fresh food.

Thanks for dinner, I managed when I swallowed the last of it. I felt his chuckle through my mind.

I know it's no pizza, but it will give you energy. He went into the small space first, inspected it to make sure no other creatures were claiming stakes, and then settled down. He lowered his head and growled softly at me.

I'm coming, I grumbled. When I settled against him, his body relaxed and he sighed. I had a moment to realize how safe I felt beside him before my mind and body shut down from sheer exhaustion.

I woke to a faint light glowing at the cavern entrance. Kieran slept beside me. Without looking, I knew that Azuria waited outside. I moved away from Kieran, careful not to disturb him, and swam out. Azuria floated in the water, her form pearly and translucent like a jellyfish. *Or an underwater ghost,* I thought.

The energy required to take my true form would freeze the water, she explained. *I hope you do not mind. As you can see, I am able to communicate with you.*

Could you talk to me this way all along? I asked.

Yes, she answered. *It takes more energy, though, so I sent you my impulses instead. You did well.* The look she gave me bordered on maternal. *Come, I want to show you something.*

We swam for a ways in silence. I watched for markers and tried to gauge distance. I assumed that what she was showing me, I would need to show Kieran tomorrow.

The water warmed slightly, and the darkness gave way to cool shades of lavender, cerulean, and emerald. Shadows of structures emerged in their glow, although there was no movement of living things save for the seaweed rocking back and forth in the gentle current.

This is the Siren home, Belle Trésor, Azuria said, sweeping her arm to indicate the entire area was a village.

Siren? As in mermaid? My curiosity was piqued. Would they be as beautiful as humans portrayed them? In books and paintings, they were such lovely creatures.

Similar, yes, although I wouldn't recommend calling them mermaids. Mermaids live in tropical waters. They tend to be more flighty and flirtatious than Sirens. Azuria shook her head with a small smile. *Both species are extremely competitive and not fond of other females.*

I'll keep my distance, I said, and Azuria laughed. Was she teasing me now? I wasn't sure. Her motives for helping me seemed clear, but I still didn't know if I should trust her. Then again, here I was, awake at the wee hours of morning, discussing the difference between Sirens and Mermaids. What next?

That's not a bad idea, Azuria agreed. *Especially since I do not know if they are on your side or not. Ken killed their leader, and as she was beloved, I'm fairly positive they are not siding with Ken unless it is in fear.*

Where is Ken? I asked. It wouldn't surprise me if he had guards waiting for us. I knew that he took the offensive much better than we did, and as he had already captured eight of our people, he must be prepared for more.

I'm not sure. Azuria's face fell and her lip trembled. In her distress, her pale image flickered in the moving water. *I can no longer sense my children very well, and in the Siren village, they are camouflaged from me.* She took my hands in hers. Considering her faint appearance, her grip was surprisingly strong. *From this point on, you are on your own. Good luck to you and your friend. Meara, I pray for your success.*

It surprised me that her power was so limited. Then again, she was dead. It would be rather scary if a spirit had a lot of power. With a gentle tug, she pulled me forward and kissed my cheek. Before she could disappear, I asked. *What do I do once I find Evan?*

Her image grew stronger once more. *Return the way you came. I will find you and guide you to Azuria.*

I blinked. She was Azuria, but then I remembered that the Blue Men's home went by the same name. How odd would that be? To have your home named after you?

She dissolved into specks of light that floated away in the murky water. My thoughts turned to Kieran. By now, he would be waking. We had a mission ahead of us. *Find Evan and get out quick. Quick and preferably alive.*

Chapter 24

Evan hurt everywhere. His muscles screamed in protest from being overworked. Yet, he couldn't stop the wide smile from filling his face. It was worth it. Vesh showed him some cool powers yesterday. By the end of the day, he was influencing the tide and speaking to fish. At first, he couldn't get the Disney references out of his head. Once he got over how unnatural it felt—he was a creature of the sea now, not a human—he stopped thinking about it.

Truth was, fish weren't all that intelligent. They mostly spoke in single words. They did manage to tell him that the mantle plume had stabilized and stopped growing. That lifted his spirits. Hopefully, he'd make more progress against Ken today.

There was no doubt in his mind that he would have to work. The fact that Ken stayed home sick yesterday was unbelievable. No way would he take off work two days in a row. Sickness was a weakness that Ken wouldn't succumb to.

A thud at his door was the telltale sign it was time to go. He didn't look in the mirror. Odds were that he looked like death warmed over from lack of sleep. By the time he was done with work, he'd look worse. Who cared? The important thing was to try and stop Ken.

He hid his surprise when he opened the door and saw Ken. The man looked worse than Evan felt.

"Ready?" Ken asked. There was no bite in his voice, which bordered on being raspy.

"Sure." Evan closed the door behind him. This close, he could see the bags under Ken's eyes and the deep lines around his mouth. He'd aged considerably in recent weeks. "Are you sure you're feeling better?"

"I'll be fine."

Ken's temper hadn't changed. With an inward sigh, Evan followed his father, boss, and at least temporarily, leader, for another day of excruciating work.

Moaning, Evan laid back on the bed. What he wouldn't give for a beer, or even better, a six-pack. The day had been hell. At one point, he thought for sure Ken figured out that Evan was fighting his efforts. The moment passed, and Ken finally called it a day. Truthfully, Evan didn't know how much longer he could keep it up. Every muscle screamed in pain as he shifted on the mattress, trying to get comfortable.

He didn't remember closing his eyes, but when he reopened them, the room was dark. It seemed he was spending more time in bed these days than anywhere else. His world revolved around eating, sleeping, and working. Surviving, that was what he was doing, just surviving.

His nose tickled, and he picked up the scents of clove, ginger, and musky perfume. Realization dawned that he wasn't alone. Deanna snuggled into him, her back against his chest. He kissed her temple, sliding his hand under the hem of her shirt to rest against her warm skin.

"Good morning," she murmured. "Or should I say, 'Good afternoon'?"

"Have you been here a while?" He wasn't surprised that he didn't wake when she came in. He could sleep through almost anything these days. His body hit the bed and shut down.

She rolled to face him, resting her hand on his side. "I stopped by when I got off work. You looked so comfortable that I decided to join you." She lifted her head and met his eyes. "I hope that's okay?"

"You can join me whenever you like." He brushed a soft kiss over her full lips that were still stained red with the heavier makeup she wore for performing. The dark eye shadow and dramatic lips made her look exotic, but he preferred her natural coloring. She was beautiful and didn't need all of that extra crap.

She raised her hand and guided him back to her lips for a longer, deeper kiss. "Did you miss me yesterday?"

"I always miss you when you're gone."

He realized that he meant it. Between the concert the day before and hanging with Vesh yesterday, he kept busy, but it wasn't the same without Deanna. She smiled at his answer. Her fingers played through his hair, creating an aching need within him.

She moved one hand down and lazily traced it across his chest, then along his collarbone. "What did you do without me?"

Evan was finding it hard to concentrate. Her head was tilted as she studied him, her eyes playful.

"I... uh... listened to Slate's band..." He cleared his throat. Deanna's hand slid down, making his stomach muscles jump.

"Did you?" she murmured. "Were they good?"

"They were..." Her fingers slid playfully along the edge of his jeans. Evan was so done with this conversation. "Oh, hell..."

He crushed his mouth to hers and felt her smile against his lips. *Took you long enough*, her voice teased through his head. She wrapped her arms around his neck and scooted closer until her body was pressed along his.

Chapter 25

re you sure this is where he is? Kieran crouched behind me. We hid behind a rock formation, the Siren settlement looming in front of us. We had been watching for hours. Although the water remained as dark as it had been when I was here with Azuria, the blues and purples from the night changed to the bright reds, oranges, and yellows of day. It was interesting that the Sirens marked the shift of time this way. Whether magic or some other power lit the buildings, the effect was breathtaking. It reminded me of stained glass or glittering jewels.

If we trust Azuria is helping us. If we don't, then this could be a trap. I didn't mean for my voice to sound bitter, but I couldn't help it. So much rode on our shoulders, mine more than Kieran's, and truthfully, Azuria hadn't given us much to go on. As she said, from this point, we were on our own. That thought petrified me. I knew very little about our enemy. *Do you see anyone?*

No. Kieran moved closer until I could feel his warmth at my back. *The whole place looks deserted.*

We know that's not true. I winced at the cramp forming in my backside. We couldn't squish behind this rock forever. At the same time, where was everyone? It was the middle of the day. Didn't they go out? Go to work? Or play? It felt like a ghost town and made my fur stand on end.

Wouldn't we be better off coming back at night?

This wasn't the first time Kieran asked me that. On one hand, I agreed with him, but Azuria specifically brought me here at that ungodly hour this morning. She conveyed a sense of urgency that we needed to find Evan today. Although she was gone, I could feel her drive pushing me forward. Like a metronome to my willpower. *Find Evan. Find my son. Find Evan. Find my son.* The sooner I found him, the sooner I'd have peace. Or, so I hoped.

We'll stick to the shadows, I decided. *We might hear something useful when we encounter some of the citizens.*

If we encounter them. His sigh was long and suffering. *Let's move, then.* He nosed me in the back. *Before someone finds us here.*

Would they recognize us as Selkies? I hadn't thought to ask him earlier. We were in our seal form, and I assumed anyone who saw us would think we were actual seals out for a swim.

I don't know. He took the lead and swam toward a shadowy passage at the back of one building. *Seals don't normally swim this deep or stay down for very long. If we can, we should avoid being spotted.*

I nodded. He explained it all earlier to me when I first panicked that we'd run out of air. Kieran reassured me that our magic made us different from the animals whose shape we took. Just as Selkies weren't truly human, we weren't truly seals either. We could breathe underwater indefinitely in seal form, and for several hours in human form. The news was a relief to me, and it explained how the Blue Men were keeping our Selkies captive underwater.

I hear voices. Kieran slid low along the wall, mere inches off the ocean floor. When he reached the end of the passage, he peeked around the corner, and then scooted back into the shadows. Without taking his eyes off the promenade, he updated me. *There's a large cave ahead to the right. I saw a few Sirens and Blue Men outside of it. That must be where most of them are.*

What should we do? Though it was tempting to hang in the shadows, doing so would not help us find Evan.

"What have we here?"

Before I could react at the deep voice behind me, strong arms wrapped around my middle and pinned my front flippers to my sides. I bucked and twisted, trying to get away, but his grip was tight.

Run, I screamed to Kieran.

I'm not leaving you.

"Get the other!" the same voice bellowed. Two large shadows overtook Kieran, though he gave a good fight. They slid a needle into his side, and his body went limp. Before I could scream, a sharp prick pierced my skin. Darkness quickly followed.

Male voices murmured nearby. The room was dark, but dry. It was strange to breathe air again. I tried to open my mouth, and then made a noise of frustration. Duct tape prevented me from moving my muzzle. I wanted to scream obscenities at our captors, but all I could manage was a soft whine. Kieran growled. His dark eyes glowing menacingly in the shadows.

Are you okay? He sounded angry, not scared, so that was a good thing.

My head hurts a little. A mild pain formed behind my eyes when I woke up. I moved to stretch and realized that they tied me down. *This really sucks.*

Tell me about it. Kieran's voice was grim. *Did you get a look at them?*

They stayed in the shadows. I tried to recall any details that might stick out. Only two things came to mind. *They seemed unnaturally large and male.*

Blue Men, then. Kieran tried to bite through his rope. It wasn't giving. *That's what I figured. Wonder where they are now?*

As if they heard us, our captors returned and flipped on the lights, practically blinding us after so many hours in darkness. Seal eyes were very sensitive to light. I wanted to change into my human form, but I didn't think I could in my current state, not without contorting my body painfully in these ropes. Hell, I couldn't even turn my head to see who abducted us.

"We're not going to hurt you."

The voice belonged to the man who captured me, the only one I'd heard. So far, his two companions remained quiet. He squatted in front of me, a safe distance away. I wanted to laugh. He was afraid of me? Even if I wanted to attack him, I couldn't wiggle a whisker in these ties. Blinking, my eyes slowly adjusted to the light.

He was rather good looking in his human form. His hair was black and spiky, and he had dime-sized plugs in his ears. A little too goth for my taste, but his light gray eyes were lovely. I gave myself a mental pinch. Why was I checking him out? Had I lost my mind?

The man hadn't moved. He continued to crouch in front of me, relaxing a little and resting his forearms on his knees. "I wonder..." His full lips parted in a friendly smile. "I've never met a Selkie before." He reached out and patted my head like a dog. "You're kind of cute."

Moving on instinct, my head jerked away from his hand and a warning rumbled in my throat. At the same time, Kieran growled low and threatening. Spiky hair ignored him, but his face fell. "I guess you didn't like that." He sat back and put some distance between us. "I'm sorry if I offended you."

I'll offend his ass to next Tuesday once I'm free. Kieran followed his statement with a rather colorful stream of curses. *He had better not touch you again if he wants to live.*

Not helping, I told him. Besides, I didn't think Mr. Plugs meant me any harm. He sounded like he was serious when he apologized. His companions moved behind him, joining in the observation party. Instead of watching them like a helpless trapped animal, I looked beyond them at the room. It was furnished like an apartment. Did Sirens live in apartments under the sea?

"Do you think that's her?" The one with the mousy, brown hair and glasses spoke. He frowned, and I wondered if he really wanted to be part of this.

Just stay calm. Kieran continued to talk to me from across the room. He was momentarily forgotten by the men. It wasn't like he could do anything anyway. He was tied down and muzzled too.

I'm okay, I told him. *I... I believe them. I don't think they want to hurt us.*

Something was going on, and I wasn't sure what it was, but I did believe that if these men wanted to hurt us or kill us, they would've done it already. They seemed to be waiting for something. Or someone.

The door flew open, and a female voice asked, "Why did you call us, Vesh? Did you find something interesting?"

"You could say that." This came from the same guy with the spiky hair.

The girl giggled and whispered to someone else. A deep laugh answered hers, and then two sets of footsteps came into the room.

"What have you done?" the new male cried in outrage. I recognized that voice. I'd recognize it anywhere. *Evan.*

Chapter 26

Meara was tied down like an animal, tape wrapped around her muzzle, her flippers pinned to her body by thick ropes. A larger seal was wrapped the same way on the other side of the room. Probably Kieran.

"Untie her!" Anger made Evan's voice shake. Deanna stepped back, and Vesh raised his hands.

"Calm down, Evan. I didn't hurt either of them." Vesh pulled a knife from his pocket, and Evan jerked it away. With inhuman speed, he turned and moved to Meara's side. Her dark eyes rolled, showing the whites. She recoiled as though she was petrified. *Damn it!* She probably was. Evan forgot that she'd never seen him in this form before.

"It's me, Meara." He spoke to her in a soothing tone, and his hands gentled while he carefully cut through the ropes. Vesh hadn't lied. Her fur was smooth underneath the ropes, her skin unharmed.

You're okay? he asked, testing their connection. If she didn't respond, he'd ask her out loud. She still looked afraid of him.

Yes. He thought he heard her sigh in relief, and her body definitely relaxed. She recognized him. *Evan, is that... is that really you?*

Yes. It's a long story. I'll tell you later. Hearing her voice in his mind made his chest pang with a mix of emotions. He'd missed her so much. More than he realized. *Can you change?*

The air shimmered around her, and then Meara sat before him in shorts and a T-shirt. Her eyes glistened with unshed tears. It was all he saw before she launched herself into his arms and clung to his neck, burying her face in his shoulder. "Evan, oh, Evan. What did they do to you?"

"Shhh… It's okay. I'm alright." He held her tight, noticing the changes in her. She was firm and muscular from training, not the soft girl he once knew.

She pulled back abruptly and turned toward the other seal. "Kieran needs to be cut free!"

"Can we trust him?" This question came from Vesh.

If looks could kill, Meara slayed him.

"Set. Him. Free," she gritted between her teeth. "Now."

The air thickened with her outrage, and Evan tasted her power. She *was* stronger and had some potent magic if her temper brought it out that strongly.

"Evan?" A soft hand on his shoulder reminded him of Deanna's presence. He covered her hand with his own and gave it a reassuring squeeze.

"Meara, meet my girlfriend, Deanna." Evan watched the tense expression leave Deanna's face to be replaced by a pleased one. He didn't mean to neglect her, but the shock of seeing Meara again affected him more than he realized it would.

Meara gave him a questioning look before smiling tentatively at Deanna and offering her hand. "Nice to meet you, Deanna."

Vesh cautiously approached the male seal, and Meara's attention turned to Kieran. When Vesh cut the last rope, the air didn't just shimmer—it *erupted* as Kieran changed. Evan had never seen a more pissed off Selkie or man. His eyes flamed, scalding everyone in the room with the exception of Meara. She ran to his side, and he dragged his mouth across hers.

So that was how it was, Evan thought. *Figures.*

"Someone better tell me what the hell is going on." Kieran kept his arm wrapped protectively around Meara. "Who are you people? Where are we?"

Deanna stepped in front of the men, much to Evan's relief. She was diplomatic and could smooth over the situation better than the guys could. Evan tensed at the appreciative look Kieran gave her. Luckily, he returned to a neutral, guarded expression just as fast.

"You're in my mother's former quarters. Underground." Deanna gestured to the plush couches across the room. "Please have a seat and make yourselves comfortable. It seems we have much to discuss."

Meara and Kieran sat next to each other on the far end of the couch. He took her hand, Evan noticed. Kieran seemed to need to touch her constantly. With a sigh, Evan sat in the armchair closest to them. Deanna perched on the side of it, facing their guests.

"Were you expecting us?" Kieran asked, first to speak as everyone settled.

"Yes and no," Deanna said after a pause. "We assumed Meara would come for Evan at some point."

Meara looked up at the mention of her name, a curious expression on her face. "You were expecting me?"

Deanna shrugged, so Evan added, "We know that your dad and aunt are captured."

Meara's eyes widened. "Have you seen them? Are they okay?"

"We haven't," Vesh answered before Evan could. "Ken ordered their imprisonment, but they are held at Azuria."

"Azuria has them?" Confusion filled Meara's voice. "Why?"

"Not Azuria, our mother. She's dead." Vesh gave Meara a strange look. "Azuria is also the name of our keep. We haven't been back since we conquered the Sirens." Vesh turned to Deanna. "No offense."

"None taken," she said.

"Ken won't allow it," Evan added, earning a nod from the other Blue Men in the room. "Only his closest followers are allowed to return there."

Kieran's expression darkened, and his free hand tapped a silent beat on his leg. The guy was wired tight like a spring. It surprised Evan that he fit with Meara, but they seemed quite close. Maybe there was truth to opposites attracting.

"What does that make you? Some kind of resistance party?" Kieran's voice dripped with sarcasm.

Vesh answered him. "Yeah, you could say that. Just because Ken is my brother does not mean I agree with his vendetta. Whatever happened between our mother and that Selkie happened years ago. There is no sense in killing innocents for revenge."

"Zane didn't kill Azuria!" Meara stood and faced Vesh.

"And how would you know?" Vesh asked slowly. "You've been a

Selkie for, how long is it again? Months?"

"I know," Meara said through clenched teeth. "Because Azuria showed me."

And that was when all hell broke loose.

Chapter 27

*F*ive people started yelling at once. The only one not saying anything was Kieran, and that was because he already knew the story.

"Stop!" I raised a hand and, miraculously, they quieted. Of course, in that moment, my stomach decided to go all grizzly bear. The guy named Vesh raised a pierced eyebrow.

"What?" I asked defensively. "I'm hungry."

"I can see why you and Evan get along so well," he said dryly and earned an evil look from Deanna and Kieran. "If you can wait fifteen minutes, I'll get us food." He stood and poked the other two guys in the back. "Come help me carry."

"Be careful," Deanna said.

He answered with a grin. "Always am."

Before he left, Vesh pointed at me. "Do not start until I get back."

The door closed, leaving the four of us. The silence in the room grew awkward. Then, Deanna rolled her eyes. "He said not to talk about Azuria. He didn't say we couldn't talk at all." She stood and smoothed her hands down her designer jeans. Her body was thin and lithe like a dancer, and I wondered if all Sirens were that lucky or just her. "Can I get you anything to drink?"

She directed the question at all of us, but Kieran stood. "What do you have?"

As he followed her to the kitchenette, I scolded myself for the ping of jealousy. He was thirsty, not interested in her.

Almost as if he was proving my point, Kieran turned back to me. "Do you want a Diet Coke, Meara?"

"That would be great." My words were nonchalant, but my heart did a happy dance. He was following a gorgeous Siren, and his thoughts were focused on me. He loved me.

"So, you and Kieran?" Evan said it like a question, and quiet enough that only I could hear.

"Yeah." No point in denying it. "How long have you been seeing Deanna?"

It was weird to talk about this. Sure, we were no longer together, but I wasn't ready to swap date stories either.

"A while," he answered with a shrug. "She's really helped me since I've been here."

I bet she has. The nasty words floated through my head before I could suppress them. Good thing I was shielding. Still, changing the subject might be good. "You've been doing okay, then? I was worried about you."

"I know." He patted my hand, and it was only a little awkward. I didn't feel any sparks like I used to. In some ways, that made me sad. I cared for Evan, but it was no longer the same.

He must have felt something similar, because he smiled at me, but his eyes were filled with remorse. "I've been okay, but Ken..." He paused and straightened. "Meara, Ken is up to no good."

Deanna and Kieran came back with the drinks. She gave Evan a blue bottle—maybe it was a beer?—and settled into his lap, leaning back comfortably against his chest.

Kieran handed me the cold can of soda and sat next to me. He put his arm around my shoulder. I guessed we were staking territories now. As a hum grew in my chest from his closeness, I realized that I didn't mind. He could claim me all he wanted.

"You were about to dish on Ken?" Kieran gestured with his drink. "What's that blue bastard been up to? I haven't seen him since he poisoned me."

I choked on my drink, the carbonation causing my eyes to water. Deanna's mouth opened in shock, and she turned to Evan, who shifted uncomfortably.

"Yeah... um... sorry about that, man." Evan's face turned a deeper shade of blue. "I didn't know."

"It's poison under the bridge," Kieran quipped, which made me jab him in the ribs for the cheesy response. He grinned and winked before turning his attention back to Evan. "Please continue."

Evan told us about the work he'd been doing at the mantle plum with Ken. When he said Ken's goal was to destroy our island, my heart stopped. How could we prevent massive destruction on that large of a scale? Months of training and for what? We were doomed.

"You said you've been fighting him. How?" Ever the optimist, Kieran latched onto the one positive piece of news in Evan's update.

"I've—" Evan started to tell us, but Deanna squeezed his knee and stopped him.

"Not now."

She jumped off his lap and hurried over to open the door. Vesh and his friends stood in the hall, arms laden with pizza boxes and carryout bags. She let them in and locked the door behind them.

"Food's here!" she announced in a voice that was too bright, not to mention, unnecessary, since we could both see and smell the food.

I watched her the entire time Evan was talking. The more he said, the more uncomfortable she appeared. She was nervous, but why? Was it Vesh or was it us?

"Hey, seal girl." Vesh held up an open pizza box. He already had a slice in his hand. "You hungry?"

"It's Meara." My response was automatic and a little scolding. He laughed. I took a slice from the box and bit in. It tasted different from pizza back home, but it wasn't bad. Who was I kidding? I was starved. They could've handed me a cold can of sardines and I would've wolfed it down like a greasy cheeseburger.

In between bites, I told them about Azuria.

Looking stunned, Vesh asked, "Why you? Why did she choose to talk to you after all of these centuries of silence?" He turned to his brothers. "Why not one of us?"

I wasn't sure whether to be offended or feel special that she chose me. In the end, I dropped it. It didn't really matter. The point was, she did choose me, whether they agreed with it or not. Then, I thought about what Vesh said.

"Centuries?" I asked, thinking I heard him wrong.

"Yes, centuries." He sounded bitter. "As in hundreds of years."

"Thanks, Einstein." Kieran was quick to jump to my defense. "We know what a century is."

I ignored the jab and tried to wrap my head around that much time. I was eighteen years old, and the Blue Men were at least hundreds of years old. Kieran, I knew, was much older than I was. How old was Deanna? She didn't seem surprised that they were talking about century's worth of time. Like me, Evan seemed to struggle with it. Of course, we were the only two recent humans in the room. At least we still had that in common.

"She told you Evan was the key?" Slate glanced at Evan, a skeptical expression on his face. "Did she say how?"

I shook my head. I'd told them all I knew. In the end, the only thing my experience with Azuria really managed to do was clear up the misconception of how she died.

"What's your plan?" Slate asked, and everyone in the room looked at him. It was the first thing he'd said since they'd captured us.

"I need to rescue my dad," I said without hesitation.

"Ah, your dad is one of the Selkies that Ken caught?" I could see the sympathy in Vesh's eyes, and my hope rose. With their help, we had a chance at succeeding. Kieran and I alone? Not so much.

"Yes. My aunt is there, too."

"And the others? Do you know them?" Slate leaned forward, his interest piqued.

"I know them all," I said. "The others are my father's guard."

Slate commented under his breath, "He should have better guards. If those are his best, you don't stand a chance against Ken."

Kieran shot him an angry glare. Vesh and Evan had almost matching expressions. I raised my hand to cut through the testosterone. "Look. Slate is right." I looked around the room, and then shrugged. "Selkies are not fighters. By nature, we are peaceful. It doesn't mean that I'll allow Ken to slaughter us." I stood and met each of their gazes. "So, will you help? If not, thank you for the meal, but Kieran and I must be on our way."

Kieran stood and put his arm around me. Vesh, who was closest to Kieran, also stood, placing his hand on Kieran's chest as if to stop him from leaving. Kieran looked down at Vesh's hand and up again. "If you like that hand, you'll remove it."

"Calm down, big guy." Vesh patted Kieran once before dropping his hand and turning his attention to me. "You, too, Meara. Who said we weren't going to help you?"

I opened my mouth, and then closed it again. I probably looked like a fish. Vesh smiled at me and gestured to the couch. "Sit, please. We need to plan and quickly."

After we sat down again, Vesh took charge as if calling a meeting to order. "If we're not gone before dawn, Ken will have Evan back at work and we won't be able to leave until nighttime. And, that gives them the opportunity to move the plume that much further." He gave Evan an apologetic smile. Evan shrugged in response. "I say we leave in one hour. All in favor?"

Everyone made consenting sounds, except Deanna. She was staring at her hands.

"Dee?" Evan covered her hands with one of his and lifted her chin. Her eyes shimmered with unshed tears.

"I'll stay here. Someone needs to keep an eye on Ken."

Evan grasped her shoulders and stared at her intently. "It's not safe. If he finds out, he'll come after you."

She placed her arms around his neck and gave him a look full of love. For a brief moment, jealousy bore its way into my heart. Then I glanced at Kieran, who blew me a kiss and made me forget all about Evan.

"I'll be fine, Evan. You know I will." Determination filled Deanna's eyes. "Let me do this for you." She looked around, capturing us all in her sights. "For all of you."

"Wait! I have something." I turned and wrapped my arms around Kieran's neck.

"I think I like where this is going," he teased. Vesh snickered and my face flamed, but I focused on my task, smiling when I held up the gold chain.

"Remember these?" I said to Evan. I hooked my thumb under the thin chain around my own neck and lifted the pearl charm. "We brought the set just in case, although Kieran and I don't need it. Why don't you see if they work for you and Deanna?"

Evan smiled one of those smiles that brought out his dimples, which managed to look cute on his face even in his blue form. For a moment, I remembered what it was like, when he smiled like that all the time, his face filled with love and devotion. That look now belonged to someone else. I unclasped my necklace and handed both to him. He clasped the pearl pendant around Deanna's neck, and the thicker gold chain around his own. I hoped that they experienced more luck and success with them than Evan and I had.

Chapter 28

e don't need jewelry to communicate. Deanna's soft voice, a mixture of annoyed and amused, drifted though Evan's head.

Not here, Evan agreed, trying to placate her. She sounded a little offended. *We haven't tested how far apart we can be before we can't hear each other. I know that these necklaces work from long distances.*

You used them with her. Deanna's bottom lip puckered.

Her pout made him want to smile, but wisely, he kept a straight face. *I did, which is how I know they work.*

It could be a trap, Deanna persisted.

It's not, Evan replied confidently. Meara would never hurt him.

You trust her implicitly? That's dangerous. Still, she let Evan fasten the necklace around her neck. It looked beautiful against her delicate collarbone.

"Don't let Ken see it," Meara warned. "He asked Evan about the necklaces in the past. He might recognize it."

"Good point." Evan gave Meara a small nod.

Vesh clapped his hands together loudly. "Now that that's all settled, should we figure out our plan? We're wasting time here."

True to his word, Vesh kept them on schedule. By the end of the hour, they had a plan and they were ready to head out. As ready as they could be.

Evan was relieved that Vesh, Dex, and Slate were coming with them. He would've helped Meara no matter what, but there was no incentive for the other Blue Men besides a mutual disagreement with Ken and his quest for revenge. It didn't matter the reason. The fact that they were helping was enough for Evan. They'd been to Azuria and lived there for centuries. If anyone could get them in, rescue the Selkies, and escape unnoticed, it was these three.

We can trust Vesh, right? Evan asked Deanna. That was his greatest fear. Would Vesh betray them? How trustworthy were his companions?

You can trust them. Deanna's voice was tender, but certain. *They will not betray you.*

"We've got a long swim ahead of us." Vesh stood and stretched. "We'd best be on our way." He turned to Meara and his expression softened. Evan ignored the twinge of jealousy. She already won over Vesh, if not the others. She was likeable, even more so in this new, stronger version of herself. Too bad Evan knew she was also extremely kissable, too kissable for her own good.

"What?" Meara asked when she caught him staring.

He shook his head and looked away. Deanna's hand found his thigh and squeezed. *You still have feelings for her, don't you?* She didn't sound upset. If anything, her voice was filled with sympathy.

A part of me always will, he answered after a moment. He covered Deanna's hand with his own. *But Meara and I? We're different now. She has Kieran, and what I have with you makes what I feel for her pale in comparison.*

It was weird talking to his new girlfriend about his old girlfriend, but strangely therapeutic, too. Deanna rested her head on his shoulder. *I understand. Be safe, Evan. I'll miss you.*

I'll miss you, too. He lowered his head and kissed her, lingering a little longer than necessary to show her how much she meant to him.

"Are you two almost done sucking face?" Kieran said. Evan held back a surge of anger. He wanted to punch the guy every time he opened his mouth. Would Meara really be upset? Kieran freaking deserved it for being annoying as hell. Evan would be doing Meara a favor if he took Kieran out, saving her from the pompous ass.

Before Evan could growl a response, Vesh stopped him. "Kieran's right. We need to go." Once again, Vesh looked at Meara. "We'll take our true form. We can swim faster that way."

She shrugged. "Fine by me. We're going to change, too."

"I'll keep an eye on Ken," Deanna said and stood. "I can tell him that Evan is sick and buy you a day. It will only work once. Be safe, all of you."

Blowing a kiss to Evan, she slipped out of the room. Vesh straightened and moved to the door. He motioned for the others to line up behind him. "Follow closely and quietly. I'll get us out of here, but we have to move fast."

With one last glance back for their confirmation, he left the room. Slate went next, followed by Meara and Kieran. Dex and Evan brought up the rear.

The hallway was deserted. Evan didn't expect anything else. He hadn't seen anyone else on this level yet. Deanna claimed that the Blue Men used it, but the only ones he'd seen here were his friends. Vesh walked quickly and stayed close to the wall. The rest of the group mimicked him. Evan didn't risk looking behind him. They had one goal—to get out.

When they rounded the corner to the stairwell, someone was there. The man looked vaguely familiar to Evan. Before the guy could speak, Vesh knocked him out and propped him against the wall. Then Vesh continued past the stairwell. Where was he going?

Evan found out soon enough. They turned left down another empty hall. An emergency exit loomed ahead. Vesh messed with a box near the door, disabled the alarm, and held the door open, motioning them through. When they were all waiting in the shadows, Vesh keyed a code to relock the door and reset the alarm.

"We're going to change forms." Vesh spoke to them all, but focused on Meara. Was he developing a crush on her? Not the wisest idea if Kieran's scowl was any indication. The Selkie looked fierce. "I recommend that you two don't change until we're outside the city walls. You blend more in this form."

Kieran and Meara agreed.

You can breathe underwater in human form? Evan asked her.

For short periods of time, she said. *No longer than an hour or so.*

Relieved she would be okay, Evan waited for the others to change. The water stirred while the three men took their true, much larger, forms. *At least I don't stand out so much now,* Evan thought. He really hated the color blue. Too bad, it used to be his favorite.

"Next stop, Azuria," Vesh announced with a flourish. No one responded as they followed Vesh out of the Siren dwelling. Each lost to his own thoughts.

Azuria—where they would succeed or they would fail. It all rode on this mission.

Chapter 29

I never thought I'd say this, but it felt good to change back into seal form. It was a more natural state for us to take in the water. We could swim faster this way. As an added benefit, instincts took over and freed me from my worries.

The swim ahead would be long, but no longer than what Kieran and I had already traveled to rescue Evan.

Evan. He swam ahead of us with the other Blue Men. It took me a good part of the night to grow accustomed to his new form. Now that I had, I could see the Evan I knew underneath. Heck, the dimples were still there when he smiled.

I was glad that he found Deanna. Okay, scratch that, maybe a part of me wished he were holding out for us to get back together. That part of me was dumb and selfish, because I had Kieran. And I loved Kieran, and I knew, deep in my heart, that I didn't love Evan that way anymore. I still cared for him. Cared—the way you did about a good friend or relative, not cared in an I-want-to-kiss-you-breathless way. That was reserved for Kieran. I felt bad for Evan too, knowing what I did about Ken being his father. Evan had it so much worse in the dad department than I did.

Kieran nosed my side. *You okay or are you lost in your head again?*

Both, I answered. *Sorry.*

It's a lot to take in. For a while, I thought we were really done for. He blew out a stream of bubbles, and I knew he was remembering feeling trapped. It was an awful feeling. *I'm not sure I trust them, do you?*

I trust Evan. That was a given. Last summer, I had my moments of doubt, but now that he explained what happened, it all made sense. *He won't betray us. I think we can trust Vesh, too, and the other two—*

Barely say anything, Kieran interjected, causing me to snort out a laugh.

Right, I agreed. *They don't say much so it's hard to know.*

We swam in silence for a while, and then Kieran asked, *What about Deanna?*

I thought before answering, putting aside any negative feelings that came from her being Evan's new girlfriend. Ken killed her mother, so if nothing else, 'the enemy of my enemy is my friend' must apply. Finally, I said, *We can trust her. She obviously loves Evan.*

Her only fault. Kieran's voice was light and teasing. *I like her.*

You would. I bumped him in the side playfully. *She's beautiful.*

So are you. He brushed along my side. *And I like you more.*

Well, that's good.

It came in a grumble, but he knew that his words pleased me, especially when he added, *A lot more.*

Kieran, I sighed. *Focus.*

On what? he asked. *The scenery?*

We passed groups of fish, rock formations—nothing unusual. Nothing we hadn't seen many times before. *Or swimming?* he continued. *Because I've got that one covered. Been doing it since I was a cub.* His voice dropped an octave and sent a shiver down my spine. *I'd rather focus on you.*

Evan smirked at me. *You two are kind of funny together.*

You can hear us? My fur was going to singe in mortification. Apparently, I wasn't shielding. At all.

In my embarrassment, I didn't notice that Kieran stopped teasing me and came to a stop. I almost ran into him. I was about to ask what was wrong, and then I knew. Vesh was the first to speak.

"Shit."

The one word perfectly summed up what was before us. The destruction was wide spread. There seemed to be no end to it, and the smell, oh god, the smell was atrocious, like month-old garbage baking in the sun. I was surprised we hadn't noticed it sooner. We must have crossed some invisible barrier, and once through, it slammed us in the face.

Vesh covered his nose and mouth. Through his fingers, he asked, "How did you handle this, man?"

Evan gave him a bland look. "I had no choice, maybe?"

"There is that." Vesh grinned behind his hand, and then coughed when he got a mouthful of rot. "Ugh. Gross. Can we get around this?"

"If we head east about a mile, we should clear it." Evan took the lead. We swam in silence, holding our breath as long as we could. When we had to breathe, it was awful. The bile rose in my throat every time the taste of decay filled my mouth. Then we were clear of it, and I gulped the clean water greedily. If I never experienced that again, it would be too soon.

"*That* is headed to Ronac?" I knew the answer even as I asked it. Ken wanted to wipe us out, and if the mantle plume reached our island, I was afraid he would succeed. Months ago, Kieran and I encountered a sampling of the plume's destruction, but it was nothing like what we just swam through. This was death, and nothing within its grasp was spared.

I'm sorry for my part in this. I tried to stop Ken and I couldn't. Evan's voice rang in my head. *I won't let anything happen to you. I will protect you and the Selkies with my life.*

It's not your fault, I told him and meant it. I didn't blame him at all. As for his promise, well, it was one that he probably wouldn't be able to keep. I appreciated it all the same.

"How much further?" Kieran asked. We couldn't communicate with humans in our seal form, but we discovered we could still talk to the Blue Men, which was convenient.

"We're within an hour of our territory." Vesh was once again in the lead. He reclaimed his position once we were back in clean water. I hadn't realized how tired I was until Kieran spoke. We'd been swimming most of the day. My head was heavy, and we were slowing.

"Once we are within their range, we must be on constant alert," Vesh cautioned. "If you want to rest, I suggest we find shelter soon."

Sleep sounded lovely. Azuria's presence permeated my mind, a cool touch at the base of my skull. She showed me a cavern that was a few minutes to the northwest of us. It would be perfect for our needs.

"Come on, guys." I swam in the direction of the cave. "I know of a spot."

"How do you know where to go?" Vesh asked.

I turned back and raised my muzzle. "Azuria showed me."

His mouth snapped shut, and he looked around with a mixture of awe and fear. The woman had been dead for hundreds of years, yet she still wrought strong emotions in her sons. She must be extremely powerful, especially to have such a strong presence as a spirit. I wondered again why she chose me instead of one of her own children.

I am not able to communicate with them. Her voice was soft and kind. *Perhaps you are a gift from my Zane.*

His name brought such intense emotions forth that I gasped.

Are you okay? Kieran asked.

I'm fine, I said. I pointed at the cave. *There's our refuge.*

The cavern was large enough to allow us room to spread out, although Kieran curled his body around mine. Within minutes, I drifted to sleep.

"You are doing well, my daughter."

Azuria stood before me on a beach. A real beach covered in fine white sand, the kind found in the Caribbean, not the gray pebble beaches of Scotland.

"Where are we?" I asked. A white, strapless sundress covered me. The sun's heat baked my skin while a light floral breeze teased my hair.

"Anywhere you like." Azuria shrugged a slim shoulder. Like me, she wore a sundress, only hers was turquoise blue—the exact shade of the water and her stunning eyes. "I thought you might like a small respite before the challenge ahead of you." She beamed at me. Then, her smile fell as her eyes grew serious. "Believe me, it will be a challenge. Ken will not give up easily."

Her bottom lip trembled, and she wrapped her arms around her waist. I wanted to give her a hug, but I wasn't sure how she would receive it, so I stayed where I was. "I wish I had known what destruction my absence would cause. Perhaps..." She trailed off, turning to watch the waves roll into the shore and smooth the sand before retreating.

"Would you have chosen differently?" I asked.

She faced me and pursed her lips. "A wise question, but one that I cannot honestly answer. I'd like to think so, but..."

I remembered the scene she showed me and the emotions. Pain cut through me like a knife. It would be hard to choose life and endure through the torture of missing your only love, especially if you were immortal. I met her eyes, and she nodded.

"You understand," she said. "And you and your Selkie share something similar, something as powerful as what Zane and I had."

I sank into the sand, letting her words settle in. Wiggling my toes into the heated ground, I sifted the granules through my fingers. The stream of sand made me think of an hourglass, which reminded me that I was still sleeping. "How much time until we need to go?"

"We have a few minutes." She sat next to me, stretching her long legs. Her toes were painted bright pink. I admired the color, and a second later, mine matched hers.

"You could make a killing in the pedicure business," I said, which made her laugh.

Frozen drinks, topped with jaunty paper umbrellas, appeared in our hands. Mine tasted like fresh peaches, one of my favorite fruits. Azuria slipped large, dark sunglasses down her head and over her eyes. "Relax, Meara. I'll get you back in time."

Leaning back, I sipped my drink and watched seagulls soar in lazy circles around us. I'd face hell soon enough. I could take this moment in paradise if Azuria was offering it.

167

Chapter 30

Someone poked Evan in the cheek. The third time, Evan grabbed the offending appendage and peered up into Vesh's grinning face. "Do you get some kind of sick thrill out of waking me up?" Evan grumbled.

Vesh shrugged. "Not just you, Buttercup." He proceeded to poke Dex and Slate and got similar reactions.

"Are you going to poke them next?" Evan motioned to the sleeping pile of fur that was Kieran and Meara.

"Maybe her…" Vesh wiggled his eyebrows suggestively, and Evan glowered out of habit. "But him? No way. I don't have a death wish."

Interesting choice of words, Evan thought. None of them had a death wish, at least that Evan knew, but they were heading into danger willingly. What did that say?

Wake up, Meara. Evan repeated it until he felt her stirring in his mind.

Is it time to go? she asked sleepily.

He didn't answer her. *Wake Kieran,* he said before cutting the connection. Evan knew she found it intrusive when he was in her head, so he tried not to do it. Who knew what Kieran would do if he discovered Evan could read their minds. It was better to let Meara deal with the Selkie. He wouldn't bite her head off, but the rest of them? Evan wasn't taking chances.

"From here, we can reach Azuria in about fifteen minutes." Vesh peered out of the cave as if he was actually gauging the distance. "I'll take us through one of the back passages that is rarely used." His face and voice filled with excitement. This was probably the most adventure

168

he'd seen in a while. "If you see any Blue Men, assume they are an enemy and take them out."

"Take them out?" Meara sounded worried.

He means disarm them, not murder, Evan explained.

Relief was clear on her face. *Oh. Okay then.*

Evan smiled at her in reassurance, but frowned when she turned away. He hoped he was right. He assumed that was what Vesh meant. He wasn't a killer, was he?

They kept to the shadows as they swam. Breakfast came in the form of unsuspecting fish. It wasn't Evan's preferred way to eat—he liked his food prepared and cooked, but the options were limited in the middle of the ocean. They needed to maintain their energy.

When Evan got his first glimpse of the underwater castle, he stopped. Since learning of his heritage, he wondered what Azuria looked like. He hadn't imagined the elegant buttresses and slim towers. Even in the underwater gloom, it sparkled like an aquamarine gem. It was an absurd comparison, but all Evan could think of was Cinderella's castle at Walt Disney World. His parents took them there when he was twelve. What he remembered most was all the turrets. Cinderella's castle seemed to be more about beauty than form. This was built much the same—elegant, not intimidating. Instead of stone and plaster, it appeared to be made of opaque glass and polished gemstones.

"Would you like to pose for a picture in front of it?" Kieran asked dryly. His voice never failed to get on Evan's nerves, or maybe it was the words that his voice formed. Evan didn't really care for sarcasm.

"Your first time to the 'ole homestead," Kieran continued, either oblivious to Evan's irritation or not really caring. "How does it feel?"

"I don't know," Evan drawled. "How would you feel with my fist in your teeth?"

"Seriously, guys." Meara swam between them and shook her head. She sounded frustrated when she said, "Could you at least try to get along?"

Evan decided to ignore them both and swam over to Vesh. He was talking in hushed tones to Dex and Slate. Vesh nodded to Evan and continued, "...looks deserted, although we know that doesn't mean anything. They could be waiting for us. Remember, be alert and ready for anything at all times." He looked past Evan's shoulder and snorted, nodding in the direction of Meara and Kieran. Evan chanced a look over his shoulder and winced. The Selkies had changed forms and were currently wrapped around each other, oblivious to the attention from the rest of the group.

"Those two are such bait," Slate said with derision. "Someone could sneak up on them right now, and they wouldn't even know it."

"Hey—" Vesh's eyes grew thoughtful. "Maybe that's not such a bad idea."

"What do you mean?" Evan asked. He didn't like the direction of this conversation.

"We could spend days determining which dungeon they've got the other Selkies in, right?" Vesh asked. Evan shrugged because he didn't know, but the other two nodded. "If we let those two get captured…" Vesh nodded toward the Selkies, who still hadn't come up for air.

"You want to let the Blue Men capture them?" Evan couldn't keep the incredulity out of his voice. "Are you serious?"

"Hear me out," Vesh said. "If we let them capture Kieran and Meara, they'll lead us right to the other prisoners."

"Absolutely not!" Evan said.

At the same time, the other two said, "Great idea!"

"You're outnumbered." Vesh smirked. "Don't worry; we won't let anything happen to your ex-girlfriend."

"You better not," Evan said. He hated the plan. They weren't sharing it with Meara or Kieran either, because Vesh thought their reactions needed to be believable. Evan had no choice except to go along with the others. In all honesty, he couldn't think of a better plan.

Chapter 31

"What do you think they're doing over there?" Kieran asked, his lips tickling my ear. Not that I minded. While I loved Kieran in either form, there was something about his strong arms wrapped around me that made me want to purr.

"Plotting against us," I said, half joking, half serious.

"You're probably right," he agreed before lowering his head and capturing my mouth. I knew we should be trying to rescue my dad or at least looking for a place to hide, but when Kieran kissed me like that, I lost all rational thought. He murmured something I couldn't understand before trailing kisses down my neck. This time, I heard his words, "God, I've missed kissing you."

Laughing, I said, "I've been with you this whole time."

"Yeah, as a seal. That doesn't count. I like your curves better like this." To prove his point, he slid his hands down along my side until they rested on my hips.

"Shouldn't we see what the others are up to?" I asked, a part of me hoping he agreed and another selfish part hoping he wouldn't stop the magic he was working on my neck. In response, he nuzzled my ear and kissed it. I sighed and tilted my head to the side. My gaze traveled to where Evan and the others were standing. How sad that I wasn't even embarrassed if they were watching us. What did that say about me? Only, they weren't there anymore. Frowning, I asked Kieran, "Where did they go? Why didn't they come and get us?"

"Hmm?" Kieran lifted his head and lazily glanced in that direction. His eyes sharpened, and he scowled. "We've got company."

I was still wrapped in his embrace and wasn't sure if I should look or pretend not to notice. "Should we hide?"

Company only meant one thing—Blue Men—and not our friends. At least, I thought they were our friends. Again, I wondered, where did they go? Why did they leave us?

"Halt!" One of the Blue Men stepped out of the shadows, a nasty-looking weapon pointed right at us.

Kieran lowered his forehead to mine and kissed my nose. "Too late."

There were two of them. One had bright red hair that stood out against his blue skin. The other's hair was wiry and gray. Both were tall and muscular. For a moment, I wondered if we could take them out like Vesh had told us. Then I realized they probably had backup waiting where we couldn't see them. Two, we might be able to take, but a small army? No way.

They bound our hands behind our backs and led us into the castle through a nearby door that I hadn't seen. Who was I kidding? I was too focused on Kieran to notice anything else, and now I berated myself for it. My hormones would be my undoing.

Kieran was nonplussed. He hummed a chipper tune and winked at me when I scowled. At least one of us was confident. *You're awfully happy about being captured,* I grumbled.

His laughter filled my head. Irritated, I turned away to study our surroundings.

I figured out the plan, and it's brilliant. I caught the excitement in his words. *I'm surprised I didn't think of it myself.*

He had such a healthy ego, maybe too healthy. Still, I was curious. *Care to enlighten me?*

They let us be captured. I sucked in a sharp breath, shocked by his words, and regretted it a moment later when I was coughing. We could breathe underwater, but water down the wrong pipe was water down the wrong pipe.

When I stopped coughing, I asked. *Why would they do that?*

We're going to lead them right to your dad. He nodded to the guard in front of us, who was currently leading us down another dimly lit hall. In other circumstances, I would have stopped to admire the design. This castle was absolutely gorgeous. I'd have to compliment

172

Azuria later. I giggled. I'd compliment Azuria on Azuria. Bizarre.

Then Kieran's words sunk in. My dad! They were taking us to my dad. I knew I couldn't get too excited. Kieran might be wrong.

I'm never wrong, he interjected.

Hey! I scolded. *Get out of my head!*

Or, they might be taking us to a different part of the castle. Too late, my hopes were up. He was probably right. They were taking us to the other Selkies.

As my mind raced with excitement, Kieran cautioned me. *Do not let on that David is your father. Act nonchalant until the guards leave.*

Easy for you to say, I said.

He turned to stare at me. *I'm serious, Meara. When the guards leave, you can feel free to hug away. I don't know what they'd do if they knew you were his daughter, so I'd rather we not tell them.*

My initial resentment at his command faded when I realized he was right and as usual, protecting me. Protecting me from myself. How sad was that?

We swam down a winding corridor. There were stairs, which surprised me, because we didn't need to use them. Had the castle always been filled with water? It grew cooler as we descended. At the bottom was a thick, metal door. The first guard moved forward to unlock it and usher us into a small, stone chamber. The second guard closed and locked the door behind us. There would be no going back that way. How would Vesh and the others rescue us?

The sound of draining water filled the room, and I realized that the water level was lowering. Within minutes, the water was gone, leaving only a wet, stone floor. On the other side of the room was an identical metal door. The guard unlocked this one as well. He roughly untied our hands and then pushed us into the darkness. The door locked behind us.

"Enjoy your stay," one man's deep voice sneered through the door.

It took a minute for my eyes to adjust, and when they did, my heart fluttered. "Dad!"

His hair was longer, and he had a full beard. Other than that, he looked the same. I tugged on the beard before I threw my arms around him. "What's with the facial hair?"

I sank into his arms while he held me close. I felt him rest his cheek on top of my head. His laugh shook us both. "I'd shave if I could, but there is no way to conjure a blade or even magically do it. Something about this room prevents us from using our powers. We can't change shape, we can't visualize clothes or anything else, and we can't conjure anything."

"Wow. That kind of sucks." I stepped out of his arms and gave my aunt a small smile. She still managed to look beautiful, even if her hair was longer and a little tangled. She didn't smile back—I really didn't expect her to—but her face softened slightly. Whether she would admit it or not, I knew she was happy to see us.

"Why are you here?" Dad asked after shaking Kieran's hand.

"To rescue you, of course." I thought it was obvious.

Aunt Brigid glared at Kieran and then me. "How do you plan to do that now that you are imprisoned like the rest of us?"

Kieran stepped closer and put his arm around my shoulder. Dad gave me a look, but he didn't say anything. "Is it safe to talk in here?" Kieran asked.

"We're not sure." My dad settled into the corner, resting his forearms on his knees and leaning back against the wall. "And before you ask... no. We cannot *communicate* here either." He made quotation marks with his fingers when he said communicate.

No telepathy? I asked Kieran to test what Dad was saying. Kieran didn't respond. He couldn't hear me. Bummer.

"What?" he asked a moment later when he caught me staring at him.

"Nothing," I said. "I just tried testing that theory. Dad's right."

"Why would I lie about that?" Dad frowned up at me, and then tapped the floor next to him. "Might as well get comfortable. They bring food twice a day."

"What do you do to pass the time?" Kieran asked.

"Sit and wait," Dad responded. I hated hearing the dejection in his voice. Was he giving up?

"That's what you do." Aunt Brigid took a fighting stance and grinned maliciously at Kieran. "Not me. Would you like me to show you how I pass the time?"

"I wouldn't advise it." Drust stepped out of the shadows, exposing his black eye. "She's ruthless."

His words belayed his actions when he bowed politely to my aunt. She smiled back. It was genuine, too. Wow. Miracles did exist. Then her eyes scanned the shadows. "What? No takers?"

Kieran raised his hands. "I'm good, thanks."

Brigid laughed darkly, sitting next to my dad. "What news do you bring, niece?"

"We have so much to tell you," I said. Circumstances could not be worse. How could I update them on everything that happened and all that Ken planned without being able to say anything important out loud for fear that the Blue Men might hear? I would write in dirt or dust, but the stone floors were relatively clean.

"It'll have to wait. Sit, Meara," Dad said. "You look like you could use some rest." I must have glared at him, because he held up his hands. "No offense, but I'm sure you've been through a lot. Take a nap. What else are you going to do?"

He was right, of course. Sitting on the other side of my dad, Kieran stretched out his legs. I curled up next to him and rested my head on his shoulder. *I won't be able to fall asleep. I'm too worried.* Those were the last thoughts I had before I closed my eyes.

>>>><<<<

The rattling of metal woke me. The door was opening. Was it dinnertime already? I squinted in the darkness. The guard wasn't carrying a tray or anything. Then, my vision cleared. "Vesh!" I whispered with excitement. They found us!

"Hey, sweetheart. You didn't think we'd forget about you, did you?" Vesh looked behind him, and then back at me. "Wake the others. We need to go and fast, before any of the guards wake."

Kieran was already stirring. I shook my dad's shoulder until he started protesting. "Dad! We need to go. Our friends are here to rescue us."

"What? Who?" His voice was thick with sleep.

I stood and tugged his hand, trying to help him to stand. "Come on!"

Kieran woke our guards and Aunt Brigid. They all roused easier than my dad. Sheesh! For the leader of our clan, he sure slept soundly.

Vesh led us through the dry chamber, where we had to reverse the process and let it fill with water. All the Selkies changed to seals. We would be faster and harder to catch in this form. When the chamber was full, Vesh opened the door and we swam up the same corridor. It appeared to be the only way in and out of the cell. When we reached the top of the passage, Dex was waiting for us.

"Coast is still clear," he informed Vesh before taking his place at the back of our group. Vesh picked up speed and turned down another corridor. We turned three more times before I saw a door. Slate was waiting by it. That was a good sign.

A relieved expression crossed Slate's face when he spotted us. He quickly swung open the door, and we filed out. As we did, Vesh told us, "We're going to swim as fast as we can for as long as we can. We need to gain some distance and find shelter. Meara, if you can contact Azuria, do it. We need all the help we can get right now. They'll be on our trail soon."

"I'll try," I said. Azuria had always contacted me, not the other way around.

Blue Men are helping us? You know them? How did you meet them? You found Azuria? Who is it? My dad fired a series of questions at me. I wasn't even sure that he realized he was doing it. After all, he had been without telepathy for months.

Dad. I kept my voice calm and soothing. *We can trust these Blue Men. They are friends with Evan. I'll explain everything later, but right now, I need to try to contact the queen.*

My dad glanced back at me sharply. *Queen?*

The queen of the Blue Men, I said. *Azuria.*

His eyes widened in amazement, maybe even respect. I didn't have time to think about that right now. I tuned out the company around me and focused on contacting Azuria.

Azuria? Can you hear me? We could really use your help.

At first, there was nothing. Then, she was swimming beside me, her long hair trailing in the water like a veil. No one else seemed to notice or react, so I assumed I was the only one who could see her.

You're right. The others can't see me. She winked at me and beamed with something like parental pride. It was similar to the look my mom used to give me when I did something that pleased her. *You did it. You rescued my son and your Selkies. I couldn't be more pleased.*

Thank you, I said. *Can you help us get to safety?*

Of course. She winked at me, then rolled onto her back and stretched out her arms. Her legs were still propelling her forward, so she remained at my side, but she held her arms straight and spread her fingers. Light pulsed from her hands in waves and shot behind our group, starting as small circles and growing larger the further away they moved. *That will confuse my other sons. The ones who want to capture you.*

Wow. I couldn't think of anything else to say, but her power was impressive.

When I am close to my home, I can harness more energy. Her laughter floated, ringing like soft bells. By the confused expressions on my companions' faces, I knew they heard it, too. She only laughed harder.

Oh, I haven't enjoyed myself this much in a while. I do like you, Meara Quinn. Her expression softened when she looked past me at the Blue Men. *My dear sons. Keep them safe. They are my pride.* She rested her hand on my shoulder; it was soft and cool. *I know you will do your best, for both my sons and your people. I can't hold this form much longer, but I'll lead you to where you can rest. You'll be safe for the night, I promise.*

Thank you for everything, I told her.

You're welcome.

"Ew! What's that smell?" I was the first one in the cave, and the rank, oily water hit me in the face.

There are a few eels that live here, Azuria spoke. Her voice was faint in my head, and her image flickered. I wondered how much longer she could hold it. *They are harmless, although their odor takes some getting used to.*

You're not kidding. Who knew that eels were the skunks of the ocean? How were we going to be able to sleep in this polluted water?

Their scent disguises yours, Azuria said and then chuckled. *My sons will not find you here. Truly, you are making a bigger deal out of the smell than it is, Meara.* Her form wavered once and then disappeared, but I heard her words. *Stay in the cave. I'll contact you again soon.*

I wrinkled my nose, looking around for the buggers. I didn't see anything. The cave appeared to be empty, although it was dotted with smaller holes like Swiss cheese. The eels probably lived in those. I heard gagging behind me, which made me smile. The guys had arrived.

"We can't stay here," Vesh complained. "It reeks."

"Azuria says it's safe," I said. "And, the eel smell camouflages our scent."

"Hopefully not permanently," Kieran muttered under his breath.

It took about a half hour, but Azuria was right. We grew accustomed to the musky odor. Dad and Brigid went to catch dinner. I warned them not to go far—that Azuria said we should stay in the cave. Dad seemed freaked out that the Queen of the Blue Men was talking to me, and neither he nor the others could see her. Still, he promised that they would stay close and on alert.

"We need to stretch after so many weeks in captivity," he said almost apologetically, but I understood. I couldn't imagine living in a cell for almost two months.

While they were gone, the rest of us staked out our spots in the cave. They came back within the hour with a variety of fish. We ate our fill, the group unusually quiet. The eels made a brief appearance, gathering up the bones and scraps. They chittered with Slate and Dex, who had bemused expressions on their faces. Bobbing their snakelike heads at the rest of us, the eels swam back into their holes.

"You can talk to them?" I asked.

"Sure." Dex shrugged. "They didn't have much to say. They thanked us for the delicious snacks."

"Can you talk to all sea creatures?"

"Most of them," Dex said.

"Not that they usually have anything interesting to say." This came from Vesh. "Fish are pretty stupid."

"Well, I'm glad the eels don't mind dining on our leftovers," I said. The remainders would've only added to the stinky atmosphere if they hadn't cleared them away. Then again, who knew what else they had tucked in those cavern walls? Best not to think about it.

With dinner over, fatigue settled it. The escape was taxing on us all. Kieran put his arm around me, and we settled in our spot. The others got comfortable, too.

"Where will we go now?" Vesh asked. He had scooted back to the wall and was resting his chin on his bent legs. He looked like a scared teenager. Where was the confident leader that rescued us from the dungeon?

The water shimmered around Dad as he changed forms. "You are welcome at Ronac," he said, much to the shock of all four Blue Men. "You kept my daughter safe and freed us. I return favors." His lips lifted in a small smile. "More than that, I now consider you friends." He crossed the cave and offered his hand, first to Vesh, then to Dex and Slate, for a firm handshake. "Friends are always welcome."

When he reached Evan, he placed a hand on his shoulder. "It's good to see you again, Evan, although I must say your appearance caught me off guard."

Evan dipped his head and turned a deep shade of indigo. He blushed more than me lately. Finally, he looked up at my dad with a smirk. "It's a long story."

"I'm sure it is." My dad patted Evan's shoulder in a friendly way. "And seeing as we have no other entertainment for the evening, I'd love to hear it, if you're willing to share."

Chapter 32

The group shifted and sought to find comfortable positions against the cave wall. Without consciously doing it, they made a semicircle around Evan. He felt like squirming under their curious stares. Not even Vesh knew the whole story about Ken. The only one Evan told was Deanna, and of course, she was not here. He hoped she was staying under Ken's radar. Tomorrow morning, Ken would realize they were gone. That was when things would really get interesting.

"So...?" Vesh prompted, motioning for Evan to begin. He had the attention of everyone in the cave, even Brigid, who he barely knew. He sighed once, crossed his legs, and started talking.

He told them about Ted Nolan, the internship with Ken, and the nightmares and headaches he experienced last summer. While he tried not to focus on any one person for too long, his eyes kept returning to Meara. The more he talked, the more dismayed she looked. Evan felt bad about that, too. What happened to him was not her fault, and he didn't blame her. She clearly blamed herself though.

When Evan got to the part with Dr. Tenuis and the clinic, Vesh's eyes widened. "Martin injected you with our essence?" Vesh gave a low whistle. "That's really dangerous, man. You could've died. That was the point where all the others did. I thought after the last one, Ken was going to stop using it."

"Apparently not." Evan snorted with derision. "Ken must've decided to take a chance on me."

"They mutated others like this?" Kieran gestured at Evan, and then snapped his hand back. "No offense."

"Yes." Vesh stepped in to explain, which was good, because Evan knew very little about the earlier experiments. "The previous males, some human, some not, died during transition. Evan was the first to succeed."

"Why?" Meara asked. It was a good question. Evan wondered the same thing. What made him different?

"Evan was the first one that Ken sired." Dex spoke quietly from the far side of the cave, but everyone turned to look at him.

"Ken and your mom—?" Kieran stopped talking when Evan glared at him.

"She didn't know." Evan explained that Ken seduced his mother by pretending to be her husband, Darren. His stomach still churned in revulsion whenever he thought about it.

"So Katie—?" Meara let the question hang.

"Is my half sister. Darren is her real father," Evan said. It felt strange to speak those words. If—no, when—he got home, would he feel like he belonged or like an imposter?

"Why can't you change forms?" Kieran asked, gesturing to the other three men. "They can, right?"

Evan was glad to change the subject. "Ken did something to lock me in this form." He hung his head and rubbed the back of his neck. The attention was starting to get uncomfortable. "I wasn't very good at changing forms before it happened. I know very little about what I'm capable of." He nodded at Vesh. "Short of what Vesh has shown me."

"You can train at Ronac," David said. "We'll give you space and privacy. I have a feeling we all need to prepare for what's coming."

Evan agreed and hoped they would have time to train. "My girlfriend, Deanna, stayed behind. She bought us some time by telling Ken that I was sick. Tomorrow morning, Ken will realize I'm gone. He won't accept that I'm sick two days in a row." Evan's chest panged from fear of Ken, who could rot in hell. Deanna better be safe. If Ken hurt her, he would pay.

"Let's rest," David said, standing and taking charge of the small group. "Tomorrow, we swim to the safety of Ronac."

"Is that the name of your home?" Vesh asked.

David nodded. The name was new to Evan, too. Meara hadn't

mentioned it. It was one of many things they failed to discuss last summer. Maybe if they had been more open with one another, they wouldn't be in this mess. Then again, maybe they would. How would he have known to stop Ken?

The group settled around the cave, some of the Selkies piling up to keep warm. Kieran and Meara were curled in the back corner. When Evan looked over at them, Meara opened her eyes and lifted her head. *I'm sorry, Evan.* Her voice was thick with regret. *I didn't know.*

He knew she was blaming herself again for his transformation. *How could you have known?* Evan kept his tone neutral. He didn't want her to cry, and she sounded like she was on the verge of tears. *What happened to me is not your fault. What happened to us…*

He paused at her soft intake of breath. She honestly thought that he blamed her for ruining their relationship? How? He was the one who pushed her away.

Is not your fault, he said firmly. *It's mine.*

He actually felt her presence relax in his mind.

I don't want you to hate me. Her words were whisper soft.

His heart broke a little. *I could never hate you.*

Kieran stirred and nuzzled into her side. In that moment, Evan was connected enough to Meara to feel her strong surge of emotion at the Selkie's touch. She loved him. Evan tried not to let the bitterness of jealousy coat his tongue.

Get some sleep, Meara. Tomorrow is going to be another long day.

They woke early and headed out, once again catching breakfast on the way. Time was closing in. It wouldn't be much longer until Ken discovered Evan was missing. He was tense and edgy while he waited to hear from Deanna. A man of faith, he prayed for her safety. Deanna was confident that Ken wouldn't know she was involved. Evan hoped she was right.

Meara swam on his right and slightly ahead. He wondered if Azuria reached out to her again. It was odd to think that Azuria was, in a sense, his grandmother. It was stranger yet that she was dead, but could appear to Meara and still had powers.

The rest of the group swam silently, but fast. David was leading the way to their island. He warned the Blue Men that as they neared it, they needed to watch the Selkies closely or they would lose their way.

"The enchantments on the island are strong," David said. "Stay alert."

The entire trip was fascinating to Evan. He saw more of the ocean than he had seen before. Creatures he had only studied in textbooks were within a hand's reach. He wished he had time to study them in their natural environment. Maybe when things settled down. Peace had to return at some point, right? Wasn't that the nature of things?

Evan kept Meara in his sight as he observed the world around him. He took David's warning seriously. It was a good thing, too, because he noticed immediately when she and the other Selkies disappeared.

Meara?

What? She sounded curious, but not alarmed.

Where are you? Evan squinted and studied the water around him. It had grown dark and murky over the last mile or so. Fish and other sea life were visible around him. Where was she?

I'm right in front of you, Evan.

Where? He saw nothing but ocean floor, although he heard her frustrated sigh, and felt her poke him in the ribs with her muzzle.

Can you see me now?

No. Bewildered, he reached out and touched her soft fur. Once he made contact, she came back into view. Vesh pulled up short behind him and asked Meara. "Where'd the others go?"

"They're right next to me," she said. This time she spoke out loud to include the others. "You really can't see them?"

"No." Vesh looked frightened and impressed at the same time. "That is some strong magic protecting your island."

"We're not even that close yet," Meara said.

They couldn't see David, but he spoke, addressing the Selkies. "Move by one of the Blue Men. Once they touch your fur, they will be able to see you like Evan with Meara. Stay in contact until we get to the island. We don't want to lose anyone."

A moment later, Evan could see all the Selkies again. Drust floated next to Vesh, Judoc by Slate, and Brigid by Dex. Brigid was not happy about the situation if her rigid posture was any indication. Poor Dex looked mortified. His skin was nearly purple with embarrassment.

"Let's move," David ordered, and everyone followed.

Holding onto Meara, the haze lifted from Evan's vision. The peaks and valleys of the ocean floor were once more in sharp focus. In some ways, it was disappointing. The landscape stretched for miles with no indication of an upward slope toward land. How much further did they have to go?

I did it!

Evan heard Deanna's triumphant cry as if she was swimming next to him. The necklaces were amazing. He wondered if Meara would let him keep them.

Evan? Are you there?

Yes. Sorry. He made himself focus on Deanna. *What did you do?*

I managed to keep Ken at bay another day. I used an evasion spell on your room. Every time he tries to approach your door, he loses focus and walks away. Her light laughter floated through his head and made him smile. *It's pretty hilarious to watch.*

That's brilliant! Evan was impressed. He didn't know that Deanna could do magic like charms. *You're keeping yourself safe?*

Of course. Her response was quick and confident. *How is your mission going?*

We rescued the Selkies. It felt strange to say it. The whole encounter had been relatively easy. Something told Evan that was the last time things would go that smoothly. *We're on our way to their home, and we'll hide out there until we form a plan.*

There was a pause from Deanna's end. For a moment, Evan thought he had lost her, but then she spoke, her voice incredulous. *They're taking you to their island? That's unheard of. No one has been there. Have you?*

No, I've never been. David offered to let us stay.

Wow. In the silence that followed, Evan waited, knowing she needed time to process everything. *How long will you be staying?*

I don't know. We can't come back until this is settled. What do you think Ken would do to us?

Don't come back, she said quickly. *But keep in touch. I think my charm will wear off by tomorrow afternoon. I can't risk casting another, but I'll tell you what's going on.*

Same here. Evan let the affection he felt for her fill his voice. *I wish you were here with me.*

I know. Me, too. Her voice was barely a whisper.

I love you, Deanna. He wished he had said it to her in person, but he wanted to say it. He didn't know what tomorrow would bring, and he didn't want to be too late.

He caught her surprise, a breathy intake of air. Then, he heard the reply he was hoping for. *I love you, too, Evan.*

Her presence vanished like the sun disappearing behind a cloud. For a moment, Evan was alone. Then Meara's voice filled the void. *Was that the first time you told her you loved her?*

At first, he was angry with her for eavesdropping, but then he relaxed. Hadn't he done the same thing to her and Kieran? Besides, she wasn't judging or teasing, she was simply asking. He nodded, but he didn't speak.

I didn't mean to listen, she apologized, *but when we're connected physically, and you're not shielding…* Evan felt the shiver travel through her body. *It's overwhelming. I can't block you out.*

Her words made Evan think that he should apologize. He didn't. Instead, he considered their connection. For some reason, it was stronger than any other was. He knew she was right. When he was close to her, he really had to try and block her out of his mind. If he didn't think about it, she was just there, especially when they were physically connected. Their thoughts seemed to mingle freely. Usually, it was fine, but when he was talking to Deanna…

I get it, she said, and he knew she heard his internal struggle. *It's the same for me. Again, I'm sorry.*

Don't worry about it. His imagination might be playing tricks on him, but it seemed that the ocean floor rose slightly. *How much further?*

Her mood shifted to something lighter. Without words, he knew she was happy for the subject change. *You see the ground's starting to slope up. It won't be much longer now.* She picked up her pace, and the rest of the pairs did as well.

Excited to get home? he asked, and then wondered, did she consider it home?

I am. You're going to love it. Ronac is beautiful.

They fell into silence, which was fine with Evan. He busied himself studying the surroundings. The gentle incline grew steeper, and soon the rocky shore was within sight. As the group came out of the water, the Selkies changed into their human forms, as did the other Blue Men. They turned and studied Evan like a puzzle waiting to be solved.

"What?" he asked defensively. He took a step back and raised his hands. "I'm stuck in this form, remember?"

"If you are, you are," David said, gripping his chin between his thumb and forefinger as he considered Evan. "I'd like to try breaking Ken's hold, though. Anyone else interested?"

"I'll help." Meara stepped forward and gave Evan a reassuring smile. Kieran moved to her side and agreed to help, albeit less enthusiastically. One by one, the others all agreed.

"You know how to do this?" Meara asked her dad.

"No," he admitted with a sheepish expression. "I've never tried anything like this before. He will cause widespread panic if we can't help him change. We need for him to look human again before we introduce him to the clan."

Human. The words were ambrosia to Evan's ears. With everything in his being, he hoped they would succeed.

Chapter 33

M *eara*. Azuria's voice floated through my head, along with the tinkling bells of her laughter. I was so happy to hear from her, I didn't even take offense that she was laughing at us. When she hadn't appeared all day, I worried that something happened. *Would you like some help, daughter? All you have to do is ask.*

I didn't know you were here, I said. *Have you been with us the whole time?*

No, I needed most of the day to restore my energy before I could contact you again. Her voice was strong, unlike last night.

I'm surprised you can get past the island wards, I said. *The Blue Men were blocked until they touched us.*

My connection to you allows me to contact you here. But that is neither here nor there, she said. *Would you like my help changing Evan?*

You can make him human? I spent enough time in his mind these last few days to know that was what he wanted. He didn't want to be one of the Blue Men. He wanted to go home to his family. I couldn't say that I blamed him. I was lucky to find my family here. In his shoes, I might feel the same as him.

I cannot make him human. Sadness coated her words. *That is beyond my abilities. However, I can help his body to change forms, despite whatever curse Ken wrought on him. Please tell your father and friends to back up. I'll need some room.*

"Make some room," I said to the group crowded around Evan. "Azuria is going to change him back to his human form."

"She's here?" Vesh asked, glancing around nervously.

She materialized next to him, dressed in a long, silvery gown with flowing sleeves. Her hair was piled on top of her head in a stylish mass of knots. *My poor sons.* She leaned in and kissed his cheek. Vesh did not react to her touch. *Tell them I love them and miss them. Could you please, Meara? Would you do that for me?* Her eyes shimmered with unshed tears when she moved her gaze from her sons to me.

"She's right next to you, Vesh." I pointed to his right side. "She asked me to tell you that she loves you, and she misses you."

Azuria wiped her eyes and nodded as I said those words. *Thank you.*

Of course, I said. *It's the least I can do.*

The shock on the Blue Men's faces melted to wonder as they considered their mother's words. The message seemed to bring them some comfort, and it certainly brought peace to Azuria. She moved from Vesh's side to stand in front of Evan. Placing her hands on his shoulders, she stood on tiptoe to kiss first his left cheek, then his right. Her voice whispered the command, *Change, my son.*

The air rippled, and Evan's image wavered like a fun house mirror. The transition happened so fast that my eyes barely registered it. Within seconds, the Evan I knew was standing in front of us. Without thinking, I ran over and threw my arms around his neck. "You're back."

He caught my waist and pulled me close. "You don't know how good it is to feel human again." His words were muffled in my hair, but I heard the relief in his voice.

Thank you, Azuria. She had already disappeared, but I knew she heard me.

Dad shook Evan's hand firmly. "It's nice to see you this way again, Evan." He turned to the others. "Let's retire to the fortress. A warm meal and soft bed will do us all some good, I think."

Evan walked on one side of me, and Kieran on the other. The tension was thick, but I couldn't think of anything to say to diffuse it. Hopefully, they would learn to get along, at least for the time it took us to defeat Ken. I knew that ultimately, that was what we were going to have to do. Sure, we rescued my dad, aunt, and the others, and yes, Azuria broke Ken's hold over Evan, but Ken wasn't going to stop. He wouldn't rest until he killed us all, unless we killed him first.

Those are some pretty dark thoughts. Kieran's words came through just as his arm went around my shoulders, pulling me close. *Don't worry about it tonight, Meara. Tonight, we should be celebrating our successes. Tomorrow, we can worry.*

I know. I leaned into his side, taking comfort in his warmth. *It's hard not to worry, though. Are we ready, Kieran?*

He stared ahead for a moment, frowning as he considered my question. *I don't think we have a choice. We'll fight, and hopefully, we'll win.*

And if we don't?

Don't think like that, he scolded. *We will.*

I wished I had his conviction. I wanted to be sure of our success. War was coming, whether we were ready for it or not.

Chapter 34

The island of Ronac was breathtaking. Evan drank in the emerald-green landscape, broken here and there by jutting rocks. As they reached the top of the hill, the fortress came into view. It was old, but that didn't mar its splendor. He could see why Meara would like living here. A few days on this island and he probably wouldn't want to leave. For the moment, he was enjoying the solid earth beneath his feet and the air in his lungs a little too much. Living underwater was not for him. The only thing that made it tolerable was Deanna.

Outside the main entrance, a small group of Selkies waited to greet them. Evan recognized Ula among them. The other two were men he did not know. One looked to be in his mid-twenties and the other in his seventies.

"You did it, girl!" bellowed the older of the two, and Meara took off in a run, launching herself into his open arms. The man wrapped her in a bear hug, practically covering her in his bulk.

"Uncle Angus." She pulled back and grinned up at him. "I told you I would!"

"That you did." He chuckled. "That you did."

Who are they? Evan asked Meara.

My great uncle Angus, she answered. *My uncle Padraic, and you know Ula.*

Ula nudged Angus out of the way and hugged Meara tightly. Then Padraic had a turn. The three moved on to David and Brigid. When the familial greetings were done, they turned to the rest of the party.

"Are you going to introduce us?" Ula asked. Evan noticed that she paid particular attention to Vesh. When he caught her looking, she blushed and glanced down.

"Of course." David took charge, although Meara was clearly about to speak. She closed her mouth, and a slight frown crossed her face. "These men will be our guests. They are Blue Men of the Minch—"

Angus' cry of protest interrupted David. Meara placed a hand on his arm, and surprisingly, the man calmed almost instantly. "It's okay, Uncle Angus," she said. "They are on our side."

David cleared his throat and continued. "Vesh, Slate, Dex, and Evan were instrumental to our rescue. They have offered to train with us and fight by our side."

"We do not like Ken's vendetta any more than you do," Vesh added. "It's time to end his reign of tyranny."

"He killed my girlfriend's mother," Evan added, noticing, but ignoring, when Ula gave Meara a surprised look. "And has the Sirens under his control. He must be stopped."

One of David's guards stepped forward. "Sir, with your permission, we would like to report back to the others on what we have learned."

David nodded to his men. "Go, but be sure to rest and replenish. We will need you at full strength in the days to come." With a curt bow, the men took their leave. David watched them go, and then turned to his brother. "Do you have enough food for a few extra mouths?"

"Always," Padraic answered with a smile. He seemed easygoing and good-natured. In many ways, he was the polar opposite of David. He even had light hair where David's was dark. As Evan glanced between the two brothers and their sisters, he didn't see much of a family resemblance. Perhaps that was the way with Selkies.

"We'll dine in my private hall this evening," David said. "And introduce our guests to the rest in the morning."

"I'll send dinner up." Padraic inclined his head slightly to his brother, winked at Meara, and then went back inside, presumably to prepare their meal. Evan's stomach responded with a growl. Warm food sounded lovely.

"Please follow me." David led them inside. The hall was cool and dimly lit by a few sconces on the stone wall. They walked to a staircase and climbed three flights. David took them to a large room full of comfortable-looking chairs. There was plenty of seating for all. The room was toasty, thanks to a crackling fire in the large hearth.

Between the cozy furniture and the warm room, Evan struggled to keep his eyes open. It looked like the others were having the same problem. It wasn't long before he lost the fight, his head resting against the soft back of the chair.

Evan woke to the soft jingle of bells. Several wide-eyed servants stood behind a large banquet table on the far side of the room. The places were already set, the table laden with serving dishes of all sizes. How long had he been sleeping? He must've been exhausted because he didn't wake at the sound of people coming and going from the room. By the way the rest of the group rubbed their eyes and stretched, he knew he wasn't the only one to take advantage of a few moments of rest.

As the smell of roasted meat and fresh herbs filled the room, his attention turned completely to the meal. It was almost comical how quickly they made their way to the table and sought seats. Evan sat next to Vesh, giving Meara some distance. By the daggers Kieran was shooting him, he knew the Selkie was not appreciating Evan's relationship with Meara. Evan didn't want to cause her problems, so he gave them space.

The food was delicious. Meara's uncle was a culinary genius. Then again, Evan hadn't eaten a home-cooked meal for several months. Raw fish was okay, but there was nothing like rich sauces and savory spices to add a little zing to the experience.

A comfortable silence accompanied their dinner as they all focused on sating their hunger. The dishes were emptied in record time. Evan pushed back from the table with a satisfied sigh, patting his now-full belly. "That was delicious."

"Thank you," Padraic said from the doorway. He crossed the room and stood by the table, surveying the empty plates and dishes with amusement. "I trust you had enough to eat?"

"It was perfect," Vesh said. "Your hospitality is much appreciated."

The Selkie chef inclined his head in a slight bow. "I am at your service. You have brought my family back to me and for that, I am grateful."

David stood. "It is late. Meara and Ula, please show our guests to their rooms. They will be in the same hall as Kieran."

"But—"

"We will meet in the morning," he continued, not letting Meara finish her sentence. Her face flushed in anger, but she remained quiet. "Tonight, I wish to speak to the Elders."

With a stiff back, Meara stood and walked to the door. Evan didn't miss Ula's sympathetic glance in Meara's direction before she turned her attention back to the Blue Men. "Come." Ula stood and waited for them to follow. "We'll get you settled for the evening."

Meara was unusually quiet as they descended the staircase and made their way to the guest rooms.

Are you okay? Evan asked.

I hate when he does that. Undermines me like a child.

To him, you are a child. His child. Evan tried to keep his voice neutral, reasonable. It wasn't the first time he had this conversation with Meara.

I don't care. Angus more or less let me run things while my dad was gone. He believes in me. Why can't my father?

Talk to him, Meara, Evan encouraged. *Show him what you are capable of.*

I've tried, she growled in his head.

Try again. This time, he made his voice firm. He wouldn't let her wallow in self-pity. She was stronger than that.

She stopped and opened a door. "Your room," she announced, not quite meeting his eyes. With a sigh, he walked past her into the small, but welcoming space.

Okay. I will try. Her words floated softly to him, and although his back was to her, he smiled. She was stubborn and proud, but she could be reasoned with. She was her father's daughter. Clearly, they shared several personality traits.

He heard the door click closed and footsteps retreat down the hall. The meal had energized him, and he found he wasn't all that tired. Exploring the fortress was probably not an option. If the wrong person caught him, it wouldn't be good for him or the others. Nothing stopped him from exploring his room, however. Besides the bed and the dresser, there was a tall bookcase with delicate seashells, a jar of colorful sea glass, and several classic novels. The books appeared to be first editions. Who knew that Selkies had an interest in human stories? A narrow window let in silvery moonlight and, looking down, Evan saw a stretch of rocky cliff that met the water a distance below. The view was beautiful.

A door to his left led to a small bathroom with a claw-foot tub. No shower, but indoor plumbing. He didn't expect modern conveniences in a building this old on an island in the middle of nowhere. Perhaps Selkie magic was more powerful than Ken gave them credit for, only it was channeled into something more useful than bloodlust and revenge. They would see tomorrow what they had to work with when they met the rest of the inhabitants.

Evan made his way over to the bed and stretched out, placing his hands behind his head and staring at the ceiling. He felt human again, and yet, not. He wondered if he could change forms on his own, but he worried about being stuck in his blue form again. He told Meara to be brave; he should heed his own advice. With a sigh, he lifted one arm above him, concentrating on his fingers. A slight tingle, and his fingers reformed to elongated blue claws. With a little more concentration, he changed them back. He could do it. He was in control again.

Relief relaxed him more than anything else had that evening. Closing his eyes, he fell into a deep sleep.

Chapter 35

"Tell me about Vesh," Ula demanded the second my bedroom door was closed. Her eagerness made me laugh. "What? He's gorgeous. You can't tell me you didn't notice."

"Okay, okay. So I noticed." I grinned at her and sat on my bed, tucking my feet beneath me. "He's a nice guy. Really. You should get to know him."

"He's single?" Between the hopefulness in her voice and the eager puppy expression on her face, when she developed a crush, she crushed hard and fast.

"As far as I know." I shrugged. "He hasn't mentioned anyone, but then again, we haven't really discussed our personal lives. You know, in the midst of rescuing everyone and fleeing Ken's wrath."

She plopped next to me and bumped my shoulder. "You could be nicer, you know. Considering I haven't seen you in weeks."

Wrapping my arm around her narrow shoulders, I gave her a squeeze. "I missed you too. Tell me what's happened since we've been gone?"

"I took over training." She raised a ginger eyebrow, daring me to challenge her.

"What about Uncle Angus?" I asked.

"He thought I should lead, and I did a good job too." She was defensive, like I would be mad. *No way!* I was proud.

"Excellent, Ula! I'm so proud of you."

"Yes, well." Her face flushed from my simple compliment. "They are all doing well. Almost everyone can shield with their energy now, and a few can throw it in combat. Arren, well, Arren is rather amazing and probably the strongest fighter and magic wielder in the group."

"Fantastic!" I was glad to hear of Arren's skills. In fact, I hoped more of the Selkies would reach his level. We could use all the trained warriors we could get. Defeating Ken and his army wasn't going to be easy. Not only did we have to contend with their strength and fighting skills, but we also had to neutralize the magic he was using to feed the mantle plume. Evan warned us that it was heading toward our island. I wondered how many more days, or hours, until it reached us. Would we be able to stop the destruction once it started? Kieran and I had seen the devastation it caused—the stench of death and decay still lingered in the dark corners of my mind. I feared it, but more, I feared for my people. What would happen to us if we lost Ronac in a fiery blaze of lava?

"Meara? You still with me?" Ula patted my arm and searched my face with concern.

"Sorry, I guess I spaced out." I gave her an apologetic smile. "What were you saying?"

"Nothing too important. More updates on our progress. You'll see for yourself tomorrow." She didn't seem offended that I zoned out. Standing to stretch, she smiled and then leaned in to give me a quick hug. "I better let you get some sleep. Tomorrow's going to be a long day."

"Thanks, Ula." I walked her to the door. "I'll see you at breakfast?"

"Wouldn't miss it. I'm curious how the rest of the clan will take to our new friends."

"Me, too." I closed the door and laid back on my bed, thinking about tomorrow. The introduction had to go well. We needed to work together to have any chance at winning. Given that we had anything from hours to a few days to determine our strategy, any time spent fighting amongst ourselves would hurt us.

I wasn't sure how long I lay in bed, staring up in the darkness and considering our options. For a while, I planned what I wanted to say to my dad. I changed my speech about fifty times. The funny thing about planning a conversation in your mind was that his responses could throw everything I imagined out the window and take the discussion into a completely uncharted direction. It didn't matter; he needed to hear me out. I was tired of being overlooked, and it was time he knew it.

Someone knocked lightly at the door. At this hour, I knew it could only be one person.

"Come in," I called.

Kieran entered and closed the door quietly behind him. He sat on the edge of my bed. His hair was damp from his shower, the clean smell of spring rain stronger than usual. I was glad he came and scooted over so he could stretch out next to me.

"Did I wake you?" he asked.

"No." His voice still gave me goose bumps. It was deep and husky in all the right ways. I inched closer to his warmth, and he placed his arm around me, pulling me against him. "How was the meeting?"

"You didn't miss much. David rehashed his imprisonment and our rescue. Angus shared what was going on here. You would've been proud of your uncle. When your name came up, he put your father in his place and told him how you have been instrumental to the training here." Kieran's lips grazed my forehead. "David's agreed to hear you out tomorrow."

"He did?"

"Yes, right after breakfast, we'll all go to the training session." Kieran chuckled. "I can't wait. You're going to give your father the surprise of his life."

"I hope so."

"I know so."

Kieran's faith in me warmed me to the core. I knew that Uncle Angus and Kieran had my back no matter what. Ula and Padraic too. Now I just had to convince my father and get him to stop treating me like a child.

"You're no child." Kieran slid his hand up my side, and then brought it back down slowly. "Do you want me to leave so you can get some sleep?"

"No." I placed my lips on his neck, kissing a sensitive spot. His pulse jumped in response. "I want you to stay."

"Always," he whispered, lowering his head and capturing my mouth in a kiss. He managed to make me forget all my worries and live in the moment. I wanted, no needed, this moment with him.

"I love you, Meara."

"I love you too."

The sharp knock was followed by my father asking, "Are you awake?"

"I am now," I called back, a little grumpily. Then my eyes flew open and, with relief, I noted Kieran was gone. After Dad caught us in bed the last time, even with nothing happening, I didn't want to experience that embarrassment again. The other side of the bed was still warm, reminding me that he woke me earlier, kissed my cheek, and said he would see me later.

"We're meeting for breakfast shortly. Hurry along." His voice was slightly impatient, but that didn't surprise me. Dad was an early riser, and he didn't understand those of us that liked to sleep in or at least lounge in bed for a little while before going to work.

There really wasn't time for lounging, though. Soon enough, Ken would realize that Evan was gone, if he didn't know already. We were fooling ourselves if we thought we had time. We didn't.

Dad wanted me to hurry, but I couldn't miss my shower. I'd gone far too long without one while we were on our rescue mission. I managed to be quick about it and, after, I pulled my hair into a ponytail, skipped the makeup, and threw on jeans and a T-shirt. Slipping my sandals on at the door, I was ready within fifteen minutes.

On my way to the cavern, I stopped and knocked on Ula's door. I was about to leave, thinking she had already gone down, when the door cracked open. Her squinting face poked out. "Yeah?"

"Didn't my dad stop by and wake you? We're all supposed to meet downstairs."

"What?" Her eyes widened almost comically. "When?"

"Now, I think."

"Are you kidding me?" she squealed while at the same time grabbing my arm and pulling me into her room. "Will that hot guy be there... um, Vesh?"

I shrugged. "I think so. After all, Dad plans to introduce them to the clan this morning, remember?"

"Help me get ready," she begged. "I have no idea what to wear."

"Wear something green," I suggested. "It brings out your eyes."

She changed into a bright green knit top and cream-colored crop pants. Unlike me, she did take time to apply her makeup and fix her hair. I tapped my foot impatiently and was about to tell her that I'd meet her down there, when she said she was ready. She picked her backpack off the bed and put it on. "If we're training, I might need this."

I nodded in agreement, once again grateful that I chose an anklet as the form for my Selkie skin when I wasn't using it. I wouldn't want to haul a backpack around at all times. It didn't seem to bother Ula. After all these years, I guess she was used to it.

The hall was full by the time we arrived. I was surprised to see that the family table was empty. Instead, everyone was seated at the much-longer table on the main floor. Kieran was there too, and he never ate with my family. He smiled when he saw me and motioned to the spot beside him. The only other opening was between Vesh and Aunt Brigid. Somehow, I didn't think Ula would mind.

Dad glanced at us curiously, but he didn't say anything. I got the impression that he hadn't planned on Ula being here. Certainly, Paddy was absent, most likely in the kitchen overseeing the preparation of the meal.

My father stood and tapped his spoon against his goblet. The room quieted. "Thank you all for joining us this morning to celebrate our safe return." Dad paused while the clan erupted in cheers. When they quieted, he continued, "We have several guests staying with us who I would like to introduce. They will be training with you and helping us prepare for battle."

Several Selkies shifted uncomfortably in their chairs, others sat up straighter, welcoming the challenge. Dad motioned for the Blue Men to stand. "Allow me to introduce Vesh, Dex, Slate, and Evan from the Blue Men of the Minch."

People broke out in protests and questions. Faces filled with shock, fear, and disbelief. Who could blame them? We had invited our enemy into our home as guests. They didn't know that we could trust these men. Dad's face hardened, and he banged his fists on the table.

"Enough!" he shouted. "These men were instrumental in our

rescue. I trust them and you will, too. We must work together or we are all doomed."

With eyes full of challenge, he surveyed the room for problems. Giving the clan a curt nod, he sat and resumed his meal. The Blue Men followed suit. Soon, the room filled with the sound of conversations and clattering dinnerware. As pep talks went, Dad's speech wasn't much of one, but I guessed it was effective enough. The question was—could we all work together? Only time would tell.

Chapter 36

reakfast was awkward at best. Evan felt sorry for the Selkies. He imagined they were confused and afraid. He noticed many of them looked to Meara. She gave them reassuring smiles, but she didn't speak up. Clearly, David was in charge. Still, Evan could see how Meara had gained the trust of their people.

The food was delicious. After two hot meals and several hours of sleep in a comfortable bed, Evan was starting to feel like his old self again. The other guys appeared well rested too. Vesh was discussing training strategies with David. Meara listened to them, her lips pursed in a frown. Dex and Slate hypothesized on how much longer before Ken came after them. Evan didn't want to know. With luck, they had at least another day.

"Are you ready?" David asked the group as he pushed back from the table and stood. "It's time to train."

He started walking toward the stairs when Meara stopped him. "Dad? Aren't you going to announce it to the clan? Aren't they training too?"

He turned back, a surprised expression on his face. "In time. I was planning to have my guards train with the Blue Men first."

"That's like ten people!" Meara said. "No. Everyone needs to be involved."

"No?" David's eyebrows rose. He didn't seem mad, more bewildered. It made Evan wonder how often anyone challenged him.

"We don't have time for that," Meara argued. "Ken might already be on his way."

She had a point. Evan was surprised that Deanna hadn't contacted him yet. Ken must know by now that they were gone.

"We need to train together," she said. "And you need to see what our people have learned."

David looked like he was going to protest, but Angus stood and moved to Meara's side, placing his hand on her shoulder. "Listen to her, David. Meara has been guiding our people in your absence. You owe it to her to see what she has done."

"Very well," David relented with a small smile.

If Evan had to guess, Meara's father was humoring her. If she thought so too, she did a good job ignoring it. She turned to address the room. The Selkies watched her expectantly.

"It is time to train," she said. "But first, I would like for you to demonstrate your skills to David. Let us go to the shore for practice."

The crowd filed out of the room. Meara followed them, so Evan and the others followed her. Angus walked alongside David. Evan couldn't hear what the old man was saying, but he assumed Angus counseled David on what happened while he was gone.

When they got outside, the Selkies were in the water, wading no more than waist deep.

"What is this?" David asked. "I forbade swimming."

"They're not swimming." Meara's voice was calm as she reasoned with her father. "We discovered that a few minutes in the water restores our energy levels and helps with training. They'll be out soon."

David studied his daughter thoughtfully. Evan could guess why. How was it that Meara, who spent most of her life as a human, discovered something about Selkies that no one else knew before? Sure enough, a few minutes later the Selkies returned to land. They lined up in a neat formation. It was obvious that they had been practicing.

"What should we demonstrate first?" Meara asked Kieran.

"Hand combat," he answered immediately.

"Very good." She faced the crowd. "We'll begin with hand combat. Pair off."

The Selkies spread out in pairs. They fought with skill and grace. Their moves were a mixture of martial arts and kickboxing. David walked through the training area, observing his people. By the expression on his face, Evan thought he was impressed.

"Stop!" Meara called and the teams halted, bowing respectfully to each other. "Switch partners."

They switched and resumed fighting. This happened three more times. Meara clearly wanted to prove their skill and show that they could fight more than one opponent. After almost an hour of training, the Selkies were not even winded.

"Take a break," Meara told them. "Weapons next."

The Selkies returned to the water, again going no further than their waists. When they came out, they bounced around energetically. The water appeared to restore their strength and vitality.

Meara and Kieran held hands and closed their eyes. A buzz of magical energy filled the air, causing the hairs on Evan's arms to rise. What were they doing? He found out a moment later when a pile of weapons appeared in front of them.

"Choose your weapon and begin," Meara commanded.

The fighting seemed chaotic at first, but then Evan saw what was happening. The Selkies were divided into reds and blues. The fight mimicked a true battle, so rather than one on one, the ratio was often one to several. They handled the weapons well. How had Meara taught them to fight like this in such a short amount of time? Where had she learned these moves?

"Stop!" David's voice rose above the clatter. "I have seen enough for now. Your skill is impressive and rivals that of my guard."

Meara stepped forward and bowed to her father. Such a formal show of respect was out of character for her. "Dad, if you please, I would like to show you one more thing."

"We really should be moving along," he said.

"Please?" She fixed him with a challenging gaze, and her jaw was set. "It's important."

"Very well," he relented and stepped back again.

With a grin, Meara turned back to the group. "It's time," she called. "Show David what you've got."

The Selkies set down their weapons and held their hands in front of them, palms up. To Evan, it looked like they were getting ready to meditate or pray. Then, one by one, a ball of light appeared, floating above their open hands. Each Selkie seemed to have its own unique color.

"What the—?" David sputtered. "How is this possible?"

"All Selkies can do magic." Kieran smiled proudly at Meara. "They just needed someone to show them how."

Meara looked uncertain as she watched her father's reaction. She gasped in surprise when he picked her up and spun her around. "I underestimated you," he said once he placed her back on her feet. "I was impressed with the combat and weaponry, but this. This is truly amazing. How did you know?"

"I didn't." She shrugged. "I took a chance."

Evan started when he realized Vesh was at his side. "You broke up with her?" Vesh asked.

"Yeah."

"You're an idiot." Vesh threw his arm around Evan's shoulder. "But you're a lucky idiot, since you managed to snag Deanna on the rebound."

"I think she caught me," Evan said, remembering how strongly Deanna came onto him at first.

"Like I said, you're lucky." Vesh turned Evan slightly, angling his head toward the petite redhead. "What do you know about her?"

"Ula?" Evan asked. He was surprised Vesh was asking. After seeing Vesh with the Sirens, Ula didn't seem like his type.

"Yeah. She's spunky. I like that."

"Ula is great," Evan said. "She's good friends with Meara. She also happens to be David's youngest sister."

"Ah." Vesh pulled on the ring in his brow and bit his lip. Then, his mouth broke into a wide grin. Evan knew he loved a challenge. "Tread lightly, then?"

"Up to you." Evan shrugged. "But I would."

David called them over. "We need to train together. You've seen what our people can do. What's the best way to proceed?"

"I can explain some things about our kind," Vesh offered. "If you like."

"Please," David said. "We need all the knowledge we can get." He motioned that Vesh had the floor.

"The Blue Men of the Minch are not a violent people." Vesh

raised his voice and addressed the crowd. His statement was met with murmurs of disbelief. "It's true. When our mother, our queen, was alive, we lived in peaceful isolation. This peaceful existence ended when a Selkie entered our territory. Some of my brethren believe that he killed our queen. They are poisoned with anger and vengeance."

"Which Selkie was it?" a man yelled.

At the same time, a female voice asked, "Did he?"

Arren's voice was the loudest. "Did the Selkie kill your queen?"

"No." Meara moved beside Vesh and spoke before he could. "The queen mother's name was Azuria. She contacted me and showed me the truth. Azuria and Zane were in love. He died when she tried to turn him so that they could be together. She killed herself because she was overcome with grief."

The crowd was silent. Meara squeezed Vesh's arm reassuringly, and then stepped back next to Kieran. He put his arm around her and pulled her close. Evan had to give the Selkie credit. Kieran took care of Meara. It was obvious that he loved her.

Vesh broke the silence and continued, "Ken, my eldest brother, is in charge. He bends the will of those who don't agree with him. Most of the Blue Men are under his control, as are many of the Sirens. Evan can tell you about Ken's plans. Evan?"

Vesh looked at him expectantly, as did almost one hundred other pairs of eyes. Evan hated public speaking. Already, he was breaking out in a cold sweat. The only thing that propelled him to the front of the group was the fact that this information was necessary. The Selkies needed to know what they would be facing.

"There is a mantle plume off the northern coast of Scotland. Ken is feeding his power into the volcanic activity, causing it to fissure and grow. He is moving the fault toward your island. His goal is to sink your home and burn you all in a fiery bath of lava."

"Meara and I have seen the destruction," Kieran said. "The damage must be contained."

"This sounds hopeless," a young woman shouted. "What do you expect us to do?"

"Fight," Vesh said. "Protect your home. We are going to show you how to defeat our kind. To do this, we must change. Do not be alarmed."

Vesh, Dex, and Slate transformed into their blue state. Evan couldn't. It was one thing to transform his hand, another to change completely. He was too worried that he would be stuck again. Vesh gave him a look of disappointment, but otherwise ignored him.

"This is our normal form," Vesh said. "We have incredible strength and endurance. We can breathe on land and under water. Our nails are sharp like daggers, as are our teeth. Avoid both in battle. Our skin is tough and difficult to penetrate, however, if you strike here—" He pointed to a spot on Slate below his ribs on the right side. "Front or back, the blow will be lethal. Remember, it must be on the right side."

He turned to Dex and tilted his head, exposing the gills on the side of Dex's neck. "You can also stab through the gills. It is not fatal, but the pain is debilitating. Because it takes weeks for us to recover from this injury, it's an effective way to neutralize us."

With a frown, Vesh glanced at the Selkies before him. "I have just told you our two greatest weaknesses. I trust you not to attack the four of us as we stand with you. When possible, I would prefer that you neutralize the Blue Men and not kill them. As I said, many are not in control of their own will."

Somewhere in the back, a Selkie started to clap, others joined in, and soon, they were all cheering.

"Thank you," David said, patting Vesh on the back. "You are a true friend."

An icy dagger of pain pierced Evan's skull. The Selkies' cheers became muffled noise in the background. He was aware of dropping to his knees, and Dex and Meara rushing to his side.

My son. Ken's angry voice thundered through his head, increasing the pain tenfold. Evan whimpered and fell to his side. *Your betrayal will be your death.*

Evan saw an army of Blue Men swimming toward the island with Ken in the lead. They were close. Too close. Evan took a ragged breath and sat up. The pain vanished, but not the vision. The island was split in half, the ground stained red and strewn with the slaughtered bodies of Selkies. He knew his face must reflect the horror he felt. Staring into Meara's bewildered eyes, he reached for her hand, clasping it between his own.

"We are out of time," he rasped. "They're coming."

Chapter 37

My heart froze at Evan's words. It was really happening. Ken and his minions were on their way to destroy us. While Dex helped Evan to his feet, I ran to tell my dad.

"Go to the highest point on the cliff," he said, addressing Kieran, Uncle Angus, Ula, and me. "As soon as you see something, contact me."

He crossed to Aunt Brigid and a few of his guard, presumably to strategize. A moment later, he ordered everyone back to the fortress. "It will be easier to spot our attackers from high ground," he said. "Surround the castle and keep a lookout. I don't want to be caught off guard."

"Sir." Vesh stepped forward and bowed slightly. "With all due respect, won't your wards keep the island hidden?"

"They should," Dad consented. "But I don't trust them in this situation. The wards were not meant to block out natural elements. If the fissure from the mantle plume has been directed at us, Ken and his followers will be able to track it, effectively neutralizing our defenses."

At those words, chaos broke out around us as the terrified clan raced to follow my dad's orders. Faces were stricken with panic and fear.

This is it, I said to Kieran. *Are you ready?*

He warmed my ice-cold fingers between his hands. I calmed at his strong and steady touch. *As ready as I can be,* he said.

Wrapping my arms around his waist, I rested my head against his chest. I needed this moment of sanity even as all hell was breaking loose. His heartbeat was fast, but steady. When I raised my head, he brushed my lips with a tender kiss.

I love you, Meara. We'll get through this.

I prayed he was right, but all I said was *I love you, too.* With a sigh, I stepped back and took his hand. *We should get into position.*

We transported to the top of the cliffs. Uncle Angus and Ula were already there, searching the white-capped waves for a sign of anything unusual. From our vantage point, I could see Dad and Aunt Brigid leading the ranks. They calmed the masses. Brigid's commanding voice could be heard on the wind, motivating the meekest of the fighters. The guard and four Blue Men would provide protection around the exterior, which allowed the less-skilled fighters to stay in the middle of the pack for protection.

Satisfied that they had our army under control, my eyes roamed the perimeter of the entire island, from horizon to shore. At first, I saw nothing. There were no boats, no mammals, no fins, nothing unusual— only the steady breaking of the waves against the shore. Then, Kieran shouted and pointed to the southwest. "Over there... do you see that?"

A thick line of steam was rising above the water about a mile off shore. The surface of the water bubbled like a boiling pot of water.

"What is it?" Ula asked.

No one answered her, because we didn't know. I had a guess. Was the fault line truly that close to us now? That amount of cold seawater should cool the lava. What would be hot enough to make the ocean boil? The vaporous column inched slowly forward. The scary part was that we could actually see it moving.

"That has to be them," I said. "I'll tell my dad."

Dad?

His response was immediate. *Did you spot something?*

Yes. About a mile out on the southwest side of the island. The sea is boiling and steaming. It's approaching at a steady pace. Fear froze my blood, but I tried to appear calm.

Can you estimate a time of impact?

The pace was about the speed that someone could walk on land. *At the rate it's traveling, it will reach the island within a half hour.*

Very good. We'll head them off at the shore. Before I could say anything, he added, *Stay up there until I call for you.*

My back stiffened. After all I showed him, after his speech about how proud he was of me, he still felt he could tell me what to do. He cut the connection before I could protest. At least anger at my father gave me something to focus on other than my fear. I'd been preparing for this or something like it ever since I came into my dad's world, but now that the moment was here, I was afraid.

"Do you ever get used to this?" I asked Kieran, knowing that he had fought in battles when defending his own clan.

"Never," he said, lifting my hand to kiss my knuckles. His dark eyes held mine. "It's okay to be afraid."

"Good." I tried to swallow my unease. "Because I am."

My teeth chattered. I couldn't remember ever feeling this apprehensive about anything. The closest feeling to this was when my mom was dying, and then, I knew what was coming and had time to prepare.

Ula stepped behind me and rubbed my shoulder. "I'm afraid, too, Meara."

"As am I," Uncle Angus chimed in with a deep chuckle. "But I'll be damned if I let some blue scumbags destroy my home."

The tension eased, and we laughed. Especially when Kieran added, "You certainly have a way with words, sir."

The laughing stopped abruptly when the ground shook violently. We tried to maintain our balance, but the vibrations were too much. Awkwardly, we fell, landing hard on the ground. Below us, I heard screams. Since the earth was still shaking, I crawled close to the edge and looked down. Several bodies were lying in broken positions. Most likely, they had been climbing down the side of the cliff when the quake struck and lost their footing. A few seemed to be recovering, but one body was not moving. From this altitude, I couldn't tell who it was, but the person was wearing a dress, so I knew it was a woman, possibly someone's wife or mother. I prayed that she was simply unconscious and not dead.

The ground trembled again, not aftershocks, because these were stronger than the first. It felt as though the island was struggling to stay together. The bubbling water was only about a quarter of a mile out now. The water churned with a mass of swimming blue bodies.

Dad, Brigid, and several of our guards stood in the shallows waiting for the enemy. The other Selkies formed ranks behind them, weapons raised. Most touched the surf to get as much energy from the water as they could before the battle. I sensed their fear, but I also saw their bravery. Through their courage, I found some of my own. These were my people. I wouldn't let them down. From here, I might be able to stun the enemy with magic at least.

There was a deafening roar as the Blue Men broke the surface of the water and raced toward the island. They held long, deadly-looking spears and well-honed swords. Our weapons were just as formidable, as was our skill. I didn't see Ken, and from this height, most of them looked the same, impossibly tall with deep blue, muscled bodies and long, clawed fingers.

Uncle Angus, Kieran, Ula, and I stood near the cliff's edge, facing the fight. We called on our magic and threw the energy at the enemy, especially those that were still in the water and the easiest targets. I smiled when we knocked several of them down, but frowned a moment later when they popped back up. It was like we were mosquitoes buzzing around them. Annoying, sure, but not deadly. Why wasn't our magic powerful enough to stop them?

Your magic cannot hurt them, Azuria's voice whispered through my head. *Their skin is tough and protects them. As Vesh explained, only your weapons, properly used, will render them powerless.*

Can you help us? I asked, excited that she might give us a winning edge.

I must stay out of this battle, Meara. I cannot fight against my sons. I will be here with you, child, and protect you as I can. I felt her kiss brush against my forehead. *I hope you understand.*

I do. How could a mother sacrifice her own children? I understood her dilemma, and I appreciated whatever protection she did give me. She had already done so much to help us.

"Why isn't it working?" Ula asked.

"It's their skin," I told her. "Azuria reminded me that the only way we can stop them is as Vesh said, either pierce their right side or their gills. Remember that."

"I'm heading down there then," Uncle Angus said. "I can't stand here and watch our people fight alone."

"I'll go with you." Kieran leaned over and kissed me hard and fast.

"Stay here with Ula. Please."

"That's not fair to ask," I said. "You're going."

His voice filled with desperation. "Please stay."

It was the last thing he said before he and Uncle Angus transported to the battle below. I saw them rush into the crowd, and then I lost them in the action.

I paced around the cliff, quickly checking the other sides of the island. They were all silent and empty. The Blue Men brought the battle to one specific point. That, at least, made things easier. Being ambushed on all sides would've made this a harder battle to fight. Then again, as the ground continued to sporadically shake and groan, I knew that their most deadly weapon had yet to be deployed. They planned to rip the island apart.

"I feel completely useless," I said, kicking a rock over the edge. Bodies swarmed below in a mass of weapons and magic. Several had already fallen from both sides. I frantically searched for Kieran in the chaos, but I couldn't spot him. "This is ridiculous. I didn't promise Kieran I'd stay. He asked me too, but I didn't promise." I paced some more, and then made a decision. "If I stay here, I'll go crazy with worry. I'm going down there."

"What can we do?" Ula asked.

"What about the mantle plume?" I pointed to the smoky pillar, now mere feet from the shore. "We should get down there and check it out. Our magic is useless against the Blue Men, but maybe there is something we can do there."

Her face lit up. "That's a great idea. We can come from the outside edge and avoid the battle. That way, you're not really going against your dad's or Kieran's wishes."

"It was never their place to tell me what to do, but I appreciate you finding a solution that makes it appear that I tried to keep their silly promise, anyway." I hugged her, and then clasped her hand in mine. "Ready?"

"Let's go!"

We transported to the far side of the cove. While we could hear the fighting near us—the clanging of swords, the grunts, shouts, and angry cries—we couldn't see anything from where we stood. That meant they couldn't see us either.

The water bubbled and brewed. It was almost here. The first earthquake must have occurred when it passed the island's wards. There was one way to determine what we were facing. We changed into seals and slid into the ocean. The temperature was raised, but not too warm, at least, not from this distance away. It might get hotter as we got closer.

It was difficult to see through the turbulent water, but I spotted two shadowy figures ahead. Of course! We never saw Ken come out of the water. He was here, feeding the mantle plume with his energy like Evan told us.

It's Ken. I pointed to the figures. *I'm not sure who is with him, but we need to stop them. It's the only way we're going to prevent the plume from completely reaching the island and destroying us.*

How can we stop them?

The only thing I could think of was to lure him away. Would he consider us to be enticing enough bait? There was only one way to find out. *Follow my lead.*

If I changed back into my human form, Ken would know who I was and that might goad him. I couldn't risk losing our seal skin, though, if it was protecting us from the heat of the plume. It would be senseless to change back and boil in the ocean.

My target was the taller of the two figures, which I assumed was Ken. I hadn't seen him in his blue form, but that man seemed to be doing the most work. I sped at him and rammed him in the back, knocking him forward and almost pitching him into the hot lava. Too bad I didn't. That would have been a quick and appropriate end for him. Ula attacked the other man in a similar fashion. What we succeeded to do was make them mad. They chased us, and we led them back to land.

As soon as I was out of the water, I changed back and conjured my dagger. Ula stood next to me with a small sword that she must have transported from the pile in the cove. Ken and the other man wasted no time attacking us. They fought fast and dirty. I defended myself and dodged Ken's blows, but I couldn't find an opening to attack. Then, I made a misstep and his claw scratched my right cheek. It burned when I touched it, and my fingers came away coated in blood. I screamed in rage.

Meara, where are you? Kieran's panicked voice filled my head.

Fighting Ken, I told him. *I've got this.*

Are you insane? He swore in a rather colorful stream. *I thought you were going to stay on the cliff.*

And risk the island being destroyed? Hell no! I crouched just in time, avoiding Ken's fist, and managed to come up behind him. *Quit distracting me. I'm fighting here.*

I tried to stab Ken under his ribs, but he turned. My dagger met his stomach instead. While it wasn't a deadly blow, he bent over in pain, glowering at me.

"I knew you were trouble the day I met you," Ken growled. "I look forward to watching you die."

"That's interesting," I said. "I was thinking the same thing."

We circled around each other, watching for weakness. Somewhere in my peripheral, I knew that Ula was still fighting the other man. I hoped she was able to hold her own. There was no way to risk taking my eyes completely off Ken. Although, minutes later when I heard her scream, I couldn't help but turn. She crumpled to the ground.

Anger surged through me. Without thinking, I threw my dagger, leaving me weaponless. It hit my target, directly in the man's gills. He crumpled next to Ula. Unfortunately, that meant I exposed my back to Ken. When I realized what I'd done, it was too late. He bent my arms behind me, stretching them almost to the breaking point. Black spots filled my vision, and my breath came out in pants.

"Who taught you that?" His words were clipped and angry. "Who taught you how to defeat us?"

"I did."

Ken whirled us around. Vesh stood before us like an avenging angel. His broad sword was coated in blood, but there was none on him. He stepped toward us, pointing his sword at Ken. "Release the girl, brother. Your battle is not with her."

"My battle is with all Selkies," Ken spat. "The fact that she is a half blood is of no consequence to me. Selkie blood still runs through her veins."

Vesh didn't take his eyes off Ken. "Azuria speaks to her. Did you know that?"

"Lies," Ken hissed. "All lies. Our mother would never speak to filth like her."

"She does speak to me," I said.

"Shut up!" Ken and Vesh said it at the same time, although Vesh's command held no bite. He was trying to help me. I realized too late that my words only fueled Ken's anger. He wretched my arms back further, and blind pain made my knees go weak. My right arm was popped out of its socket, and the left wasn't faring much better.

"Let her go!"

I recognized Evan's voice before I saw him. My pain was nothing to my fear. *Oh god, no.* I couldn't handle it if something happened to Evan. He ran to Vesh's side, and the two of them slowly advanced on us. I felt Ken's indecision. At the last minute, he threw me to the ground and raised his sword.

The island shook violently, and although I was thankful I was already sitting, the movement shot pain through my arms, causing me to whimper. A loud crack resounded and the ground split, leaving Ken and I on one side with the two unconscious bodies, and Evan and Vesh on the other. The chasm was deep and full of red, hot lava.

"It's begun!" Ken laughed gleefully. "It's only a matter of time now before this island sinks in a fiery bath."

Ken was so busy gloating that he didn't realize I had recovered my dagger. My left arm was bruised, but okay. It wasn't my dominant hand, but it would do. Before Ken could turn, I thrust the dagger into his neck, and he crumpled. "Over my dead body, you bastard."

I kicked him before returning my attention to Evan and Vesh. They watched me with a mixture of respect and awe. "What? Never seen a girl kick butt before?" I asked them. I tried to be all Laura Croft badass, but with one hanging arm, I wasn't sure I pulled it off. When they continued to stare, I asked, "C'mon, how do we stop this thing?"

"It took Blue Men power to create it. I imagine our power can destroy it, too," Evan said. "I was able to undo Ken's work in small amounts before, but this is much bigger. Vesh, can you lend me a hand?"

"Sure thing."

They knelt at the edge of the fault. Evan held his hands over the fissure. Vesh covered Evan's hands with his own. A stream of bright blue energy flowed from their joined hands into the chasm. The lava began to cool and solidify. It was working. We grinned at each other in relief. Unfortunately, it was a moment too soon. The ground shuddered and groaned, then the solidified lava cracked and the red liquid bubbled through, fighting against the magic.

Evan and Vesh increased their power. The blast of magic hit me in the face. The ground solidified again, and then the process repeated itself. By the tired expressions on the guys' faces, the hot lava was winning.

"The magic is too strong. Ken must've recruited help and been feeding the plume for days. I—" Evan faltered, his voice cracking with emotion, his face beaded in sweat. "I'm not sure we're powerful enough to stop this."

"Let me help." I stepped forward. The air was so thick with power that I felt like I was moving in slow motion. Would this be it? Would my magic help destroy the plume or would the magic of the Blue Men destroy me as it had my ancestor, Zane? It was a risk I had to take. The lives of my family, my people, were at stake. If my life could save theirs, it was worth it. We couldn't lose so many. We couldn't lose our home.

I placed my hands on top of Vesh's and drew on my power. My bright orange energy mixed with theirs to create a sickly purple brown. It didn't look promising. At first, nothing happened, and then it started to work. The lava cooled again, but more than that, the ground began to seam together. My heart rate quickened with excitement. We were doing it!

Then the magic backlashed, and I couldn't hold back a scream. My body was on fire, inside and out. Heat prickled along my skin. Was my body tearing in half? It felt like it.

Evan looked up and held my gaze, gritting his teeth. *Hold on, Meara. Hold on if you can.*

I clenched my jaw and focused beyond the pain. I thought about Kieran, my dad, my aunts, my uncles, the triplets, and yes, even Arren. Then I thought of Mom, Grandma Mary, and Grandpa Jamie. They would be proud of me.

My power flared and for a moment, the pain subsided. Our combined power burned brighter as we fought against the mantle plume.

The ground healed inch by aching inch until it had almost reached the water's edge. Then our power flickered and started to fade. We were exhausted. We couldn't fight much longer, so we were going to lose.

From the corner of my eye, I caught a mass of red curls. Then Ula's hands covered my own. The energy changed, blazing white.

"Ula, don't!" I shouted, but it was too late.

Her face crumbled in agony, but her eyes pierced mine. "My choice, Meara. This is my home, too."

The white energy poured into the fault. The ground stitched itself together as we watched until only a slight scar remained. We couldn't see into the water, but I was confident that the ocean surface was healing too. The combination of equal parts Selkie and Blue Men seemed to be the secret ingredient. The question was—how much longer would we have to keep at this? I didn't have much more in me, and Evan and Vesh had been at it longer than the rest of us.

From below, Evan made a strangling sound. I looked down and gasped in shock. If Vesh and Ula hadn't been sandwiching my hands between their own, I would've broken the connection by accident. The color was draining from Evan's body. His hair was white, his eyes gray. His skin was slowing losing its pigment. He was desaturating like a black-and-white photograph. Was he dying?

Don't let go, Meara. I'm okay. I sighed in relief as Evan's voice slid through my mind. *Azuria is here with me. She told me it's okay.*

Azuria? Why wasn't she showing herself to me too? Was she telling him the truth?

To my right, Ula made a soft noise. Her hands slid off mine, and she collapsed on the ground. I was focusing so much on Evan that I didn't notice what was happening to Ula. Her skin was now the same turquoise as Azuria, her long, curly hair a deeper shade of that color. I glanced between Evan and Ula in confusion. It was like the color that drained from him had siphoned into her. How did that happen? What did it mean?

When Ula fell, she broke the connection. The magic stopped flowing. The earth was still, but so was Ula. I dropped beside her and placed my ear against her heart. With relief, I heard it beating, steady and strong.

"Ula?" I tapped her cheek lightly. "Can you hear me?"

Her eyes fluttered and opened, and I jumped back. They were the same bright blue as Azuria. Her face was both foreign and familiar. My vision split, and I saw a double reflection—Azuria's face superimposed over Ula's. Then, Ula's normal coloring returned, bleeding through the blue. What happened to her?

"Is she okay?" Vesh stood over us, supporting Evan. His skin was still smooth and youthful, but his hair was pure white. When he raised his head and looked at me, his eyes were light gray, almost silver. If it didn't look so alien, I would've thought his new eye color was stunning. As it was, I was once again reminded of a muted photograph.

Ula blinked a few times, her gaze moving from Vesh to Evan and back again.

"Can you sit up?" I asked her.

"I'm fine." She sat up and brushed off her jeans, frowning at them as if she were confused by what she was wearing. On the ground where she had been lying was a pile of ash.

"Your backpack!" I pointed at the remains. She frowned and twisted to look behind her. The back of her shirt was stained dark from the ash. Her Selkie skin was gone, burnt to nothing. What did that mean?

She glanced up at us, and her expression cleared. She didn't seem worried, if anything, she looked pleased. "You've done so well. You all have." She offered her hand to Vesh. "Help me stand, please."

The Ula I knew would never have the confidence to ask her crush to help her up. She certainly would be more worried about her skin. This was not the same girl; I knew it in my heart. Vesh did as she asked, offering her his hand. She took it, and with a fluid movement, she stood. Her image shivered and wavered in the setting sun, flickering from Ula to Azuria and back again.

Azuria? I asked.

Yes. Yes.

In an echo, I heard both Azuria and Ula's voice. Now, I was scared. I took Ula's shoulders and peered into her eyes. The eyes that stared back at me were ageless and alien. "What have you done with my aunt?" I whispered.

The figure that had been Ula whispered back in an odd, monotone chant, "I have changed your aunt into something new, something more. She is the new queen of the Blue Men. This moment begins an age of peace."

The dual image wavered again, and then split in two. Azuria stood beside Ula in her spirit form, wearing a benevolent expression. She kissed Ula's cheek, although Ula appeared not to notice, then she approached me.

You saved your people, you gave me the opportunity to save my sons, and you freed me to be with Zane. Thank you, Meara. She kissed me, and it felt like the flutter of icy butterfly wings on my cheek. *I will be forever in your debt.*

She stepped back and sighed, closing her eyes. Her peaceful expression turned to joy. *I can see him. I can see Zane. He is beckoning to me.* She opened her eyes and grinned. The first real moment of happiness I had seen on her face since the vision she showed me of her time with Zane. *Goodbye, Meara. You will live long and well. Your offspring will be blessed. These are my gifts to you.*

I felt her blessing settle on me like a warm embrace. Her image slowly faded until all that was left was the sea beyond. Azuria was gone.

Chapter 38

*E*van couldn't remember the last time he was this exhausted and disoriented. It was worse than when he had mononucleosis freshman year, worse than when Ken was conducting all those experiments on him last summer, and even worse than the last few weeks he spent working with Ken on the mantle plume. A slight buzzing filled his skull, and everything was out of focus. He shook his head, trying to clear it.

"What happened?" Evan asked. "I feel so strange."

Ula's beaming face swam into view. She wrapped her arms around him, much to his surprise. Since when did they have any kind of relationship? He glanced at Meara in confusion, but she was staring out at the ocean with an odd expression on her face.

"You were magnificent, Evan," Ula said. "You have saved your people and the Selkies." She kissed his cheek, but her eyes were sad. "You gave the most precious of gifts, but it is one that you cannot have back. Your essence is gone. You are no longer one of the Blue Men."

"What do you mean?" After all that happened in the last few months, he was finally adjusting to his new life. It didn't mean he stopped praying to be human again. While his new body offered some advantages, like breathing under water, it frequently felt more like a curse than a gift. Did she say what he thought she said?

"You are completely human." Ula confirmed his question as though she could read his mind. "With a few alterations."

She shaped her hands into a circle. A reflective bubble formed between them, the surface as smooth as glass. Evan stepped closer and stared at his reflection. His hair was white as snow and his eyes were pale gray. Tentatively, he touched his hair. The white made him look much older. "What happened?" he asked.

"When your essence drained from your body, your pigmentation went with it," Ula explained. "Unfortunately, I can't change you back."

"Why would you be able to?" Vesh asked, his voice bewildered. "Can Selkies normally do that?"

"She's not a Selkie anymore, Vesh." Meara's voice trembled with emotion. She watched her aunt with a mixture of pride and uncertainty. "Your mother changed Ula into something else."

Ula touched Evan's hair and continued as if Meara hadn't spoken. "I understand humans have products that can change your eye color and hair."

Seriously? Was she telling him to buy contacts and use hair dye? Evan fought the urge to laugh at the absurdity of it. He wasn't troubled by it. Like Ula said, hair and eye color could be changed. The fact that he was human again was the reward. If the cost was white hair, so be it as long as Deanna was okay with the changes. Would she continue to love him?

"You are still you, Evan." Ula smiled at him. "She will love you the same."

Evan nodded, too surprised for words. Ula could read his mind! She never communicated with him before, and she had the chance. Why now?

Vesh studied Ula carefully. She met his curious gaze and asked, "Something on your mind, Vesh?"

"I know I only met you yesterday," Vesh began. It was the first time Evan had seen the other man appear nervous or unsure. "But you seem... different... than before."

Ula laughed, and the air filled with the music of tinkling bells. "I am different. Evan's essence has changed me."

Standing in the middle of the group, Ula closed her eyes and raised her hand. The air shimmered around her as her human façade melted away. Wearing a shimmering gown of aquamarine with a silver crown on her head, Ula stood before them. There was no mistaking that she was the new queen of the Blue Men of the Minch. Power poured off her in waves. Despite his now-human state, Evan could still feel it.

Ula looked like herself—petite with long, curly hair, and more—her skin and hair were the aqua blue of the Blue Men. She also exuded more confidence and sovereignty than she did as a Selkie.

"My queen." Vesh bowed deeply to her. When he straightened, his expression was pained. "May I speak freely?"

"Of course, Veshian," she said. "You have that right."

He seemed to consider his words. "I know you are my queen, I feel the rightness of it, but you do not look like my mother. Your appearance favors the Selkie, Ula."

The bells rang again, and her face lit with joy.

"I *am* Ula. Azuria transferred her power to me, which fundamentally changed me and made me your queen. She also shared select memories with me. Things I will need to know to rule the kingdom, but your mother has finally moved on. She is at peace." Ula smiled. "We will have time to discuss the technicalities of the transformation later, although some of the details are even unknown to me. Right now, our first order of business is to stop this ridiculous war."

With a confident stride that Ula didn't previously possess, she marched toward the battle sounds on the other side of the cove. The rest of the group followed in stunned silence. Evan wondered how Ula was feeling. He was still reeling from the news that she merged with Azuria. Ula seemed calm and poised, but was it a façade? He couldn't imagine what it felt like to acquire someone else's power and memories. He shivered uncomfortably and decided he got the better outcome of the two of them.

When the group crested the peak, the scene that greeted them spoke of death and loss. Bodies from both sides were strewn along the ground, limbs bent at odd angles, blood darkening the earth. It was eerily similar to Evan's earlier vision, except in reality, there were as many Blue Men casualties as Selkies. Evan couldn't spot Dex or Slate in the blur of fighting figures. David, however, was surrounded by three Blue Men, fighting with an impressive amount of skill and power. Brigid wasn't far from him. She cut through a crowd of Blue Men and rescued several of her people from losing battles. From what Evan saw, she was unstoppable.

Next to him, Ula surveyed the wreckage, her expression grim.

She took a deep breath, raised her hands, and clapped them together. Thunder rumbled in the distance, and the scene below froze like she hit the pause button on a remote control.

"Enough!" she cried. "Enough blood has been lost from misplaced hatred. Blue Men of the Minch, I am your queen." Her voice crested in waves over the unmoving figures, her magic palpable. "Come to me now."

The Blue Men unfroze, blinking astonished eyes and stumbling around as if they were waking from a dream. In a large swarm, they made their way to Ula, dropping their weapons and ignoring the Selkies. Were they compelled or did they move of their own accord? Evan felt no pull from her words, but then again, he was completely human. The Blue Men stopped before her and fell to their knees, many of them crying.

Ula moved through the men, touching their heads or shoulders, kissing their foreheads. "Sons of Azuria," she said. "You have been misled by anger and fear for far too long. Azuria chose me to restore peace. It's time to return to a more-loving existence."

After she acknowledged each individual, she returned to her place at the front of the group. "Selkies are not our enemy. As proof of this, your queen has been reborn of both Selkie and Blue Men blood."

"Please forgive us!" several men called from the group. Many wore ashamed or distraught expressions.

Ula smiled benevolently. "I forgive you, for you did not know the truth, nor did you have free will unless Ken deemed it so." The men relaxed and settled at her words. She held their rapt attention. "It is time for you to return home. Prepare for my arrival." She blew a kiss their way and the Blue Men disintegrated, including Vesh, Dex, and Slate.

"What did you do?" Meara asked. "What have you done with our friends?"

"Sent them to Azuria," Ula answered with a frown. She seemed confused as to why Meara questioned her. "They are all safe. I assure you."

Tears shimmering in her eyes, Meara stared at the woman who was her aunt and friend. "Are you leaving with them?"

With a look of understanding, Ula pulled Meara into a hug. "I am their queen. I have to go. It doesn't mean that I won't keep in touch. You know I will. You are my best friend, and I adore you."

Meara yelped when Ula tightened her embrace. This made Ula frown. "You're hurt." She placed her hands on Meara's shoulders, more gently this time. Meara bit her bottom lip as cool blue light traveled from Ula's hands and down Meara's arms. The light faded, and Ula stepped back with a smile. "Better?"

Meara rolled her shoulders. "You healed me. Thank you."

"You're welcome." Ula squeezed Meara's hand, and then stepped back. "We'll talk when this is all over. We have much to discuss. Right now, I have one more Blue Man to deal with."

Skirt swirling around her ankles, Ula turned and went back toward the fault. Evan assumed she meant Ken. Had he regained consciousness already? Meara dealt him a powerful blow to the gills. Of course, if Ula could freeze an entire battle, she could probably wake an unconscious man with no problems.

Once she disappeared over the hill, Meara announced, "I've got to find Kieran!" She ran down the slope into the sea of Selkies, some of the fallen were beginning to regain consciousness. Evan didn't see Kieran in the mass of bodies. For Meara's sake, he hoped the male Selkie was unharmed. One individual did catch Evan's attention. Brigid stood and scowled fiercely.

"Cowards!" she shouted, shaking her sword above her as she searched for the enemy. "Where are you? Show yourselves!"

"They're gone," Evan told her. "Their queen sent them home."

"Azuria?" A few feet away from Brigid, David sat up and rubbed his forehead. "I thought she was dead."

"She is. They have a new queen." Ula could explain it to them.

David blinked rapidly, and then squinted at Evan. "Is that you, Evan? What the hell happened to you?"

"Long story."

"Do you plan to share it?" David asked.

"I'll fill you in later. You're safe now. The war is over, and Azuria has returned. Care for your people, David. They need you." The words tumbled out as Evan began running toward the cove where Ula had gone. He wanted to see what was happening with Ken.

Ken lay unconscious on the ground. The angry set of his jaw and deep furrow marks on his face were softened into something more humane. Ula knelt next to him, talking in hushed tones. She finished and leaned down to kiss his forehead. "Awake, eldest son of Azuria."

Ken's eyes fluttered open. His initial confusion was replaced by awe. When Ula stood and offered him an outstretched hand, Ken took it and let her pull him up. "Mother?" he asked, clearly seeing something in Ula that took the rest of them much longer to notice. He shook his head as if to clear it. "Not my mother, but our queen. How?"

"Evan gave his essence, and Azuria made me your new queen. I am not your mother, Ken, but I have her power and share some of her memories." Ula's back was to Evan. If she sensed he was there, she gave no indication. When she spoke again, it was to reprimand. "What you have done, Kennaught, is terrible. You destroyed many innocent lives and planned for more death. Is this how your mother taught you to live?"

"But the Selkie," he stammered. "The Selkie killed her."

"No." Ula held Ken's face between her hands, staring into his eyes. "You are wrong. Zane loved Azuria. He died when she tried to change him so they could be together. Azuria took her own life in her grief."

"Liar!" Ken's face distorted in rage. "My mother would never abandon us." His eyes narrowed, and he sneered at her. "Why should I believe you? You are not my mother. You're a Selkie. You may have fooled my brothers, but you don't fool me!"

"If Azuria didn't trust me," Ula said. "Why would she share her essence and memories with me?"

"You forced her! You tricked her, and now you're trying to influence me!" He pulled his hands away and ran to the fault line, which was now a healed seam in the rocky shore. Although Ken's arms shook with exhaustion, he dropped to his knees and tried to feed his energy to the mended fissure. "The Selkies must die! You all must die!"

Ula's eyes filled with tears. She slowly made her way to stand before Ken. "I hoped it would not come to this. You are, after all, the eldest son, and at one point, you were a great man. I am sorry to see you broken." Ken was so gone in his quest for vengeance that he didn't seem to hear her words or acknowledge Ula when she bent over his bowed head.

"May you find peace in eternal rest." She kissed his forehead, and Ken collapsed to the side. After she chanted a few words that Evan couldn't understand, Ken's body disappeared.

"Is he—?" Evan was afraid to ask.

"Dead? Yes," Ula answered. Although her back was to Evan, she didn't startle when he spoke. She must've known he was there the whole time. When she did turn, she was wiping the tears from her cheeks. "So much senseless loss. Centuries of hatred that stemmed from a love story that ended tragically."

"Love and tragedy aren't that far apart. The same pattern has been repeated through history," Evan said.

Ula frowned. "How do you mean?"

"Think of Romeo and Juliet," he said. "Fear of failure might dissuade some couples, but I think, when you have hope, true love is possible. Love is the strongest magic of all."

Ula gave him a genuine smile and slipped her arm through his. "You're wise, Evan." She leaned her head on his arm, looking out to the sea. "I'm sorry you had to sacrifice so much."

"I don't consider turning human again much of a sacrifice," he admitted. "The hair and eye color will be harder to explain, but as you said, there are ways to cover it."

When Ula didn't respond, Evan looked down at her. She was focused on the water, which reflected the fiery reds and oranges of sunset. Evan paused to appreciate the display. Since returning to land, his thoughts had been consumed with Ken and battle strategy. Now that the war was behind them, he relaxed and admired the sunset. Ula gasped and glanced up at Evan with a coy look.

"Someone is coming and looking forward to seeing you," she said mysteriously.

She pointed out to sea. The sun was now a sliver of orange blaze on the water, highlighting the frothy waves. In the setting light, flashes of brilliant jewels glinted, popping up between the whitecaps. Then, Evan caught a tail, and another one. *Deanna*, he thought, and his heart raced.

The Sirens came in all their colorful glory. With Deanna in the lead, it seemed that their entire community was rushing to the aid of the Selkies. When they neared the shore, the girls changed, walking out of the surf on human legs. Unlike the Selkies, they couldn't create their own clothes—that was why they had the dome at Belle Trésor—but Ula helped to dress them. A wave of her hand, and the Sirens were covered.

Evan barely noticed the others. He couldn't take his eyes off Deanna as she ran to him. He wanted to meet her halfway, but his feet were frozen. He was too afraid of her reaction to his changes. What if she no longer loved him?

"Evan!" She threw herself in his arms and kissed him, leaving him no choice but to catch her and kiss her back. He buried his face in her hair and breathed in her warm, spicy scent.

"I missed you," he murmured against her neck.

"We came as soon as we could." Her voice was breathless, excited. "Ken had us under an enchantment. When it broke, we raced here."

"That quickly?" Evan asked. Ken only died a half hour ago. How did they swim that fast?

"The enchantment broke when Meara neutralized him," Ula explained. She must've read his mind again. He was getting used to it.

Her explanation made more sense to Evan. He knew the Sirens could travel far in a matter of hours. Heck, Ken had them working in northern Scotland when they lived near France. That alone was quite a commute!

"Will you quit your job now?" Evan asked Deanna. Now that she was here, it dawned on him that he wouldn't be able to return to Belle Trésor with her. What if she didn't want to live on land? The only option would be to break up, and Evan didn't want that.

Ula gave Evan a measured look. If he didn't know better, he would think she was silently scolding him. "Or you may keep the club," she offered to Deanna. "Our gift to you for all the Blue Men have done to your kind." She smiled, but her eyes were serious. "I know it doesn't make up for your mother's death, but perhaps having control of the club will give your people purpose and help them heal."

"Thank you," Deanna said. "It is a generous gift, and we accept. I will, however, be putting others in charge. I'm going away for a while."

"Oh?" Ula asked, although the smug look on her face told Evan that she had an idea of where Deanna was going. He wished he knew.

Deanna's head rested on Evan's shoulder while her hand rubbed his back. "I'm planning to enroll in college. I heard this cute guy with white hair and gray eyes goes there." Grinning, she looked up at Evan. "If that's okay with you?"

"You want to come to school with me?"

She nodded happily, and he imagined what a normal life with her would be like—studying in the library, going out for pizza, and introducing her to hockey. They could take the time to get to know each other. He could expose her to all the great things about living on land; show her around like she had done with him in her home. He bent down and kissed her.

"I'd like that," he said. "Very much." Then a thought occurred to him, and his smile faltered. Before she chose him, she needed to know he was completely human now.

"I don't care if you're a purple seahorse," Deanna said, interrupting his thoughts. She threw her hands on her hips and pursed her lips. He didn't mean to annoy her, but apparently, he had. "Well, okay, maybe I would care if you were a purple seahorse, but it's *you* I love, Evan, not the type of being you are or aren't."

"You can still read my mind?" He wasn't getting any kind of signal or messages from her.

"I guess I can." She grinned happily. "Score one for the Siren!"

Evan laughed and pulled her close. As she buried against him, he realized that everything was going to work out just fine.

Chapter 39

Bodies lie scattered on the ground, broken and bloody. It was both raw and devastating to see that much blood. The stench of sweat and death filled the air. I tuned it all out with a singular focus—Kieran. I had to find him. I couldn't breathe until I knew he was okay.

Although I no longer needed it, I gripped my dagger in my hand. It was my security blanket. If I focused on the feel of the blade in my hand, it kept the nightmares at bay. My eyes sought out the larger, male bodies, and with equal parts of guilt and relief, I rejoiced at each one that wasn't him. Thankfully, many of the downed Selkies were injured, but not dead. The injuries would need time to mend, but they would heal. If Kieran were dead, my heart would never recover.

Arms wrapped around me, and reflexively, I spun and raised my knife. It was lucky that Kieran had fast reflexes. He caught my wrist, stopping the blade from slashing his chest.

"I survived the battle with no marks, but you almost took me out." He smirked at me and let go of my hand.

"Don't sneak up on me then!" I scolded, but there was no bite in my words. With a sob of relief, I threw my arms around him and buried my face in his chest. He hugged me back just as intensely, kissing the top of my head.

"You fought Ken," he said. "What were you thinking?"

"Stop the mantle plume, save the island."

"You're crazy." He kissed me. "And incredible." He kissed me again. "And mine."

This time, his lips met mine in a long, slow kiss. There was no need to rush. We found each other. We survived. We were going to be okay.

As the night grew long, the injured were transported to the gathering room near the kitchen. It became our temporary sick bay. Paddy and his staff offered to care for them. The final count was twelve Selkies dead. Any loss was painful, but I was numb. Among the twelve was Uncle Angus. He was my friend and my champion. At times, he believed in me more than my own father. How often had I gone and sat in his room, swapping stories about human life? We were the same, he and I, and now he was gone.

Kieran's shirt was wet from my tears, but he held me tight and stroked my back while I drained my emotions. Wracking sobs turned to sporadic hiccups. I was spent, for the moment.

I looked up when I felt a firm hand on my shoulder. Dad stood there, his own eyes red and watery. Without a word, I left Kieran's arms and went into his. Dad hugged me tight, and I hugged him back. Uncle Angus was gone. Ula was... something else now. My family was dwindling almost as quickly as I found them.

The tears started again, and Dad comforted me. "It's okay to grieve, Meara."

"Why?" I asked. "Why Uncle Angus?"

"He was protecting me." Arren stepped from the shadows. His eyes were swollen, one bruised and bloody, the other from crying. A sling supported his left arm. He was in worse shape than many of us. "I thought I was being brave, but I was stupid. I rushed two Blue Men at once. I would've died if Angus hadn't stepped in front of me. He took the blow." Arren's voice cracked on a sob. He coughed and regained his composure. "He was a great man and a friend. I... I'm sorry." Again, his voice cracked, and he began crying in earnest. "If you want to exile me, I understand."

Dad met my eyes. *Talk to him*, he said. *He'll listen to you.*

I crossed the room to Arren, my head spinning. Was this the way of war? Senseless violence struck like a typhoon and left a wake of death and injuries. The survivors remained to wonder why and relive with guilt every decision that they made.

"Arren," I said, keeping my voice soft and soothing. "It was Angus' choice to help you. His choice, not yours. I don't blame you, so don't blame yourself."

He wouldn't meet my eyes, but he nodded and wiped his nose on his sleeve.

"Are you staying down here for the night?"

With a shrug, he shuffled his feet.

"You need to stay here," I told him firmly. "You could have a concussion." I searched the room and spotted an empty bed close to the fireplace. "Follow me. I'll get you settled."

I led him over to the simple cot, unfolding the blanket. He hiccupped and swayed on his feet. "Sit down and take off your shoes."

Like a small child, he did what he was told, but nothing more. Inwardly, I sighed, but with a gentle voice, I said, "Now lie down and I'll cover you with this blanket." He did, and I tucked him in. "Close your eyes."

I sat on the edge of his bed and held his hand. At first, I didn't know how to help him fall asleep, but then I remembered a lullaby my mom sang to me when I was young. I might have been a little off key, but he didn't seem to mind. By the time I reached the end, he was breathing deep and evenly.

Dad and Kieran still stood together on the other side of the room. They appeared to be having a serious conversation. I let them be and headed to a table in the back of the room set with sandwiches and drinks. There were no bottles or cans, but several kinds of punch in bowls. I poured a cup of a pretty, orange drink that smelled like melon and honey. My throat was raw and scratchy from crying, and the cool liquid soothed it.

"Where is Ula?" Brigid picked up a sandwich, inspected it, then put it back and picked up another. That one must've met with her approval. She took a bite and looked at me expectantly.

"I haven't seen her for hours," I said. I couldn't begin to explain to Brigid that her sister was not the same. Ula would have to explain it herself.

"I'm here." Ula spoke from the doorway. Once again, she had red hair and green eyes.

"Where have you been?" Brigid asked. "You missed practically everything."

"Oh, I did. Did I?" Ula's eyes danced with mischief.

"Is Evan with you?" I asked.

"Yes," she said, adding vaguely. "And others. Where is your father?"

I pointed across the room, and Ula left to talk with him. Who else would be here with Evan? Ula sent the Blue Men home. I wished I had been able to say goodbye to Vesh, Dex, and Slate. Hopefully, I would see them again.

Dad, Ula, and Kieran kept glancing our way as they talked. "What do you suppose they're saying?" Brigid asked between bites. She was already on her third sandwich. I guessed fighting gave her an appetite. It had the opposite effect on me. My stomach was queasy. It was enough to sip the sweet, cold drink.

Finally, Dad motioned for Aunt Brigid and me to join them. She snagged two cookies off a plate on our way. When we got there, Ula said, "I have something to show you." She exchanged a knowing glance with me before transforming. Like before, she changed into a long, flowing gown of ice blue. On her head was a small, silver crown. Her skin, hair, and eyes became aqua.

Dad's mouth hung open. "What happened to you?"

"I am the new queen of the Blue Men," Ula said.

"Azuria? How?" Dad asked in confusion.

"I'm not Azuria." She patted her chest. "I'm Ula. Your sister, remember?"

For once, neither Brigid nor my dad had anything to say. Kieran reached up and touched her crown. "You look kind of badass, Ula."

His statement broke the tension, and we all laughed. Then, she said, "I'll go let Evan and the others know that they are welcome to stay tonight." She glided across the room and into the hall, her movements more graceful than before. She held herself regally, which made sense since she was now a queen. A queen! When I first came to Ronac, she insisted she was one of the weakest of our kind. Now, she was powerful and something completely unique—a blend of Selkie and Blue Men. The first of her kind.

Chapter 40

la had been gone about twenty minutes, and Evan was getting worried. David wasn't going to turn them away, was he? If they had to, the Sirens could swim home, but they looked exhausted. Traveling here as quickly as they did took a lot out of them.

"What's taking her so long?" Deanna asked.

"Good question," Evan said, and then he caught the flash of blue at the entrance. "Look. She's coming."

"I'm sorry to keep you waiting," Ula called as she approached. "I needed to talk to my brother first. You are welcome to stay at the castle. I'll show you to your rooms." She led them inside and up to the second floor. They went to the same hall where Evan stayed with the guys the night before. Hard to believe it had only been a day ago, so much had happened.

"You may need to share rooms." That was the truth. Deanna brought many Sirens with her. At least forty women stood in the hall. Evan was too tired to count. "And there is a large room with a fireplace in the middle here." She pointed to a door that Evan didn't notice yesterday. "There are no beds inside, but you'll find plenty of comfortable chairs and couches."

"Thank you," Evan said, speaking for them all.

"Are you hungry?" Ula asked.

According to his stomach, Evan was always hungry, but he didn't want anyone to go out of their way for him tonight. Food sounded good, a bed sounded better. "I'm okay."

"We're fine," Deanna told Ula. "Thank you for everything."

"Sleep well," Ula said. "I'll return to get you in the morning for breakfast."

Evan stood with the Sirens in the hall watching Ula leave. At first, no one moved. Then, Deanna asked, "Which room is yours from last night?"

Leaning against the door, Evan grinned. "This one."

"What are you waiting for? Let's go in."

The rest of the Sirens watched them with growing interest. "What about them?" Evan asked.

Deanna's eyes widened in mock horror. "You want them to join us?" Laughing, he rolled his eyes. He loved how she could lighten the mood. She leaned in and kissed him before adding, "They'll be alright." Without taking her eyes off Evan, she called, "Won't you, girls?"

Those were the magic words that got everyone moving. With murmurs of consent, the Sirens dispersed by twos and threes into the rooms, some giggling or casting last-minute, knowing glances at the couple.

When the hall was clear and all that could be heard were soft whispers behind closed doors, Deanna asked, "Now can we go in?"

With a flourish that earned an amused squeak from her, Evan opened the door and drew her inside.

Chapter 41

"Meara!"

Evan's voice stopped me in my tracks. With all the extra mouths to feed at breakfast, I was helping Paddy serve our guests. I hadn't even noticed Evan enter the room with the Sirens, although it was funny to see him with a crowd of women. I couldn't help thinking of them as his harem. I was sure he wouldn't mind the reference.

"Hi, Evan," I said. "Did you sleep okay?"

I asked the question without thinking, and then my face grew warm when I realized that he probably spent the night with Deanna. I hoped he didn't answer me honestly. I didn't want to know.

"Yeah, thanks." He grinned and touched my cheek. "You always blush so easily."

"Yes, well…" I silently pleaded with my skin to cool quickly. Why did it always have to betray my feelings? I was a walking emoticon—"She's embarrassed, she's embarrassed."

His charming smile and kind eyes undid me. "I wanted to say goodbye," he said. "In case I missed you later."

"When are you leaving?"

A lump formed in my throat, though I tried not to let him know how upset I was. Losing Evan again would be hard. Not because I wanted to get back together. I didn't, but part of me would always love him. He was a great guy, and I really cared about him. "How will you get home?"

"I can get him to Scotland." Deanna came up behind Evan and wrapped her arms around him. She was even prettier out of the water, and she looked at Evan like he was her hero. Truly, he was. He saved us all.

"And from there?" I asked.

"I'll catch a flight home," Evan said. "Deanna is coming to Canada with me."

"I can't believe I'm going to fly!" she said, bouncing on her toes.

I wasn't sure how she planned to blend in with skin and hair the color of spearmint gum, but they would figure it out. I hugged Evan and kissed his cheek. "Take care of yourself and keep in touch, okay? You're always welcome here."

"You can visit us, too," he said.

"I'd like that," I said. "What are you going to do when you get back?"

It would be hard to go from the world of underwater wonders to the mundane of everyday life. Last year, I worried about coming home with my dad. Now I couldn't imagine living a normal human life. Unlike me, Evan had no choice, but he seemed okay with it.

"I'll go back to school and finish my degree." He gave me a crooked grin, and his dimples flashed. "Someone needs to keep the waters safe for you."

"True," I said. "Keep an eye on those mantle plumes."

He shuddered. "I hope I never see one again."

"How about you, Deanna?" I asked.

It was obvious they were in love, but could she stay on land? Did Sirens have the same constraints as Selkies?

"I'm going to school with Evan," she said. "I think I'll take some business courses. After all, we just inherited a bar."

"You did?"

"The queen... oh, um, Ula gave it to us. The one that Ken owned and made us work at." She laughed and shook her head. "It's a dump, but with some work, it could be a respectable establishment."

"Deanna's got big plans," Evan said proudly.

"That's great." I gave Deanna a hug too. "Now, I really need to come and visit. We could get some pizza, maybe catch a movie." *And see my grandparents*, I thought. I was sure they worried about me. Too much time passed since I last saw them, and they weren't getting any younger. As a Selkie, I had a long lifetime ahead of me, but human lives were short. My leaving abruptly after graduation would have hurt them too. They probably felt like they lost their daughter and their granddaughter at the same time. "Look in on my grandparents, okay? Let them know that I'm fine."

"I will," he said. "I'll keep an eye on them. Don't worry."

My eyes filled with tears, and I gave him a watery smile. "Thank you, Evan. For everything."

"You don't have to thank me." His voice thickened with emotion. Deanna placed something in his hand, and then stepped back to give us a moment of privacy. "I only want the best for you. I think you can have that life now. Right?"

I nodded. "And, you? Are you happy?"

"I am. I really am." His gray eyes, both familiar and foreign, locked on mine. "Don't grieve for what I lost. I didn't want it to begin with."

With a laugh that was more of a wet snort, I wiped my eyes and tugged on a section of his snowy, white hair. "Even this?"

"Okay." His face broke into a grin. "I could do without the grandpa hair, but I can deal with it."

Throwing myself in his arms, I hugged him tightly. I would miss him so much.

"I love you, Evan." It felt right to say it, as right as it felt to be in his arms. This time, though, I knew it was the deep love of friendship, nothing more.

"I love you, too, Selkie girl." He took my hand in his and placed my grandparents' necklaces in my open palm, curling my fingers over them. "These belong to you."

"I gave them to—

"I couldn't possibly keep them," he interrupted, his eyes searching mine. "They are one of your only connections to your grandparents, a family heirloom. Keep them, use them, or don't… Heck, pass them on to your kids."

Swallowing the lump in my throat, I gave him a sad smile and kissed his cheek. "Thank you."

He nodded, swallowing hard, but not speaking. As I watched him return to Deanna, I clasped the pearl around my neck. It felt smooth and warm against my skin. Somehow, I knew it would always remind me of Evan. He was a good man, and I hoped this wouldn't be the last time I saw him.

A few more goodbyes were exchanged, and then Evan and the Sirens were ready to leave. I followed them out and stood on the shore, watching them depart. Some of the girls smiled and waved, while others hurried off, seemingly relieved to leave our island. When the shore was empty, I transported back to the hall.

Ula was talking to Dad, her palm resting on his cheek. "I must go to Azuria. The men await me to honor those we lost."

"Won't you stay and grieve with us first?" Dad asked. "These are your people too."

"You're right," Ula said. "I'll stay, but I must leave immediately after."

One of my father's guards approached and asked, "Shall we make preparations for the final blessings, sir?"

"Yes, please see that it is done," Dad told him. He placed a hand on my back, guiding me toward the door. "As the bodies are prepared, Meara, it is our job to comfort those who grieve. Come with me."

I motioned for Kieran to join us, taking his hand in mine and finding comfort in his touch. Funny how at first love felt like a fire, but now it was a warm blanket. He was quiet as we walked, waiting while Dad and I stopped and met with our people. We listened more than talked, providing hugs and a shoulder to cry on. I was shocked when I found Arren and his friends grieving together. He lost more than the friendship with my great uncle—their pretty friend with the blonde curls died in the battle too. They told stories about her kind heart, and I regretted that I hadn't spent more time getting to know her. Going forward, I would find the time to spend with them. They were close to my age, and they needed friends and guidance. With Ula leaving, I needed friends, too. The teens wanted to know more about the human world, and I could share that with them. I vowed to find the time to do that, in honor of their lost friend.

We finished making the rounds. The bodies were laid out on the beach, adorned with shells and wildflowers that the women and children had gathered. My father stood in front of everyone as they formed a semi-circle around him, facing out to sea.

In an ancient language, he spoke words I didn't understand. Kieran translated for me, his words flowing in a soothing tempo through my mind.

From the depths of the blue, you were born.
From the depths of the blue, you return.
May your spirit ride the tides out to sea.
May the ocean ever be your company.
May the fish and mammals sing your praise.
May we honor your memory throughout our days.
Peace to your spirit, old friend.
Peace until we meet again.

"That's beautiful," I murmured. Kieran wrapped his arms around me and pulled me back against his chest. Together, we watched as one by one, the bodies were slid into the sea. Dad called on the wind to change the tide, and they floated away, sinking below the waves and disappearing out of sight.

"What will happen to their bodies?" I asked. The question seemed morbid, but important. I hated to think of my uncle becoming fish or shark food.

"At the point you saw them sink, their body disintegrated into the water. There is nothing left of them now. Their spirits have rejoined the ocean."

Odd as it was, that comforted me. I liked the idea of my great uncle jumping with the dolphins or swimming with the turtles. I knew he was at peace, and therefore, I was, too.

"We have blessed the dead." Dad spoke quietly, but his voice carried over us all. "Let us now return home and feast in their honor."

Ula stepped forward. "I must leave you now and return to the Blue Men. From this point forward, our kingdoms reside in peace." Tipping up, she kissed Dad's cheek. "Call when you need me, brother."

Then she turned to me. I focused on the sweet, loving face of my aunt as she hurried over to me.

"You have done well, Meara. You will make a fine leader one day." Leaning in, she whispered in my ear. "I'm still open for ice cream dates, so don't be a stranger."

I laughed and stepped away from Kieran to hug her. "I'll miss you, Ula."

"I won't be far away," she promised, hugging Kieran next.

After Ula exchanged a few more words, hugs, and tears with members of our clan—including Paddy, which I expected, and Brigid, which I did not, she slid into the water. We watched her depart until all that remained was the churning tides.

Dad led the clan back to the castle in a slow and solemn march. No one transported. No one spoke. I watched them go, content to stay in the sun. It warmed my back and arms, adding to the dreamlike state I was in. The day had a surreal quality to it. Ula was gone. Uncle Angus was dead. My head was reeling as I struggled to come to terms with it all.

Kieran stood behind me, quietly watching. He opened his arms, and I fit my body against his, finding peace in his embrace and breathing in his comforting spring rain scent. "Are you okay?" he asked.

I asked myself that question over and over again. I'd come to the realization that I was. "Yeah," I said, wrapping my arms around his neck. "I am."

He lowered his head and met my lips in a long, delicious kiss. When the kiss ended, I lost myself in his deep, dark eyes. "I love you, Kieran Peter Voda."

His lips quirked in response. "I know you do." With that egotistical smile I had grown to adore, he picked me up and swung me around. "I love you too."

When he set me down, his face grew serious. "You do realize the worst is not over yet?"

My heart skipped as I stared at him. "What do you mean?"

"Now that I've gone and fallen in love with you," he said. "You have to meet my family." He tilted my chin up. "After all, my father will not let me take a mate that he hasn't met."

If he weren't holding my jaw, my mouth would fall open. He was ready to make a lifetime commitment to me.

"You don't think I'd let you get away now that I have you, do you?" he murmured before taking advantage of my silence and capturing my lips again. Warmth slowly built from my toes and spread through my chest. Kieran wanted to pledge himself to me, and I wanted that. I wanted a lifetime with him. I loved him. I loved him so much. He was my equal in every way, respecting my strength and opinion. We were good together. No, we were better together.

I felt my mouth widen in a foolish grin. "Bring it, Kieran. I'm ready for anything."

His laughter rumbled in his chest and through mine as he wrapped his arm around my shoulder, and we started walking to the castle. A feast was underway—one last gesture to honor the dead—and Dad would be looking for us.

I twisted and looked back at the ocean. The water continued its steady dance of advance and retreat, bathing the rocks in its moisture. Life was like that, I realized, often a slow and steady rhythm, but sometimes a storm. I didn't know if Kieran and I would stay at Ronac or go to live with his family, but we would be together. I'd proven that I could face and conquer the storms. Now, it was time to enjoy the dance, bask in the love that surrounded me, and live. I was looking forward to that.

I tugged on his arm, and he raised his eyebrows. "Would you say the swimming restrictions have been lifted?"

"I believe so. Why?"

"Race you to the water?" I challenged.

With a flash of teeth, he took off, calling back over his shoulder. "You're on."

Laughing, I chased Kieran across the ground, changing into my seal form before the water touched my skin. He was in the lead, but I was confident I would catch him.

THE END

Epilogue

1 month later

"Do you see him yet?"

Dad leaned against my doorframe with his arms crossed. His face was full of amusement. I didn't even hear him knock. He caught me staring out the window, once again, while waiting for Kieran to return.

"What else should I be doing?" I asked. "It's not like I'm taking a suitcase."

"I'm not criticizing you," he said, although his grin told me how silly he thought I was acting. "I'm sure you're excited to meet Kieran's family."

"I am," I admitted. "But I'm more interested in seeing Kieran again."

Kieran left a few days after Uncle Angus' funeral. We decided it was better if he went home alone to Alkana and caught up with his family. He promised to return within the month and then I was going back with him so he could introduce me to his family. My stomach jumped with nerves and excitement. It didn't stop me from grinning back at my dad.

"I'm not sure I'm ready to let you go." His face grew serious as he crossed the room and pulled me into a hug. "After all, you only returned from Azuria two days ago."

I looked up at him and rolled my eyes. "I was gone a week, Dad. That's nothing."

Visiting with Ula was a blast. The first thing she did was drill me for information on how things were going back home. She missed all of us. Once I learned about her world, I was surprised she even had time to miss us. She was super busy as the new ruler of the Blue Men.

I told her that Brigid had moved into the apartment next to Dad's, the one that belonged to Uncle Angus. She started helping Dad with the day-to-day functions of the clan, too. There was a rumor she started seeing one of the guards. Ula wanted details on that, but all I could tell her was that I saw Brigid walking on the beach with a man one morning. I was too far away to determine who it was, so I had yet to confirm the gossip. In any case, she was less edgy and smiled more these days. To Ula, that was confirmation enough.

"You'll miss the next Elder meeting," Dad said, breaking through my reminiscing with his teasing.

"I think you and Aunt Brigid will carry on fine without us."

I kept my voice light, but a part of me was a little sad that I would miss my first Elder meeting. After realizing how much my leadership helped with the battle, Dad held a small ceremony the night before Kieran left for California and swore me in as an Elder. When I told Ula, she squealed and pulled me into a bear hug. Then we celebrated with too much ice cream. Brain freeze aside, it reminded me of old times, complete with a discussion of guys. It seemed that Vesh was not intimidated by her new royal status. They started seeing each other privately. From what Ula said, things were going well. Her eyes lit up when she talked about him. Over the course of the week, I noticed how much they watched each other, even when the other wasn't looking. Vesh had it just as bad as Ula, which was great in my opinion. They made a cute couple. By the time I went home, I was satisfied that Ula was happy. That was what mattered most.

Dad leaned forward and rested his arms next to me on the window ledge. Together, we watched the cresting waves and soaring gulls. It was peaceful, although my eyes wouldn't rest. I continued to search the horizon for any sign of Kieran. Then, movement in the distance caught my eye.

"It's him!" I squealed, turning to run down to the cove and greet him.

Dad caught my arm and leaned down until our eyes were level. "Be careful out there." He tapped the silver bracelet on my arm. When Ula left, she gave me hers so I could communicate with my dad. "Send a message when you arrive."

"I will, Dad."

"I'll miss you."

"I'll miss you, too."

This time, I hugged him, and he kissed the top of my head. "I love you."

"I love you, too."

He let me go, and I raced out the door. Once I was outside of the fortress, I transported to the shore. A moment later, a magnificent seal with large, chocolate eyes emerged from the water. The air shimmered and then Kieran was standing there. His dark eyes drilled into mine. My heart raced in response. I thought that over time, the intense way he made me feel would start to fade, but it was as strong as ever.

"How's Ula?" he asked, placing his sealskin, now in its baseball cap form, in his back pocket. The light tone in his voice directly contrasted with the smoky expression in his eyes.

I ran into his open arms. I'd never tire of the feel of his strong arms wrapped around me. In his warm embrace, I looked up and smiled. "She's made a lot of progress. The strait is peaceful once again."

"Any reports on Evan?"

I knew Kieran really didn't care how Evan was doing, but I was touched that he asked all the same. "Evan and Deanna enrolled a few days ago, and they found an apartment near campus. I guess they'll start taking classes next semester." I smirked. "Evan caved in and dyed his hair. I guess his mom really flipped out when she saw him."

"He should've dyed it before he went home. How did he explain to her?"

"He...um, he..." Kieran ran light kisses along my neck, making it hard for me to concentrate and form a complete sentence.

"Yes?" His voice filled with humor, and his wicked mouth moved to my ear.

My knees weakened. With some effort, I focused enough to get my thoughts together and out of my mouth coherently. "He told her it was a reaction to the chemicals he was exposed to while working on the mantle plume. She thinks he was in a hospital all this time detoxing."

Kieran paused with his kisses to consider. "I suppose that's as plausible as anything."

"Whatever." I hit his arm playfully. "It was a good explanation and you know it."

His face grew serious. "I missed you."

"I missed you, too." I leaned up and kissed him. I missed his kisses a lot.

"Do you need rest?" I asked. "Do you want to go inside and eat or something?"

We originally planned to leave as soon as he got back. I hadn't considered how much swimming that meant for him. I wondered if he was up to it.

"I ate plenty on the way here." He laughed when I made a face. "Unlike you, I prefer my food fresh."

"So, you're ready?" I asked.

"If you are." As usual, he left the decision to me. "Did you say goodbye to your dad?"

I nodded. "We said goodbye just before you got here. I told him that we're leaving right away." Running my hand across his collarbone, I smiled when he shivered. "I know you're anxious to introduce me to your family, but can we make a stop first?"

"You want to see your grandparents, don't you?"

"I miss them," I said. "And I know they're worried about me."

"Of course we'll stop," he said. "It might do my father good to wait a few extra days. He is anxious to meet you, though. So are my siblings."

"What did you tell them about me?" I teased. "Should I be nervous?"

"Only good things." He winked. "They'll love you as much as I do."

I rose up on my toes and kissed him. "I love you, too."

Taking my hand in his, he said, "Shall we?"

We walked toward the ocean, the waves welcoming us in their ever-flowing embrace. As the water lapped over my bare feet, a shiver of anticipation traveled up my spine. I exchanged one last grin with Kieran.

We dove in.

Acknowledgements

First, I'd like to thank my parents, Dennis and Mary. If it weren't for you, I wouldn't be here today (in more ways than one!) Thank you for your love and guidance. You've always believed in my dreams, and I am forever grateful for you.

Thank you to John, Dori, and Nate, for letting me have the family computer most evenings and weekends. You know how important this dream is to me, and without your support, I wouldn't be able to achieve it. Even if I'm zoned out in writing, you know that I love and appreciate you!

Next, my beta readers...you all rock! You had great feedback and caught those little errors that disappear when I look at my manuscript. I'm so glad you loved the conclusion to Meara's story. You've been a great help, and your review of my manuscript means more than I can say.

Thank you to Clean Teen Publishing, the CTP street team, Nerd Girls, Cynthia Shepp, and my readers and fans. This book would not be what it is without all of you. I appreciate everything you do!

About the Author

Kelly Risser knew at a young age what she wanted to be when she grew up. Unfortunately, Fairy tale Princess was not a lucrative career. Leaving the castle and wand behind, she entered the world of creative business writing where she worked in advertising, marketing, and training at various companies. Currently, she works full time as an eLearning Instructional Designer, fitting her creative writing into the evenings and weekends.

She's often found lamenting, "It's hard to write when there are so many good books to read!" So, when she's not immersed in the middle of someone else's fantasy world, she's busy creating one of her own. She is the author of the Never Forgotten series—Never Forgotten, Current Impressions, and Always Remembered. She also contributed to the Fractured Glass young adult science fiction anthology.

Kelly lives in Wisconsin with her husband and two children. They share their home with Clyde the Whoodle and a school of fish.

www.KellyRisser.com
www.Facebook.com/AuthorKellyRisser
https://twitter.com/kar2b
authorkellyrisser@gmail.com

CPSIA information can be obtained at www.ICGtesting.com
Printed in the USA
LVOW11s1052080515

437753LV00002B/9/P